PRAISE FO

"The camaraderie of a small town is captured in all its glory in this story of rediscovered love, lies and deceit. Trust comes in small doses and is lost just as easily as the clever plot unfolds, especially when unusual characters provide surprises."

—RT Book Reviews on *Sweet Tea and Secrets*

"Fabulous, fabulous read! Be sure to have a tissue with you as you read this sweet book. [*Life After Perfect*] is full of emotion and heartfelt struggles of love and life."

—Tabitha Jones, *A Closet Full of Books*

Until Tomorrow

ALSO BY NANCY NAIGLE

The Adams Grove Series

Sweet Tea and Secrets

Out of Focus

Wedding Cake and Big Mistakes

Pecan Pie and Deadly Lies

Mint Juleps and Justice

Barbecue and Bad News

Standalone Books

Sand Dollar Cove

InkBLOT, cowritten with Phyllis C. Johnson
under the pen name of Johnson Naigle

The Granny Series

cowritten with Kelsey Browning

In for a Penny

Fit to Be Tied

In High Cotton

Under the Gun

Always on My Mind: Pick Your Passion Novella 1

Come a Little Closer: Pick Your Passion Novella 2

The Boot Creek Novels

Life After Perfect

Every Yesterday

Until Tomorrow

NANCY NAIGLE

Montlake
Romance

This is a work of fiction. Names, characters, organizations, places, events, and incidents are either products of the author's imagination or are used fictitiously. Any resemblance to actual persons, living or dead, or actual events is purely coincidental.

Text copyright © 2017 by Nancy Naigle
All rights reserved.

No part of this book may be reproduced, or stored in a retrieval system, or transmitted in any form or by any means, electronic, mechanical, photocopying, recording, or otherwise, without express written permission of the publisher.

Published by Montlake Romance, Seattle

www.apub.com

Amazon, the Amazon logo, and Montlake Romance are trademarks of Amazon.com, Inc., or its affiliates.

ISBN-13: 9781477848609
ISBN-10: 1477848606

Cover design by Lindsey Andrews

Printed in the United States of America

To Andrew:

For reminding me to trust the journey, because even when it looks all wrong, the reward may be better than ever imagined.

Thank you for being such a wonderful part of my journey.

PS—I know what you're saying right now.

"I do what I can." And you always do. I like that in a guy.

Chapter One

"He was all wrong for me anyway." Flynn Crane lifted her coffee cup to take a sip, hoping to hide her disappointment, but Angie knew her better than anyone else. She'd see right through her.

"You didn't think he was all wrong for you a week ago." Angie pushed her dark hair behind her ear like she was known to do when she was aggravated.

How many times over the past two years had she sat at this very table having the same discussion with Angie? Was she ever going to learn? It was exhausting for her. She could only imagine how tired Angie was of this rerun. Probably even more so now that Angie was happily married to Jackson Washburn. Angie hadn't even been looking for love when she met Jackson.

"Are you getting ready to tell me you told me so?" Flynn tugged the afghan around her, tucking the sides between the kitchen chair and her bottom to get warm. Darn furnace had gone out the same day she kicked Brandon out. Talk about bad timing. If the problems around here kept mounting at this speed, Crane Creek Bed and Breakfast would need a crane just to lift the list of to-dos.

"No, but it was more than just me who was raising flags on that guy's intentions. Megan and Katie had their concerns too."

"I know. I should've listened." Flynn sighed. It was true. Was it her biological clock going cuckoo or her hopeless romantic side that kept getting her into trouble? "Is it too much to just want to be happy?"

"You don't need a man in your life to be happy."

Flynn kept her mouth shut, afraid that if she opened it right now, it might also open a trail of tears and she was absolutely positively not going to cry over Brandon.

"I'm sorry he wasn't the one, but I promise you the right guy is out there." Angie leaned forward, hugging her mug. Probably to keep warm.

"Do you need another blanket? A sweatshirt?"

Angie laughed. "No, I'm fine." She took another sip of her coffee and set it down carefully. "Flynn, this is going to sound harsh, and I promise I don't mean it that way. Do you know what you want? I mean really want?"

Flynn lifted her chin. Good question. She'd thought so, but now she wasn't sure her man trouble wasn't more out of habit than desire. "I know what I don't want. He's gone and good riddance." It had been her choice, but darn if it didn't still sting a little. One thing was becoming painfully clear. Finding love in Boot Creek seemed impossible.

"What *do* you want, Flynn?"

Angie had been Flynn's best friend since the first time she'd come to Boot Creek to stay with her grandparents. Way back when Mom had still been alive. Almost as far back as she could remember. The distance made for huge gaps between school years and summer visits, but the friendship had withstood time and distance.

Angie pulled her feet into the chair and shifted the blanket over her legs. "What I mean is you've made so many changes." She swept her hand in the air. "This place for one."

This place. It had turned out to be a lot more work than she'd expected. The tired old bed and breakfast she'd taken over from her

2

grandparents needed constant attention. It was like a puppy you had to grab and race outside every time it went to sit down, for fear it would pee on the new rug. You couldn't leave it for a moment or else something might go wrong.

"I love this place, but it is becoming a money pit." The fact that she and her best friend were sitting here in the kitchen drinking coffee under blankets because the furnace was on the fritz was one more jab on a bad day.

"It wouldn't have been so bad if you hadn't stopped taking reservations."

"I couldn't rent out rooms while Brandon was fixing things." Okay, that wasn't exactly true. And Angie knew it too. "Fine. I could've rented at least one or two of the rooms if we'd been strategic about the renovations. But he was fixing things here, there, and everywhere, with no real plan." That's what had hit her in the bank account. She'd finally had to change the website to show no vacancy. "Up until then I was fine. This place had been staying full, and repeat customers were telling new ones. I should have taken control of things when Brandon got started and made a plan."

"My point exactly," Angie said. "You never operate without a plan. What got into you? Are you being true to your dreams or just being whoever it is you think these guys want you to be?"

She sipped the blend of coffee spiked with Kahlúa, Baileys, and Amaretto. The warmth sent a toasty surge through her. The family recipe could chase a chill better than Grandma's crocheted afghan, and it worked a miracle on a broken heart too.

Good thing too, because she needed both today. Didn't make that bitter pill go down any better though. Angie made a good point. What *had* she been doing? She'd promised herself last year that she wouldn't try to change a man again. She'd made good on that, but darned if she hadn't sacrificed her own needs and wants to make that so. A nervous giggle escaped. Flynn tried to stifle it, because it wasn't funny. It was embarrassing.

This was one of those days she wished Mom was still around. Mom and Dad had had the perfect relationship. It's why she'd always dreamed of one just like it. It wasn't until Mom died that Dad had gone middle-aged crazy and moved away. Granpa said that it was just too hard for Daddy to deal with her, since she was the spitting image of her mom. The last she'd heard, he was up in Canada somewhere. She wondered what he'd think about her running Crane Creek Bed and Breakfast now.

Angie placed her hand on Flynn's arm. "You okay?"

"Can we quit talking about my love life for half a second?"

"Sure." Angie shrugged, or was that a shiver?

"Are you sure you're warm enough? I can get you another blanket."

"No. I'm fine," Angie said. "Are you sure Brandon didn't sabotage the furnace to get a free ticket back?"

"He wouldn't do that." But it did get her to thinking. Had it started acting up before then?

Angie lifted her brow.

"Okay, fair enough. Maybe he would, but he was handy to have around." But she had to cut her losses. He'd turned a two-week job into a six-month one, and it had become clear it was more for extended free room and board than time with her.

"There are other handymen around, and they won't cost you near what you paid Brandon." Angie pulled her feet underneath her. "You need to be the leading lady in your life story, and he practically moved in before the first date."

"That was out of convenience. He was working all hours."

"I think it was his plan all along. Find a job with freeloader potential."

"You give him too much credit. I'm not sure he was smart enough to be that conniving."

"Well, there is that, and he was good looking."

"Can't deny that." It was those steely blue eyes that had almost had her melting to her knees when he first shook her hand. "New rule number one—no one moves in unless there's an engagement announcement in the paper."

"That's a good one. You deserve a smart guy. Don't settle."

"I didn't know I was." She spread her arms wide. "Instead of an *A* for *Adultery*, my scarlet letter will be *D* for *Desperate*. Not flattering no matter how you dice it."

"Flynn, don't shortchange yourself. You're beautiful, brilliant, and you can do anything. You are the catch. Brandon, and the last four guys you've dated, have all been users. I hate seeing that."

"It's easy to see now. You were right. Again." She lifted her mug in the air with a polite salute, although admitting she was wrong was never easy. "I know it, so why does part of me miss him? Just a teensy bit. Why is that?"

"Because you're mourning the loss of the guy you loved in your mind and heart. We both know that is *not* who *he* was."

"He said right from the beginning he didn't want a girlfriend." She leaned her head into the palms of her hands. "I should've listened."

"We've all made that mistake before, Flynn. Sometimes we hear what we want to hear. Don't beat yourself up."

"It just seemed like we had so much in common. He was fun."

"Fun is good, but he was having fun on your dime."

Dimes that were quickly running low since Flynn's severance had run out, and she'd been dipping into savings since she'd put the "No Vacancy" sign up on the website.

Angie got up and topped off her coffee as she continued, "Look, it just so happened his hobby was what you needed around here at the time. So it wasn't a total loss, but he had it made. He piddled around like a kept man while you cooked, cleaned, and paid for everything. Too bad I'm married. Sounds like a good gig."

Flynn balled up her napkin and tossed it at Angie. "Real funny. He had some good points too. He's an amazing furniture maker, and I'm going to miss his kisses."

"Kisses are easy to get."

Even now, the thought of his lips on hers made her insides dance. "I needed a handyman way more than a boyfriend. If I'd been smart, I'd have kept things at that."

"Someone else said that. Who was that?" Angie put her mug on the table. "Oh yeah. That was me."

"Was that a passive-aggressive I-told-you-so?"

"Pretty much."

Flynn had to laugh at that. Only a best friend could make you laugh at yourself for being an idiot.

"Well, not all that passive," Angie admitted, "but it's the last time I'll mention it. I promise." She crossed her heart between giggles. "And I promise when you're ready, the right one will come along."

"Easy for you to say, since you married the last good guy in four counties." Angie and Jackson's wedding last year had tossed Flynn's yearning for a husband and family into overdrive. No question about that.

"And I wasn't even looking for a relationship." Angie clicked her fingers. "See, I was only focusing on myself and taking care of Billy when I met Jackson. I'd finally become comfortable with my own life, struggles and all. Take care of yourself first, Flynn. Maybe the right guy will walk right into your life too."

"That will be easy, because I'm pretty much done with the whole dating thing. I feel like all I've done is date and make mistakes." Or was just too darned tired of trying so hard. Either way she needed a break. "I'm not even sure I'd recognize Mr. Right if he walked up and handed me a business card with that title."

"Quit trying so hard. Just relax and take that list of things you don't want, and use it to help you figure out what it is that you do. Let your guard down, but not too far."

"I need a GPS to navigate the path to love, because apparently I'm lost. Let your guard down. Not too far. Look, but don't look. Be open. Don't change him. Don't change me. Give, but don't be taken." She sighed. "I want a man with a real job. No more of these guys who are freelancing around."

"You do know Brandon not being the right one has nothing to do with his job, yes?"

"Yeah, but it didn't help either." She stood and walked over to refill her coffee. Getting a man was easy—they waltzed right into her life, sometimes uninvited. The problem was they all seemed right at first. She could see herself in anyone's life, but finding the one man that fit into her life correctly seemed impossible. "Or maybe I was meant to be alone." She stopped mid-pour. "Do you think that's it? I'm supposed to be alone? I can't even picture that."

Angie shrugged.

"I should concentrate on the bed and breakfast for a while." She might be wasting precious time trying to find her perfect match. From here at the kitchen table, she could see into the den. Thoughts of a young girl and boy playing with blocks strewn across the rug taunted her. Being an only child, she'd always wished for brothers and sisters. Probably why she wanted a husband and children of her own so badly. Then again, she didn't need a husband to make that happen these days either. "That den needs a fresh coat of paint."

Angie nodded. "Something bright, but that keeps to the time period of the house."

The thought of the walls in a brighter, fresh, springy hue lifted her mood. And maybe it was time to think about the things that were important to her and how she'd achieve those things alone. "Exactly. It would cheer things up around here."

"And maybe you."

"I could definitely use a little of that," Flynn admitted. "I'm going to have to hire someone to finish the work that Brandon started. I need to get money rolling back in. If I don't get this straightened out, I'm going to have to go back and get a real job to catch up." She sat down, plopped her elbows on the table. "This whole place needs some attention. Just like me. And neither of us is getting it."

"Stop with the pity party. You always get plenty of attention; it's just not always the right kind."

She straightened and patted the table in a drumroll. "I'm going to treat this B&B like one of those million-dollar banking projects that I managed and get it up and running—on time and on budget."

"That's the Flynn I know!"

"Besides, I can't let my grandparents down. They are counting on me to carry on the taking care of the business they've built. I'm all the family they've got left. How could I ruin their dream of traveling now that I've taken the place over? Being able to help them do that is my biggest life accomplishment so far."

"I've heard you say that before. So make it work. If anyone can do it, you can. You're an awesome businesswoman."

"Business is business. I'm going to focus on the B&B, and I'll be so busy that there won't be room for any romantic mistakes."

"You might as well build in a plan B for when you meet someone." Angie's smirk made her look like one of those exaggerated emojis.

"I hope your face sticks like that," Flynn said. "Didn't you just hear what I said? That's over. Finished. Complete."

"And crazy, because you're a hopeless romantic. You can't help yourself."

"I have to find a better way to deal with that." Flynn leaned forward, leveling a stare into her best friend's eyes, then stabbed a finger into the air. "Here's my plan B. Promise me. The next time I say I think I've found the one, you'll tell me to repaint the den. Or buy new hardware for the kitchen, or something that will take a week or two, so I can get over that idea before it becomes a problem."

"Fine." Angie cocked her head, her eyebrow arching. "Don't go to extremes, though. It's not all or nothing, just slow down a bit. You need to let these guys earn your trust, instead of giving it to them. Get past the dating honeymoon period so you can see any red flags. Then maybe you won't have so much invested if the next guy turns out to be a Mr. Wrong too."

"Like Brandon."

"He was a charmer. You were a major catch for him, and I do think he liked you, but he's a user. This place was his dream home. Once he moved in, and you were still paying him top dollar for work he'd have done for free just to hang out with you, he knew he had a first-class ticket on the gravy train . . ."

"In his defense, he's very good at what he does. Did you see the craftsmanship of the bathroom vanity? And I just showed him pictures of what I liked. It turned out amazing. You can't find that kind of stuff online or at the local home improvement store."

"It's beautiful. But you paid a fortune for it, and it took him five months to do it. He needed you. And he milked that job. You know it."

"Probably."

"Probably? He used you, and he never made you a priority. Remember the night you asked him to come out to dinner with us, and he said he was too busy but then texted you all through dinner?"

Angie was right. That had ruined her fun, and she'd been down-right rude to text with him while she was out with her friends. "I was an idiot."

"But you're not. You're one of the smartest women I know. That's what makes me crazy."

Flynn felt tears of frustration tickle her lower lashes. She made the same mistakes over and over and over again in her personal life. "I'm great with business. I suck with men."

"True."

"And I have to take responsibility for some of that. Sure, Brandon may have had less than honorable intentions all along, but I *let* him take advantage of me. I had an inkling something was amiss and ignored it."

"When you're lonely, anything seems better than nothing, but it's not. And you have so much going for you. Please don't let him shake your confidence."

Flynn didn't bother to wipe the hot tear that ran down her cheek. If she did, another would likely follow anyway. "I've wanted to be married and have children for so long that I've never even reconsidered if that's what I still want. I need to figure that out."

"I think that's a great idea." Angie placed a hand on Flynn's arm. "Be happy alone for a while. You're great company. Ask me. I'm your best friend. I know."

"Thank you." Flynn pulled her hands into her lap. "I'm exhausted from dealing with it all."

"And when you think you want a houseful of kids, just come get Billy for a day or two. He's just one kid, and he wears me out."

"I love Billy."

"I know you do, and he loves you, but a few days and you'll find out what being tired really is." Angie stood, folded the blue-and-red-striped lap blanket, and laid it over the side of the chair. "Get some rest. Spoil yourself a little. It'll be cheaper than paying him . . . I didn't say that." She laughed. "Okay, that was my last jab at the situation. I need to get home to Jackson and Billy. You sure I can't talk you into coming over to stay with us until you get the heat fixed?"

"No. The fireplace will keep the chill off. I'll sleep out here on the couch." North Carolina was having one of those warming trends following a week in the forties. The sixty-degree temperatures were cool, but not unbearable.

A week ago it would have been a whole different story.

She got up and walked Angie to the door. "Thanks for coming over. I know you're tired of hearing my romance-gone-wrong woes."

"You've had more than your fair share, but I will always be here." Angie lifted her jacket from the wooden hall tree and slipped it on. "That's what friends are for."

"Oh, wait," Flynn said, turning and racewalking back to the kitchen. She picked up a container of brownies that she'd packed up for Angie to take home. "Here you go."

"And this is why Billy adores you. He loves your brownies."

"I think he just likes that I put blue sprinkles on the top of them." Flynn's phone chirped from the other room. Her insides leapt at the familiar sound of Brandon's text tone.

"His favorite color. Call me in the morning." Angie glanced toward the other room. "And don't you dare text Brandon back. He's not worth it."

"Not a chance." Flynn raised her chin, feeling strong enough to actually ignore him tonight.

Angie waved as she jogged out to her car.

It had been an exhausting day. At least she'd sleep well.

As Flynn walked down the hall, the familiar text tone sounded again from her phone in the kitchen. That *not a chance* she'd so strongly uttered just moments ago echoed in her mind, but she was already moving toward the sound.

~

She picked up the phone and stared at the message.

Brandon: Wondering What You're Up To Tonight . . .

Not exactly a declaration of love or an apology. Either one would've wooed her right into a conversation. The lackluster text was a blessing.

The furnace being on the fritz was a legit reason to talk to Brandon. He could probably fix it for half the price of the local HVAC guys, but was it worth it? He'd smooth-talk her right back into the situation she'd just nixed. Plus, all the way out the door he'd restated that he'd always said their relationship was meant to just be fun. And fun wasn't what she was looking for. She could have fun with her girlfriends and spend a lot less money doing it.

She picked up her phone and stared at the partial line of text on the display. The ellipsis taunted her. What else did he have to say? Was there anything that he could say that would matter?

But if she looked, he'd know she'd seen the message. She took in a breath, and then laid her phone back down.

Like the whispers from a hopeful angel on one shoulder and a devil on the other, thoughts whipped back and forth.

He's a waste of my time.
But he makes me laugh.
He's probably horny.
But he sure is a great lover.
He's handy and I have stuff to fix.
He's not the one for me.
What if I never find the one for me?

Self-doubt crept in. Being with the wrong guy was *not* better than being alone. Maybe she'd prove that to herself if she'd ever stay alone for more than a few weeks.

Her phone sounded again.

Brandon: Is Something Wrong?

Seriously? He knew very well what was wrong. They'd talked it to death this morning until she finally got him out the door and then texted about it practically all afternoon. There was no sense rehashing it.

She turned off the sound on her phone, hoping it would be easier to ignore if she didn't know about the messages.

If she were smart, she'd block his number completely.

She wasn't there yet. A little piece of her still needed to know he wanted to talk to her to give her the strength to not talk to him.

The relaxed feeling she'd had just a little while ago had vanished. The kitchen project she and Brandon had planned to start next would have to wait. Maybe that was for the best anyway. Now that she'd have to fix the furnace, that would bite into the money she'd set aside for the upgrades, and there was no way she'd compromise on the kitchen renovation.

She got up and headed down the hall toward the smallest of all of the bedrooms in the house. The room that had been her mother's room when she'd come back home after graduating college. She'd once thought about turning the carriage house into her living quarters. Close enough to take care of guests, but roomier—more private too. Then again, being here in the downstairs of her grandparents' B&B held fond childhood memories, and there was a closeness to Mom here that she couldn't seem to let go of.

She stopped in the doorway of her office. It had been her grandparents' library, and Flynn had spent hours in this room as a little girl, poring through the books in the floor-to-ceiling bookshelves. She hadn't changed it much, except for adding a few of her own favorite books.

In here, the thick wall of books silenced the world. This was her special spot to escape from the noisy family gatherings. Hiding in this room had been like closing herself off in the turret of a castle, or ducking into a cave to escape the bad guys, or hiding away in a cottage by the sea. She stepped inside, quietly closing the door behind her like she had all those years before, reliving, for a moment, all of those memories and imaginary friends from between the covers of these books. The room still felt safe.

Memories of the hours spent coloring pictures in here at the heavy wooden davenport desk made her smile. With its hidden drawers on one side, the desk was magical. Her imagination would take off, inspiring creative and fantastical thoughts.

After Mom died, it had become tradition for her to leave a drawing for her mom's parents beneath the inclined desktop like an Easter egg waiting to be found. It was the one thing she could do that seemed to put the brightness back in her grandparents' eyes.

When Flynn had moved into Crane Creek Bed and Breakfast, the first thing she'd done was check the desk compartment. Three of her drawings had still been tucked inside.

Finding those memories had seemed like a sign that she was supposed to have stepped in and taken over Crane Creek Bed and Breakfast from her grandparents when she had. She wanted to carry on the legacy for them just like they'd always planned. It was part of why she'd left most everything the way it was. Her parents' wedding picture and several treasured others of her mom still graced the shelves.

As a little girl she'd tallied income and receipts for her granddaddy during the summers, pretending she was the owner. Even back then she'd pictured herself running the B&B with a husband and children. One child at her side, and one on her hip. How she thought she could do all of that and run the B&B was humorous now that she knew how much work went into the day-to-day operation of this place.

The antique desk wasn't functionally the best choice; she could actually use a bigger desk for all she had to deal with, but the memories outweighed the practicality. This treasure deserved a place in their family forever. And since she was the last one in the family, it was hers to care for.

And there was that familiar pang in her gut. The constant reminder that there was no one else to follow in her footsteps when she reached her last tomorrow. *Yet*.

Chapter Two

Ford Morton pulled a long-sleeve shirt over his T-shirt, then layered a hoodie, and finally his jacket. Layers were a must in Alaska in late October. His muscles felt tight after the long afternoon of work. On cold days like today, the warm temperatures inside Glory Glassworks were welcome, making the icy temperatures outside feel more like a much-needed thaw.

In the summer, the glass shop melted off pounds as quickly as it turned solid glass into a pliable medium. Even in Alaska, glassblowing was as hot and sweaty as any full-contact sport he'd ever played. A real workout. Maybe that was part of the allure.

Ford ducked outside, hunching forward, tucking his chin down into the collar of his jacket. Chicagoans bragged their wind could cut your face, but the wind off the Alaskan harbor made that look like a spa treatment. Today the wind sliced at his skin with every long stride he made down Factory Street, instantly cooling the sweat at his collar.

Buildings along this block were once part of a huge fish cannery that had gone under years ago. For a while the buildings thrived from the tourism the cruise ships brought to port, selling trinkets and novelties, but over the past five years since Ford had lived here, he'd watched the businesses disappear one by one, leaving the block more empty than occupied. "For Lease" signs filled several of the windows.

Ford's skin reacted to the chill, feeling suddenly a size too small for his body. But the rush of fresh air into his lungs after a full day in the studio always brought an appreciation of what nature delivered on a daily basis.

A Tennessee boy born and raised, he'd turned thirty here in Alaska, and living here was worth the expense of traveling back to spend time with family a few times a year. He'd reclaimed his soul here. In a way, he owed Alaska his sanity. If he'd stayed in Nashville practicing law, he'd have been a bitter, unhappy man. Helping big corporations beat the system and guilty people dodge justice was big-ticket stuff for the law practice his dad was so proud of, but it nipped at the edges of Ford's moral compass. Leaving it all behind had been easy—even if it had been at the expense of his relationship with his father.

He'd left the shop early, but days were so short this time of year that it was already dark.

He shoved his hands into his pockets as he headed for the Manic Moose Saloon. As he acclimated to the cool weather, he picked up his walk to a jog, ducking into the side door of the saloon behind a group of guys that worked the dock.

Ford pulled the heavy wooden door closed behind him. Hand carved by a local artisan, the same one who'd done the custom door on Ford's house, the scene of an old, weathered fisherman standing in hip waders fly-fishing only got better with time. The wood had silvered from years of drastic weather changes. In the background, a bear eyed the shiny pink salmon swimming toward the fly dancing in the water.

A puff of cold air followed Ford inside.

"Hey, man. Heard you're flying out this week."

Ford turned toward the comment. Chet stood talking to some folks at a corner table. Chet's father had owned this place back when it was still called the Slippery Rascal. Now Chet and his wife, Missy, ran the joint, and lived upstairs.

"You heard right."

"Abandoning us for good?" Chet made his way around the bar and pulled a draft of IPA for Ford and slid it to him.

"You know better than that. Just going down to North Carolina to run some glass workshops for the PRIZM Glass Art Institute."

"That's where you ran off to last summer when your friend got married. Right?"

Ford took a sip of the cold beer. "I visited the glass shop while I was in town."

"If you don't come back, I want first dibs on your house." Chet poured a drink. "Not that I could afford it."

"I'll be back before you realize I'm gone, just thirty days."

Chet eyed him. "Yeah, right."

"What?"

"Seen that look before. You're going down to find a girl."

He was set to argue, but that would just be a lie. "What if I am? What's so wrong with that?"

"Seen it too many times. Never lasts long. The only women that make it up here are the ones born and raised into it. This place ain't for those dainty types. If you find one you like down there, I suggest you stay there."

"I'll be back." He chugged half the beer. "I'll do some work, spend some time with friends, and then I'll be back. One way or the other."

"That long-legged blonde you talked about after the wedding lives down there too, don't she? That one of the friends you plan to spend time with?" He'd air quoted the word *friends*.

Why did air quotes always make him feel awkward?

Ford narrowed his eyes and pointed a finger in Chet's direction. "You're supposed to forget that stuff at closing time."

"Heck no. I'm going to write a book with all the shit you customers tell me, one day. Going to be a bestseller too. Probably buy the whole town with the money I'll make and never work another day in my life. Might be how I pay for that fancy house you built." Chet let out a laugh as raucous as a drunken pirate.

"I hear you. You and I both know that Missy won't be having any of that. You'll have to work just to keep her in—"

"I heard my name," Missy said, swatting Ford on the butt with her bar towel. "Don't be talking about me."

"Wouldn't dare." He reached over and gave her waist a squeeze. "How you been, girl?"

"Great. Heard you're headed out of town."

He'd just made final plans two weeks ago. "Of course you did. Can't keep a secret around here."

"Well, it won't be the same without you."

"Glad I'll be missed." He loved living here. He'd never felt so alive as he did the first week he'd been in Alaska. The grandeur of the open space, the power of the seasons, and the wildlife brought out the alpha in a man's soul.

"Heard you're leaving out of here for a few weeks," a redheaded guy said as Ford peeled off his coat.

"Just a month. Doing an in-residence stint at a glass shop down in North Carolina." He'd be telling this story over and over until the day he left. Small towns. They were the same no matter what part of the country you were in.

"My wife still thinks you're like the Picasso of glassblowing or something. Congratulations. Sounds like a big deal."

"It's pretty cool," Ford admitted. "Plus, I have friends down that way."

"Let me buy you a going-away shot," the guy said. Ford could not bring his name to mind. Embarrassing in their small town. "Don't ever understand why anyone would leave this time of year. Finally got rid of the tourists and got our town back. Best time of the year if you ask me. Must have been one helluva offer."

"Pretty much." Ford couldn't argue with him; the offer *had* been too good to turn down. Despite the cold and snow, this was Ford's favorite time of year too. Tourists were nonexistent, so he got to spend time on his craft and stock up on the inventory that would carry him through the next year. He needed that productive time. But being in new surroundings inspired creativity, and this year he hoped to make something that would finally separate him from the other top glassblowers.

That restless need had been nagging at him lately.

No more teaching tourists how to make simple glass balls, now that the cruise ships had paused their schedules until next spring. He could go wild and create new designs—real showpieces that brought in real money that would continue to grow his savings.

Ford settled into his regular seat. Missy set a shot in front of him. She nodded to the foursome at the table across the way. "Jack Daniel's from over there."

"Thanks, Missy." He tossed it back and set the empty shot glass back on her tray. "Can you bring me another beer, please?"

"I'm on it, handsome."

The whiskey mellowed him. Being pretty much snowbound through the winter had its advantages. But he was over spending nights alone. Not that he had to be alone, but having someone in his bed he had no intention of keeping there had gotten old a long time ago. He longed for someone to share the dream with. To plan, to collaborate with, build a family with. Someone to laugh at his more stupid ideas, and high-five and hug him for the good ones.

The house had been a high-five idea even if he didn't have anyone to share it with. Yet.

"You selling your place?"

"Just a rumor." Ford spun around. "Junior. How've you been?"

"Great. Business is good," said the wiry man. Junior might've been his name, but he had to be at least seventy years old. His shock of gray hair always looked like he'd just rolled out of bed, even on Sunday morning in church. "Heard you were leaving town."

"Just a month. I'll be back." This was already getting old.

"Damn. I'd give up my storefront to buy that place of yours."

"Thanks. I'll take that as a compliment," Ford said. He'd invested in a nice property up on good, high land with decent roads. Three years he'd bartered with friends to get that place just right. Junior had done three carvings for him, including the front door that had taken him almost a year to complete. "All that's missing now is the perfect woman."

"No such thing, Ford. You gone crazy or something? A woman will just ruin that place."

"I don't think so." When he'd been offered the artist-in-residence spot in North Carolina, he hadn't had any intention of accepting it. Giving it a couple of days to not insult them, he'd been surprised when he'd been inundated with dreams of the long-legged girl he'd met last summer at his old school pal Jackson's wedding in Boot Creek. She'd snuck into his dreams and then into his daytime thoughts.

He still remembered the moment he laid eyes on Flynn Crane. He'd been thirteen hours overdue for sleep after one long layover in Denver to get to North Carolina. Hungry and exhausted when she started talking about home-cooked breakfast, he'd thought she was flirting and talking about the morning after. Even tired, he hadn't found that a bad proposition, because damn, she'd looked fine.

His ego had taken a blow when he realized all that talk was because she was the innkeeper where the wedding party was staying, *and* the bride's best friend. Couldn't love and leave the bride's best friend. So he'd tucked that attraction away.

But once it had reignited, he found himself considering the residency. It had been a good offer.

And he hadn't been able to shake the memories of how her hair had smelled, how her fingers tapped his when he danced with her. How her every curve looked perfect under the satiny bridesmaid dress.

Rather than the polite no-thank-you to the folks out at PRIZM, he found himself plotting and planning that trip to North Carolina and the possibility of bringing Flynn Crane back into his life.

He took a sip of his beer and shook his wandering mind back to Junior who was still rambling on.

"Guys outnumber the girls plenty around here. Finding one who isn't taken is hard. And the ones that are available aren't the type you want anyways."

Ford laughed. It sounded harsh, but it was pretty accurate. "Junior, you're getting cynical, man."

"Truth hurts."

Five years had flown by. He liked wintering in Alaska. There was no place quieter that he'd ever found. The only improvement he could imagine would be having a special woman to share it all with. Back in Nashville during their college days together, Jackson had been one heckuva wingman. Hopefully, being married to Angie hadn't ruined that skill for his best friend.

"Mm-hmm," Junior said. "That long pause just then. I know what that means. Means you're thinking you're going to bring back a woman. I know that look."

What was it with people? Did he have an I-need-to-get-laid label stuck to his forehead or something? "You're just looking for something to talk about."

"I'll put a hundred bucks on it right now that if you bring some mainlander back, she won't stick around."

"Oh, I'll take that bet." Ford stuck out his hand. "If I do bring someone back, it'll be for all the right reasons." And saying it out loud gave it life.

Missy swept past him with a tray of drinks. "Hope you're going to come back. I kind of like having you around here."

"Not you too," he said. "You know me. Why would you even say that?"

"Because we've seen it so many times before." She placed the drinks in front of the guys telling fish stories just behind him. They never stopped talking. "And as good looking as you are, someone will snag you."

"Yeah, yeah. Your dear husband said the same thing." It bothered Ford that the locals still thought of him as temporary around here. He'd been here long enough that he considered this home.

Missy turned and blew him a kiss as she skittered past in the other direction.

What the heck did that mean? Ford shrugged his shoulders and turned back toward the bar.

Missy and Chet were about as different as Alaska and Florida, but somehow their relationship worked. She bubbled with life in her compact five-foot frame, and Chet's moose-sized body was filled to the brim with a dry-witted humor that swung from funny one day to cranky the next, making you wonder sometimes if he might end it all and not open the next day. But the Manic Moose Saloon was open every day no matter the weather.

Missy swung around the end of the bar with an empty tray and patted Chet on the tush as she passed behind him. Chet gave a playful grunt that sounded more like a horny hog.

"I'm not one of your statistics. I'll be back," Ford said. He tapped two fingers on the bar for another round.

"Whatever you say, man." Chet raised a bottle and gave Ford a generous pour, then leaned over the bar. "You decide you're not coming back, you'll get one helluva price on that place of yours. People ask me about your place all the time. I could sell that place in a week."

"Just finally got it fixed up the way I want it. Why would I leave that now?"

"Not everyone is cut out to live here. You fit in like you're one of us, but that's unusual."

"Don't see why. This place gives me more in return every day than I could ever hope for. The beauty. The people. The inspiration. The solitude. It becomes a part of you."

"Gets in your blood. I know what you're saying, but my Missy has a good eye for what's going on with people. I swear she can tell when a man is ready to settle down, and she's always right about it. Kind of witchy freaky when you think about it."

"I think all women think they have that gift," Ford said with a laugh.

"No. I'm serious. She said just last week that she thought you were going on that trip of yours to rekindle a flame, that's why I brought it up."

He didn't say anything. What could he say? She was right. Sort of. He hadn't met a prettier girl than Flynn—her long legs and flowing blonde hair made him think of beautiful mermaids in the sea.

"Love ain't enough to make a woman fall in love with this lifestyle."

"It's a good life." He wasn't sure he bought that line of thinking. Love was love, and it didn't have to be in the city limits.

A blast of cold air rushed through the bar as the guys off the fishing boat *Katie's Ring* came filing in one by one, shouting obscenities; the fishermen rolled in like high tide on a full moon. So many greenhorns made their way as far as this town to hop on boats in hopes of quick, easy money, but most found out quickly just how unforgiving the ocean was. And working it wasn't for sissies.

Trash talk about their Pacific salmon haul tonight being better than the others set the bar humming. That kind of smack could get a greenhorn in a fight in a hurry, as if Captain Andrew'd ever hire one. Seasoned fishermen didn't have much of an appetite for newbie braggers who basically stole from their potential take. Andrew amped up the volume as he ordered a round of drinks for the house.

Chet's lips stretched into a lopsided smile. "Case in point."

Folks around here loved Andrew. It was uncanny timing that he'd been the one to walk in just then. His breakup with Katie had been the talk of the town for a solid year. That Jersey girl he'd brought home after a week in Vegas had been driving him nuts with all of her nagging and neediness. When he finally got the balls to cut her loose, he used the money he'd saved to spend on her engagement ring to put toward the fishing boat of his dreams. Being married to the sea seemed to be suiting Andrew just fine. And the men on his fishing vessel were more like family than most.

If Ford was wrong about Flynn then he might end up with a boat himself called *Could've Been Married* the size of a cruise ship.

But he wasn't into those high-maintenance girls who spent all their time getting their nails done and shopping. His picture-perfect mate was the girl next door. The one who would throw her hair in a ponytail and a ball cap to get the day started, like Flynn when she'd been zipping around that bed and breakfast. Jackson had even made a comment about her being a good match for him. He should've paid more attention to it while he was there.

Now he was stuck thinking about how her pretty long legs would've felt wrapped around him on a cold winter's night.

He still wasn't exactly sure how he was going to manage seeing her without flat-out telling Jackson. He pulled his phone out of his pocket and texted.

Ford: Will Be In Your Neck Of The Woods Wednesday.

Jackson: Here? North Carolina?

Ford: Took The Artist-In-Residence Gig.

Jackson: Great. We'll Pick You Up.

Ford's lips twitched. Angie had been eager to introduce him to Flynn last year. He hoped like heck she was still in a matchmaking mood.

Ford: Was Going To Rent A Car For My Stay.

Jackson: Don'T Bother. You Can Drive My Old Truck. Send Your Flight Info.

Ford: On It. Thanks, Man.

And just like that, the possibilities of tomorrow felt a bit like the Northern Lights: unpredictable, but bright and worth the wait.

Chapter Three

Flynn sat at the desk and updated the long list of to-dos. To her credit, it wasn't a list, exactly. No, she used a pretty high-tech spreadsheet with pivot tables, so she could sort by type of repairs, cost, and priority.

She adjusted the priority on the few things that would get this place back up and open for business. She needed guests, and that meant she needed the plumbing finished in the suites, pronto. The new toilets for all three bathrooms upstairs had been bought months ago. Brandon had taken all three of the working toilets out of the house that day but had never gotten around to installing the new ones. Guests would forgive a dripping faucet, but there was no getting around not having a pot to pee in. No matter how old the house was, a chamber pot was not a charming feature.

Install all three new toilets.
Replace faucet and showerhead in Blue Ridge Retreat bathroom.
Fix leaking sink in Crane Suite.
Finish the flooring in the third bathroom.

Things like upgrading the heat and air system and installing new windows would pay for themselves over time in energy efficiency, but they could wait for a while.

Turning her lengthy to-dos into *ta-daa*s seemed like a daunting undertaking, but it didn't take her more than twenty minutes to have the tasks recategorized and prioritized into a doable plan. When her grandparents had handed over the reins to Crane Creek Bed and Breakfast, it was because they wanted to keep it in the family. They'd trusted her, and that had given her a renewed purpose after the unexpected pink slip.

Rich and Suzy Crane would never have left to travel the country had Flynn not gotten laid off from the consulting firm when she had.

She'd driven up from Charlotte that night, not really knowing what else to do under the circumstances. She'd expected a little commiserating and a good you-can-do-it speech from Granpa. Instead, they'd talked about dreams and her future, and the next thing she knew they were writing up an agreement for her to take over Crane Creek Bed and Breakfast.

Everything had fallen right into place. She'd transferred a large chunk of her savings to them as the down payment. A month later she was in business, and they were packing up a manageable-sized RV to live out their golden years doing whatever they wanted, wherever the mood struck them. First stop, Florida for the winter.

There was a lot more to running a bed and breakfast than she'd given her grandparents credit for. Despite their warnings, she'd thought it would be like endless entertaining. Nope—it was a lot of preparation and constant upkeep, and her years in the corporate world weren't much help. But Flynn loved it. She truly felt it had been her calling all along.

She lowered the screen on her laptop, noticing the date on the calendar to her right.

Friday after next was circled in bright red.

Because her grandparents had been worried Flynn hadn't known what she was getting herself into, they'd insisted on an escape clause in their agreement. Friday after next was the date they'd revisit the situation and roll back or continue with the purchase.

Until just a few weeks ago, she'd thought it was a ridiculous suggestion that she might reconsider. But lately, with all of the repairs needed and then the mismatch with Brandon, maybe it wasn't so crazy.

Can I handle all of this by myself?

Could I really leave all of this?

Going back to work would be so much easier.

But the plan I just rearranged is doable. Completely doable.

Flynn leaned back in the big leather chair and stretched. It made her tired just thinking about all the things that needed to be done around here.

Her phone rang, and her heart hitched at the familiar ring tone.

Speak of the devil. Brandon.

She reached for the phone then yanked her hand back.

No.

With the mounting list of repairs in front of her, it would be even harder to resist him. There wasn't one thing on her list he wasn't capable of doing.

But if Brandon had really been trying to help me, he'd have had this whole list knocked out months ago.

She turned her phone over, letting the call roll to voice mail.

Trying to steel herself against listening to his message, she raised the screen of her laptop and logged into her online banking account. The numbers depressed her. Her checking and savings accounts had begun to dwindle over the last two months since she'd had to close off reservations, and her investments portfolio had taken a beating the past quarter too.

It was bad timing.

She had to invest in the B&B even if that meant spending most of her savings. Even if she took the escape clause route, she surely couldn't return the place in worse shape than when she got it.

Yet she'd always pictured raising a family in the town where her mom had grown up. Where she herself had spent the best days of her own childhood. But she'd dated just about every eligible bachelor in town and no one seemed right. Maybe her dreams for a family weren't meant to be. Maybe this place was all she'd ever have. Was that really so bad?

There were worse situations.

Her phone rang again. The area code was from back in Charlotte. Was Brandon calling from someone else's phone? If he was trying that hard, the least she could do was answer.

"Hello?"

"Hi, Flynn. It's Darcy. How have you been?"

Flynn's posture sagged. Had her hopes danced that quickly at the chance Brandon might be trying to rekindle their spark? Stupid. That's what that was. Just plain stupid. "I'm great." Big fat lie, but she wasn't about to tell her old boss that.

"Things are great here too. We just took on a huge project. We need someone just like you. You tired of playing house yet?"

Flynn laughed politely. "I'm not sure you'd ever be able to afford me, Darcy. I know all the dark, dirty secrets. Remember?"

"I know. That's exactly why I need you. If my money is right, are you available?"

"That's the cart before the horse, don't you think?"

"Not really. I budgeted enough to woo you back."

Now that sounded tempting. "Things are pretty amazing with the B&B. I can't even imagine leaving this, but I'm listening." Flynn could picture her mom's frown at the lie. It was only a half lie though. Business had been great, until it wasn't. There were just a lot of things to fix. Okay fine, just two minutes ago she'd been imagining leaving it all behind. Mom never had approved of lies of any color or size. Little white lies were still lies in Mom's book. She glanced heavenward and nodded a silent apology.

She listened to Darcy's offer, and the details of the project. It was a temporary assignment. Six to ten months tops with a bonus for delivering early. She'd completed this type of project dozens of times. It was totally in her wheelhouse.

Ten minutes later Flynn sat at the desk feeling more torn than ever. The number that Darcy had rolled out was a good thirty percent higher than Flynn would have asked for. Plus, they'd pay for a corporate apartment so she could commute back and forth to Boot Creek on weekends if she wanted.

When they'd laid her off, after the dedication and endless hours she'd put into making her project successful, it had stung. And Darcy's response hadn't helped either. "Nothing personal," Darcy had said. "It's simply a head-count exercise."

Could she ever trust them again after that? It was why the B&B had been so attractive. She wouldn't have to work for anyone else. She had complete control of her future.

She underlined the extra-large salary she'd written on the desk pad in front of her.

Why am I even entertaining this offer?

If she went back to work now, she could explain the short absence from the workforce. Too much more time and it would be like starting over again.

Her life was at a crossroads. If she only knew what tomorrow would bring, it would sure make these decisions a whole lot easier.

The doorbell rang, and Flynn jumped from her chair. She jogged to the door, happy for the welcome reprieve from those thoughts.

The mailman shifted his bag on his shoulder. "Need you to sign for this one."

She scribbled on the form and then took the letter and placed it on top of the stack of magazines and advertisements he'd handed her.

"My niece mentioned you were closed for business," he said. "Everything okay?"

Her mouth went dry. How many of her neighbors had noticed she didn't have any customers? "It's fine. Just working on some renovations."

"Rich and Suzy always kept this place filled even when they had projects going on. Did I ever tell you about the time they had to bring in one of those 'posh potties' trailers for showers and bathrooms because the plumbing had busted in the front yard?"

Everyone had told her that story. That and the one about the time the President of the United States was passing through and the Secret Service had parked a decoy car here. Even had the look-alike sleep overnight. The blue bedroom at the top of the stairs was dubbed the Presidential Suite because of that. "I remember. Too bad they hadn't updated all of the pipes when that happened. I probably wouldn't be replacing all the plumbing now if they had."

"I'm sure Rich had his reasons," the mailman said.

She regretted the snarky remark. Her guess was that he didn't want to shut down and lose the room rate. But Flynn had done the math. If she rented posh potties for the time they'd be out of commission, it would end up costing her more than the income from those rooms, and that was not something she was willing to do. Although there was always the long-tail view. Happy customers meant repeat customers, and even if she only broke even during renovations, repeat customers were something to appreciate.

Flynn started to back inside, pulling the door closed.

"Flynn?"

She looked up and saw Megan coming up the walkway. "I thought you'd be up to your ears in packing for your trip to California this week," Flynn said.

"I am." Megan scrunched her pretty face, then caught the edge of the front door and dipped inside behind Flynn. "Was hoping you could help me package up the last of my candle inventory if you have some time. The place is in a complete mess. I'm feeling a little overwhelmed."

"No problem. All I have is time right now."

"What's that mean?" Megan's brown eyes widened.

"No customers. No help."

"I heard you and Brandon . . ." Megan made a cutthroat gesture.

"It wasn't quite that dramatic, but yeah, it's over."

"Are you sad about it?" Megan cocked a hip. "You don't really seem sad."

Flynn sighed. Maybe she wasn't. "I think I'm more sad about the idea of not having someone than I am that Brandon wasn't the one."

"I wasn't a Brandon fan. You know that."

"I do."

Her look said I-told-you-so, but those words didn't come out of Megan's mouth. "For sure. Anyone who gets between you and your friends, or you and your family, is not the right one."

He had done that. Brandon had made excuse after excuse to not spend time with her friends. "This place needs some life in it. I need to get these rooms filled."

"You do love taking care of your guests."

"I was thinking about kids." It wasn't like this was the first time she and Megan had talked about this. She was probably tired of hearing about it.

"Of course you were. You can have my quota of children too."

"I'm beginning to think that's never going to happen for me if I don't get busy."

"Don't be silly. If you want children, you'll have them. You don't need a guy in your life to make that happen. You could adopt. What is it that you want? The relationship or the children?"

Flynn bit her lip. "The answer should be both, shouldn't it?"

"Well, yeah. No. Maybe? I don't think there's really a right or wrong answer," Megan said. "I will say this, though. You think this inn is a lot to handle alone? Honey, raising a kid by yourself is no picnic. Talk to Angie about that. Billy is about the best kid in the whole world, and raising him alone wore her out. Having Jackson in her life is the best thing that ever happened to her."

"I know. Jackson's great, and now you've got Noah. Maybe I'm just feeling left out. I'm so over looking for the last good guy in a pile of duds. I'm tired. Confused. Lonely."

Megan rolled her eyes. "And dramatic?"

"I'm not being dramatic. I'm just trying to be realistic." Flynn hesitated. Should she even mention the job offer?

"What?" Megan cocked her head. "What aren't you telling me? I know that look."

"I had an offer to go back to work. My old boss called with a *very* nice offer."

"That job sucked the life out of you. You love this place."

"There's so much to fix around here."

"Brandon let things pile up on purpose. He knew he had a good thing going. We'll find someone to help you out. In the long run it'll be way cheaper than your live-in handyman."

"It's not just the B&B. It's this little town. If I'm not going to find a Mr. Right, then I'd at least like to be somewhere that I could do things. Everyone here is part of a couple. Angie and Jackson. Katy and Derek. You and Noah. I'm the odd man out."

"Nothing manly about you."

"Thanks for that. Some days I wonder if the guys realize that I'm a woman."

"They do. Be patient. If you'd quit hooking up with the wrong guys, maybe the right one would finally have a chance to come along. Trust me, you're going to meet somebody that deserves you. And you'll have this business right back where it was in no time." Megan brushed her hair from her face. "I came here to get you to help me, but what can I do to help you?"

Flynn hated to put her troubles on Megan. She had her own stress right now, but no one knew her better. "Help me figure out what I'm going to do next. Remember the stupid escape clause my grandparents

33

insisted on? Maybe it wasn't so stupid. That discussion comes up Friday after next."

"You're really considering not sticking it out? That's so not like you."

"Harder than this is telling my grandparents that they need to put the place up for sale. I feel like a failure."

"That's why that clause was put in the contract in the first place."

"I don't want to let them down, though. They were counting on me to carry on this legacy for them. It's what we'd always dreamed about. You've got to help me sort all of it out."

"You could always sell the business, name and all. That way it's still in existence. Everyone wins. I'll call Winona down at the realty office and get her to come over and appraise the house."

"That would be great. I worry about my grandparents being able to enjoy the retirement life they've started to live if I decide not to go through with the deal. I hate to let them down. We've had this plan forever, for me to take over this place. You know that."

"I do."

"Maybe I jumped on it too soon after I got laid off. It seemed like the perfect timing. The perfect solution, but now I'm not so sure."

"Then let's get your ducks in a row before you make any hasty decisions."

"I'm going to miss you like crazy. Who else would ever listen to me babble in circles when I'm stressed and confused?"

"Me. On the phone. In person if you come visit."

"I will if I can get away." She let out a sigh.

"Quit frowning. Everything will come in the right time. We just have to believe that. Trust the journey. I mean really . . . who would've believed I'd be packing up and moving to California? *Ever?* I'd have called you crazy if you'd said that to me."

"I never thought you'd leave Boot Creek. It's going to be a lot harder for us to be your new scent testers for your candles. You'll be hard-pressed to find a nose like mine out there in California."

"I can mail samples to you."

"You've got an answer for everything."

"Flynn, you need to figure out what you want, because I can promise you this—if you know what the goal is . . . there *is* an answer to everything." Megan snapped her fingers. "Listen to me preaching. I came for a reason. I need packing tape and your help."

"Those things I can do." Flynn walked to the kitchen and came back with a two-pack of packing tape. "Let's go." Flynn grabbed her keys from the hook next to the door, and just as they opened the door to leave, a loud thump followed by a hiss stopped them both midstep.

"What was that?" Megan asked.

Flynn closed her eyes, leaning her head against the door. "It can't be good."

Chapter Four

Ford wiped down his tools and put them back on the rack. The end-of-day ritual of cleaning up his workbench set the stage for the next day's creativity.

He picked up his phone and checked his messages, then snapped a picture of his latest creation and posted it to social media. His mom posted a comment immediately.

No surprise. Five o'clock here meant eight o'clock back in Nashville. She'd be perusing the Internet while Dad worked in his office at home.

This time the compliments were earned, though, because this piece was extra special. The color, texture, and shape had formed in his mind so clearly that he'd only hoped he could translate it into reality. Glass wasn't always as cooperative as his imagination. The piece had come together so flawlessly that at each step he just knew something was going to go wrong. But it hadn't, and there was no question he'd created his best work of art to date.

"Ford, I'm glad you're still here." Winston Ziegler, the owner, walked over and parked himself against the table filled with colored bits of glass.

"I was just packing it in for the day."

"I like the new piece." Winston admired it, leaning in closer to check out the details. "This might be your best showing yet."

"Thanks, Winston." A compliment like that from him meant a lot. He'd been a great mentor the last couple of years. And the reputation of Glory Glassworks Gallery had put Ford on the fast track to being able to make a living blowing glass. He'd even been contracted for specialty items like the huge vases used in a photo shoot at the Biltmore for a holiday magazine spread. "I just took it out of the annealing oven an hour ago." Ford glanced at his signature markings. He was proud of this piece—unique in design and scale. "I'm thinking about doing a series of these to sell next spring. What do you think?"

"I think you'll do really well with that." Winston ran a hand along the stubble under his chin.

Ford's ears perked up; maybe it was his short time as a lawyer that had given him the knack of sensing when people were not being completely honest with him. "But?"

"No buts. People will be in line to buy these. They always love your stuff."

"Then we'll both benefit. Right?"

Winston let out a breath. "We need to talk."

"What's wrong, man?"

"We're shutting down," Winston said.

"For how long?"

"I need you to get your personal stuff out of here before you leave town."

"But I'm leaving tomorrow night. What's going on? Are you firing me?"

Winston lifted his hand. He looked tired. Worried. "No, Ford. It's not like that."

"Then what is it like?"

"Maizie isn't well. I need to take her down to Seattle where we can get her better care. I know it's not much notice, but I can help you move all of your things up to your place."

"Can't you just have someone handle the shipping from here while you're away?"

"No. That won't work."

He locked his knees. "Do you need me to stay and run the place? I can stay."

"Ford, I wish that was an option, but I'll be honest, I've got this place overmortgaged, and I haven't been able to make the bills. I have no choice but to shut her down."

"How about I buy it?"

"That window of opportunity slipped by months ago. I don't think they're going to let me do that."

"Winston? Why didn't you say anything? I might've been able to help."

"I kept thinking I'd find a way out of this mess." Lines etched Winston's face as he frowned. "I'm sorry. I know this isn't convenient timing. You need to move everything you possibly can tonight, because I have no idea how fast things are going to happen. They could padlock the place, and if they do, I don't want you to lose any of your stuff in the midst of it," Winston said. "I've got some boxes in my office. I'll help you get everything moved. We can fill up both of our trucks."

"Don't worry about that. I'll get my stuff moved." Ford's gut ached like someone had sucker punched him. "I can't believe this is happening. You. Maizie. Y'all have been so good to me. I want to help."

"There's nothing you can do. I appreciate it, though. I really do."

Ford grappled for some way to help. Something to say. "Will you keep me posted if anything changes? Even if I'm still down in North Carolina. Call me if they let you put this place up for sale. I'll come right back."

"I've got all of your information. I'll keep you posted. Let me get you those boxes."

Ford watched Winston walk out. His shoulders slumped like a boulder rested upon them. This changed Winston's life too. He wasn't sure who he felt sorrier for at the moment.

He packed up the bulk of his tools and took them out to the truck. The back of his SUV filled quickly with the number of things he'd accumulated. He saved the backseat for his most expensive pieces. The rest would have to wait until tomorrow. Hopefully the bank wouldn't beat him to the punch.

With the fragile cargo, Ford drove as carefully as he could up the hill to his property.

An army-green '54 Ford sat parked in front of his house. He could see Benson's tall silhouette moving around the house, closing the vents on the foundation. Ford had hired him to winterize the place in case he was gone longer than expected. There was no way he'd risk letting anything happen to this place after all the work he'd put into it. Besides, Benson needed something to do.

"What's all this?" Benson asked.

"Bad news."

Benson straightened. "You got fired?"

"No. They're shutting down."

"Why would they close down Glory Glassworks Gallery? Ziegler loves that place."

"Not by choice. Bank is foreclosing on them."

"Shit. That's the fourth business in the past two months to take a hit."

"It's tough all over," Ford said. "Bad time of year."

"Only going to get worse. You'll be gone when we're all stuck here with neighbors that have no jobs."

"I'll only be gone a month." Ford tossed a set of keys to Benson.

"Word down at the Moose is you'll be gone for good."

If Ford had to guess, Benson had fired up the gossip a while ago by telling folks he was winterizing the place. Ford probably could've gambled on things being fine this time of year, but he'd never really been a betting man. "They are just acting like gossipy old women. I'll be back. You can count on that. Hold the fort down for me."

"I've got it under control." Benson eyed him. "You really are coming back, aren't ya?"

"I said I was, didn't I?" It had taken Ford a long time to feel accepted in the small Alaska town, but he felt like one of them now. But all this talk about one simple trip to North Carolina was kind of ticking him off.

"No one expected you'd stay as long as you have."

The bets placed on how long he'd last hadn't really been all that secret. And truthfully, he'd almost been ready to throw in the towel when he heard about the wagers. "I'll be back. Do you think I busted my ass for two years building this place only to leave it behind?"

"Well, you got no job to come back to."

"I'll figure something out."

"You better, because I don't see you as the hunting and fishing type."

"I've done my share over the years. You seem to forget I grew up in Tennessee."

"Nashville ain't Alaska. What? You going to hunt for dinner with a guitar?"

"Not every part of Tennessee is Nashville. My parents had a farm on the outskirts of town. I know my way around this kind of stuff."

"Right." He slapped Ford on the back. "And yet you paid me to come winterize your house for you."

Ford shrugged off the comment. The only reason he'd paid Benson to winterize his place was to help Benson out. A heart attack had sidelined the guy from his usual fishing season. But Ford would never tell Benson that. Some things you did just because they were the right things to do.

And now that the glass shop was closing, there really wasn't any reason for him to rush right back after his visit to Boot Creek. Maybe he'd add a short visit to see his parents onto the end. Mom anyway. Dad would make himself scarce. The man had not and probably never would forgive him for not following in his footsteps.

Benson pulled his coat on. "I've got to get on home. It's meatloaf night. I'm never late on meatloaf night."

Somehow Ford doubted meatloaf was on the heart-smart meal plan Benson was supposed to be following, but that wasn't for him to worry about.

The sound of Benson's old pickup truck chugging down the lane echoed in the distance. Ford waited until he was out of sight to start unloading his stuff. The last thing he needed was old Benson having a heart attack trying to help him carry the heavy boxes into the house. The man had been more like a father to Ford than his own the last few years.

He carried each box from the SUV to the house, filling the right corner of the living room; there was plenty of space left in the huge living room. Not that you needed a lot of room to entertain in a small town in Alaska, but one day this would be where he and his family would celebrate birthdays, anniversaries, and holidays.

Pride swelled in him as he looked at every tiny detail like someone who'd never seen it before. He'd spent the last two years on the finishing work. He'd modified the wood and iron stair railing to include small colorful blown-glass inserts. The huge stone fireplace wasn't unlike most found in log homes, but he'd personally picked out the tree the mantel had been carved from. Junior had turned it into a one-of-a-kind piece of art with the intricate relief carved scene. And the carefully planned back-lit gallery niches highlighted more of his work. Even the chandelier had been his own creation, sending beautiful darts of color around the room.

If anyone had told him back in college that he'd be living in a log home in Alaska one day, and his college education was just a piece of paper in a frame, he'd have called them crazy, but that was okay by him.

He was quite certain all of the guys he went to college with were in debt eyeballs deep with the expensive homes and cars, not to mention the high-dollar shopping and day spa habits of their too-blonde, spray-tanned wives.

To be fair, though, any woman seeing this house for the first time would be impressed. A few gentle feminine touches wouldn't hurt though.

His dad could make smart-ass remarks about Ford giving up a good career to be a starving artist, but Ford knew better. He was far from starving, and no one would ever talk him out of his life in Alaska. This place was paid for. When money ran low, he simply worked harder to sell more glass or took on special consignment work.

With all of the boxes inside, he picked up his itinerary from his desk. Tomorrow night he'd be on a flight to Raleigh. Thank goodness he'd taken that gig.

He unpacked his glass and arranged the pieces on the floating shelves in the middle of the room. He stepped back, seeing the clear improvements in his new work as compared to the pieces he'd cherished up until tonight.

What would happen if the bank auctioned off Glory Glassworks Gallery? The place would probably sit empty for a while. No one would want to do anything with it in the winter.

Getting a loan to buy the gallery shouldn't pose a problem, though his bank account was still lean from all the work he'd put into the house. If push came to shove, he'd be able to take out a mortgage on the house to pay for the business. He'd often dreamed of the day he might own his own glass studio. Maybe this was his lucky year.

Only, having his dream become reality at the expense of his friend's misfortune just didn't feel good. But Winston would go to the ends of the earth and sacrifice everything for Maizie. Ford knew that the business was the least of Winston's worries right now.

Chapter Five

The loud bang-clunk that had come from the back of the house had Flynn and Megan making a beeline toward the kitchen. The smell of smoke hung in the air.

"I don't think this is good," Megan said, waving a hand in front of her face to clear the cloud.

"Smells electrical." Flynn followed her nose to the basement door. "It's coming from here." She reached for the door handle.

"Haven't you seen a single scary movie? What if something is on fire down there?"

She retracted her hand and pulled out her phone and dialed 911.

"Boot Creek Dispatch, please state your emergency."

"This is Flynn over at Crane Creek Bed and Breakfast. There was a loud bang and there's smoke coming from my basement."

"We'll send the fire truck right out. Please leave the building."

She ended the call. "Come on." Flynn grabbed Megan's hand and then her purse as they rushed out of the house and stood on the lawn.

A moment later sirens blared down Main Street.

The bright red fire truck pulled to the curb. Firemen hopped out and headed inside as the captain stopped to talk to Flynn before directing the team.

Neighbors lined the street, craning their necks to see what was going on.

Flynn folded her arms across her chest, feeling like everyone was wondering what she'd done wrong. It hadn't helped that the captain was an old buddy of Granpa's. Megan, bless her, satisfied the curiosity of the onlookers.

It felt like a long time before any of the firemen came back out of the house, but when they did, they had their helmets pushed up and were talking easily. The captain met the guys at the stoop and then walked over to Flynn.

"It's safe to reenter. The smoke was coming from one of the fuses on the electrical panel. That old wiring could use some attention. We've cut the power to that section."

Her heart sank.

Megan's look brightened. "That's great news, right? I mean that can be fixed way easier than a fire."

"Not really." Flynn's eyes glassed over. Even though she'd made a plan to get the B&B back up and open for business, this was going to delay that plan. "There's no way I can afford new wiring and a furnace on top of all of the other problems around here if I'm not bringing in any money." Flynn fought back tears. "Would you mind if I meet you back over at your house in a little while? I think I need a little time to get my head around this."

"Sure." Megan hugged Flynn. "It's going to work out. Don't let it upset you." She turned and started down the sidewalk. Her house was just a couple of blocks away. "Come on down whenever. I'll be packing for a while."

"I won't be long. Call me if you think of anything else you need me to bring."

Neighbors peeled back from the curb as the fire truck moved down the street.

Inside, Flynn closed and locked the door. Not that anyone would come in, but she needed to be alone with her thoughts and with this place. But first, she needed to get the power back on safely.

She pulled out the huge binder Granpa had put together over the years. Just about every trick in the book was in that huge honkin' thing. She easily put her hands on the phone number for the electrician and dialed him.

Small-town pluses were on her side. The electrician would be here in the morning, and he'd told her not to worry, that he'd have her back in business in no time, reminding her that he'd been working on the wiring on this house since he was her age.

Flynn went into the living room and sprawled out on the couch. She loved this place, but this many things going wrong had to be a sign of some sort. And on the tail of that random offer from her old boss? Like the red flags she'd ignored with Brandon, was she simply turning her back on a clear message?

If there was one thing she did believe in, it was listening to the universe when it was sending signals. And these had been real live smoke signals. They may not have burned the house down this time, but if she didn't start paying attention, who knew what could happen next.

I need to use that escape clause.

She was in over her head.

This was a sign that she needed to move in another direction. She picked up her phone and mustered the strength to call her grandparents. On the third ring her grandmother picked up the phone.

"Gran? It's Flynn."

"Hey, sweetheart. Your ears must've been burning."

That and the house.

There was a muffled sound as her grandmother pressed her hand over the phone. "You won't believe who it is, Rich." Gran's voice came back on the line, strong and bouncy. "It's so good to hear from you."

"How are things going?" Flynn pasted a smile on her face. A trick she'd learned early in her career to sound happy on the phone. It usually worked with clients. She sure hoped Gran didn't pick up on her real mood.

"Never better. Your grandfather bought a fancy golf cart."

"Granpa golfs?"

"No. Goodness gracious, no. He's not the athletic type at all, but we've found our dream place. You won't believe it. They don't allow cars! Just golf carts. Isn't that absolutely charming?"

Flynn's throat tightened.

"Wait until you see him riding around in it. He's like one of those NASCAR drivers. I've been calling him Richard Petty. Get it?"

"I get it," Flynn said with a laugh she didn't feel.

"I told him if he doesn't stop grinning like a wild man, he's gonna get bugs in his teeth."

"She did say that!" Her grandfather's voice rang in from the background. "I'm not afraid of a few bugs. Protein. That's all those are."

"Don't be gross, Rich." A hearty chuckle came across the line. Flynn wasn't sure she'd ever heard them this lively. "He's a hot mess. You should see this place. It's perfect. And we have you to thank. If you hadn't taken over the B&B, we'd never have found this new phase of our lives. Now, honey, you called us, what's up?"

She sat down on the couch feeling like a complete failure. They'd been so generous to trust her with their hard-earned reputation at Crane Creek Bed and Breakfast. And the special family sale price of the inn was one heck of a deal. She'd dreamed of it too, but in her dreams she'd already had a husband to help, and children. How would she ever find a husband or find the time to have the family she'd always so desperately wanted if she was tied down to this place . . . in this little town?

Selfish?

Daddy was selfish. She'd promised herself she'd never be like that.

"I . . . well . . ." It wouldn't take long for them to hear about the fire. She couldn't keep that a secret. "I wanted to let you know before you heard from your old neighbors that the fire truck was here a little while ago."

"Oh, goodness. Flynn? Is everything okay? You're not hurt, are you?"

"No. I'm fine. Megan was here. I called the fire department immediately, but everything is fine. Turns out there's some faulty wiring."

"The wiring? I told your grandfather we needed to fix that."

"You were right," Flynn said.

"That's not good. That'll cost a pretty penny to fix, but your grandfather and I had already put money aside for new wiring. We knew it needed to be done."

"I'm worried maybe I'm not cut out for this, Gran. So many things have gone wrong. I hate to let you down."

"Don't be silly. It takes time to get into the groove, but you're doing a great job. Our old clients have been raving about you and your fabulous cooking. Now, you get to work, and I'll get your grandfather to call the electrician and get all of that taken care of for you."

"I've already called the electrician. He'll be here in the morning."

"We will help pay for that. Don't you worry about a thing."

"Are you sure? I don't want to jeopardize your new plans."

"Of course I'm sure. Your grandfather is so tight he squeaks, but we've had the money set aside for years for that work. This one is on us."

"How will I thank you, Gran?" *And how can I let them down?*

"Don't be silly. Just be happy, sweetie."

Happy? Flynn hung up the phone feeling trapped. So trapped she could barely breathe. Keeping the Crane Creek Bed and Breakfast in the family was important. She loved the house and the people in this town, but she sure did miss having some free time, and the slim pickings of available men in this small town depressed her.

If she sat here any longer, she'd probably just roll up into a ball like a roly-poly and cry herself to sleep. In the dark. With no electricity and a mountain of trouble.

No. There'd be no pity parties tonight. She grabbed her coat and walked down the street to Megan's. The old gas station that Megan's dad had given her was still one of the coolest homes in this town. And now Megan was moving away. Another reason things looked less than bright right now.

Flynn knocked on the door and walked inside. "Where are you?"

"In the candle shop," Megan called from the back.

Flynn followed the long hall back to the space where Megan poured and stored her beeswax candles for her business, Balanced Buzz. Boxes with the cute little beeswax and bee logo were stacked near the rear garage door ready for shipment to customers. Others were marked for shipment to California.

Megan wielded a tape gun with precision across a large cardboard box and then slapped a label on the top. "You okay?"

"I've been better." She walked over and started folding a flat into a box. "The electrician assures me he can get the power on tomorrow. We'll see."

"That's great news." Megan scooted the box across the floor with her foot. "I just got off the phone with Angie. She can't come tonight. Jackson just sprung on her that Ford's coming into town, so she says she needs to clean her house."

"From the wedding? Alaska Ford?"

"Yep. He took an artist-in-residence job around here somewhere. He's stopping in to stay with them for a couple of days. I don't know why she's bothering to clean. I doubt some dude from Alaska is really going to notice a little dust and fingerprints."

"Be nice," Flynn said. "He's a good guy."

"Y'all seemed to hit it off last year. Maybe *he* is your Mr. Right."

"He lives in A-freaking-ice-cube-laska. Remember?"

"Noah lived in California and we worked things out."

"That's different."

"How so?"

"Because you can do your job from anywhere. I can't do my job from Alaska."

"Maybe he'll move back here. Or you could run a B&B in Alaska."

"Stop. My focus is on me." She grabbed a box flat and started taping it into shape. "I spoke with Gran before I came over. They're so happy . . . My grandfather is even cruising around in a golf cart. Can you even picture that?"

"Not in a million years."

"Exactly. They are like teenagers again. It's kind of cute. I didn't have the heart to tell them that I might have to go back to Charlotte to work just to pay for the place."

"You're not going to do that." Megan stepped over and hugged Flynn. "Don't do something you can't undo. Girl, I love you, but I'm not sure you know what you want."

"I do know what I want. I just don't know how to make it all happen."

"What's the problem?"

"I like running the B&B, and it was making great money before I got sidetracked on all of the upgrades—"

"And with Brandon."

"True. I should have just concentrated on making the repairs that were needed instead of going hog wild. I can make it work, but it's a little isolating. I'd like some flexibility in my schedule. Otherwise, I don't know how I'm ever going to meet someone. And I know you keep telling me to cool it, but eventually I'd like to be in a couple."

"I've told you before that you could block out dates that you're not going to host guests."

Why didn't I do that? Probably because I was afraid the last customer might be the last *customer. I didn't trust that there'd be a steady stream . . .*

and there always had been. "That sounds ridiculously easy, but I could do that. I just never have."

"Wasn't it you that used to tell me how to manage my calendar to allow for the things I wanted to do?"

Megan was right. Flynn had given her that speech a million times. "Do as I say, not as I do?" She had to admit that was a harder piece of advice to follow now that she was in business for herself too.

"Use your own advice." Megan loaded another box. "You know how I felt about love. I wasn't looking for it. Didn't even think I wanted it. I was perfectly happy doing my own thing. But Flynn, when I'm with Noah I feel more like myself. Like my best self. I don't feel like I'm compromising or even having to try."

Flynn tucked candles into a box. "So what you're saying to me is to quit trying so hard, and let things happen."

"Yeah. It seemed to work for me." Megan squatted and scribbled a list of contents down the side of the box in a smelly Magic Marker. "I want this feeling for you so much."

Flynn's eyes teared. It was the same advice Angie had given her. "Thank you, Megan." She hoped the sound of the tape being strapped across the box hid the choke in her voice. "I'm going to miss you."

"Good, because I'm already missing you. If you're not working a new job, then we can have fun whenever I'm in town. There's time to figure all of this out." Megan sat on the box. "I really think things are going to work out for you right here in Boot Creek."

Flynn started packing supplies, carefully tucking wads of newspaper between items to protect and keep them from shifting. "I can't drag my feet too long. That top-dollar job won't last long."

"Just give it one month," Megan said. "That's when I'll be back in town for Mom's birthday. If you want to throw in the towel then, I'll even help you pack."

"But the date on the calendar is just a week away."

Megan cocked her head. "You know your grandparents would reschedule that for you."

"You're right." All she had to do was ask, and they hadn't brought it up yet anyway. "I can do that." She held out her hand and Megan shook it. "I'm going to focus on chipping away at this list and getting the electrical and furnace taken care of. If I can get the reservations opened back up by the end of December or early January, then I'll be fine. If not, it's time for a change." She had no idea what that change would be, but something had to happen.

Chapter Six

Ford pulled his duffel bag from the overhead compartment. Flying from Alaska to North Carolina was a haul, and the only thing on his mind was getting somewhere that he could stretch out after being cramped all day long.

He hitched his bag over his shoulder and made his way closer to the continual "buh-bye, buh-bye, thank you for flying with us, buh-bye," then headed up the jet bridge. Following the signs, he texted Jackson.

Ford: On My Way To Baggage Claim.

Jackson: Already Here.

As Ford rode down the escalator he spotted Jackson. Ford responded with a chin nod.

"Thanks for coming to pick me up," Ford said. "Angie didn't come with you?"

"No, she's making dinner. She's worried to death you're going to be starving after being in the air all day." Jackson grabbed his gut. "Girl loves to cook. I swear I've put on like twelve pounds since the wedding."

"That's usually a good sign," Ford said.

"Not good. Great. I wish I'd found and married her three years earlier, even if I am getting a gut." Jackson patted his stomach. "I knew she was the one the day I met her. Still can't believe how lucky I am."

Ford didn't have any trouble meeting girls, but he'd yet to meet one that turned his head and kept his attention the way Angie had done to Jackson. Even Angie's cute friend.

"I can't believe you hadn't mentioned the glass shop gig sooner. Were you going to try to come to North Carolina without contacting me?"

"I know you and Angie are still in the honeymoon stage. I didn't want to be a bother."

"There's always room in my life for friends, and Angie feels the same way."

Three short horn blasts rang out from the back wall, and the conveyor started chugging in a circle as luggage spit out of the chute onto the belt. People converged on the baggage area like it was filled with gold coins, practically elbowing one another to get a front spot to hurry and wait for their bag to make its way to the roundabout.

Ford crossed his arms and hung back as the others rushed by.

"So, what else is new in Alaska? Still no special someone in your life?"

"Not yet. Just work, and now there's really not much of that."

"What do you mean? You must be doing something right to get this gig down here at PRIZM. Angie says that's kind of a big deal to get asked to teach."

"Yeah, that's all good, but the glass shop I was working for back home suddenly shut down."

"When did that happen?"

It still didn't seem real. "About twenty hours before I headed here."

"Whoa. What are you going to do?"

"Catch up with you. Take a little downtime. Fish or something. I wish I could buy the glass shop, but Winston isn't sure the bank is going to let him sell. It may go straight to foreclosure."

"That might end up a better deal for you anyway."

"Maybe."

"So how did this opportunity at PRIZM even come about?"

"I went and visited their shop while I was here for your wedding. You probably don't remember. You were kind of sidetracked."

"Tell me about it." Jackson shook his head. "The wedding. The surprise room for Billy. Y'all really made me a superstar with that truck bed. He loves that room."

"We had a great time working on that. Must've been what inspired me to kick things into high gear when I got home. Not that a year is fast, but I did finally finish my house."

"Get out! That's cool. Guess we've lost touch a little since the wedding. Sorry."

Ford shrugged it off. "I didn't call you either. We were busy. Nothing new."

"True. Hope you brought pictures of your house. You know Angie is going to want to see them."

"I did."

"So, you're really going to make a home there?"

"Didn't realize that was news."

"I thought it might lose its charm after a while. And honestly you never were one to sit around and do nothing, so it's kind of hard to imagine you stuck inside all winter."

"There's plenty to do. I feel more alive there than anywhere I've ever been." Ford lifted a finger for Jackson to hold his thought, jogged over to the conveyor, and pulled a royal blue backpack off. He lifted the handle and rolled it behind him. "Let's get out of here." Ford headed for the big glass doors.

Jackson dug in his front pants pocket and led the way outside. "I'm parked just across the way."

They crossed four lanes in front of the terminal to the parking garage.

One click of the key fob and Jackson's brand-new Ford dually blinked a hello with its lights.

"New truck?"

"Yep. Needed it to tow the new horse trailer we bought."

"Angie is letting you teach Billy how to ride?"

"And her."

"That girl is perfect for you."

"Told you, didn't I? Noah and Megan are doing great. Austin is already married. That only leaves you, my man. And we all thought you'd be the first of all of us to get married."

"Maybe I'm the luckiest of all." But that was total BS. He wanted what Jackson had.

"I'm here to tell you no one feels luckier than me," Jackson said.

The look on Jackson's face bore out the truth of his words. Ford wasn't usually the jealous type, but darn if he wasn't feeling just a little envious right now.

"Angie told me to let you know that you're welcome to stay with us while you're in town."

"I couldn't do that. There's a dorm across the street from the Art Institute. I didn't check that out when I was there last year, but it's supposed to be nice."

"Billy can camp out in our room. Angie was already changing the sheets for you when I left."

"I couldn't kick Billy out of that cool pickup truck bed."

"Sure you can."

"Not because of him, but because of me. I'd leave here wanting one, and I'm afraid it might be a little hard to woo a woman with a pickup truck bed in my master bedroom."

"That could be a problem." Jackson started up the truck and pulled out of the parking garage.

Ford leapt at the chance to bring up Flynn. "I was going to book a room at the B&B we stayed at last year for the wedding, Flynn's place, but the online app said there were no vacancies. She must be doing really well."

"She's been doing some remodeling." He merged onto the interstate and then gunned the engine. "I'm sure she'd be willing to let a friend stay, though."

Jackson looked at him across the truck.

"What?" Ford said.

"I guess I wouldn't be a friend if I didn't warn you that Angie already invited Flynn over for dinner with us tonight. Hope that doesn't piss you off."

Piss me off? Hardly. Just made the long, tiring day worth it. "Not at all. It'll be good to see Flynn. She's a nice gal."

"Not bad to look at either."

"Oh, I remember." Ford regretted it as soon as the words left his lips. "She's not seeing anyone?"

Jackson shot him that look. The one when a guy knows you're fishing for information, but he let it go. Which worried Ford.

"Just broke up with some guy, from what Angie said. I think he was part of the renovation problems."

"Too bad," Ford said.

When they got to the house in Boot Creek, they hadn't even gotten out of the truck when Billy ran outside to greet them. "Daddy Jack!" Billy leapt into Jackson's arms and hugged his neck.

Ford walked around the front of the truck with his bags. "How are you doing, Sport?"

"My name's not Sport. I'm Billy. You don't remember me?"

Ford laughed. "Yeah, I think I remember. Aren't you the really cool guy with the pickup truck bed?"

Billy did a fist pump. "Yes!"

"I thought that was you."

"Mom's making her baked spaghetti for you. You're going to love it."

Billy grabbed Jackson's hand. Ford leaned in. "You let him call you Jack? You beat the hell out of a few guys for doing that, if I recall."

"When he came up with Daddy Jack, it flat-out melted my heart. Don't you dare try it though. I'm pretty sure I can still kick your ass."

Ford had been touched by the enthusiasm of Billy's greeting too.

They hadn't even gotten to the door and he could already smell the garlic and tomato sauce. His stomach growled. He hadn't had anything but a protein bar, almonds, and a chocolate chip cookie all day long.

"Something smells like heaven in Italy," Ford said.

Angie set the plates she'd been carrying to the table on the counter as they entered and ran over to give him a hug. "I'm so glad you're here. At least this time I can treat you like a real guest, since I'm not up to my eyeballs in wedding plans."

"Last time was great. Best wedding I've ever been in. Guess Noah's will be next." He glanced over at Flynn. She looked taller and even prettier, if that was possible. And this time instead of a bridesmaid gown she was in jeans and a long-sleeve T-shirt. His kind of girl. "Flynn. It's great to see you." His breath hitched a little when he said her name. He hoped she hadn't noticed. "You look great."

"Thank you. It's good to see you too."

Flynn didn't seem all that excited to see him. Maybe that attraction he'd remembered from last year wasn't quite as strong as he'd remembered.

Angie walked over to Billy. "Go wash your hands, Billy. We're about ready to eat."

Billy ran from the room.

Jackson said, "Ford told me he tried to rent a room at the B&B but the website showed you were booked."

"I don't want to impose," Ford interjected.

"I can't very well rent rooms with all of the bathrooms out of commission."

"What happened?" Ford followed Jackson and Flynn into the dining room and took a seat. "Water line break?"

"Not even something that difficult. The toilets need to be set and I have new fixtures. My handyman took an unexpected exit."

Must be that boyfriend. "Oh. That happens. Doesn't sound like what you need done will take all that long. We can do that while I'm in town," Ford said, glancing over to Jackson. "Heck, I can do that without Jackson's help."

"Wouldn't that be nice," Flynn said with a nervous laugh. She sat down and put her napkin in her lap. Billy climbed into the chair next to her.

"I always get to sit next to Flynn," Billy announced. "I'm going to marry her when she's old enough for me."

"I hope everyone is hungry," Angie said while trying to stifle her giggles over Billy's claims.

"I'm hungry enough to eat a bear," Ford said, swiping his hand in the air like a claw to get a rise out of Billy.

"A polar bear," Billy said with his eyes wide.

Sitting here at this table tonight felt like everything he'd dreamed of. Simple. The family. The home-cooked casserole. The playful banter with Billy. "Polar bears can get to be nine hundred pounds. I might not be able to eat a whole polar bear."

"Oh?" Billy's eyebrows pulled together. "Maybe just a polar bear sandwich then."

Ford scratched his head. "With french fries, maybe. There's always room for french fries, right?"

"And ketchup."

"Oh, heck yeah." Ford raised his hand for a high five.

"You're the coolest guy ever." Billy tilted his head, as if he was pondering something very important. "Are you an Eskimo?"

"Nope. I'm just a guy from Tennessee who lives in Alaska."

They all laughed.

"You should have been here the other day. I was a pirate for Halloween. A pirate could eat a whole polar bear." Billy put a hand over his eye and hooked his other hand. "I even had a patch."

Angie reached over and patted Billy's hand. "Want to say grace for us?"

"Yes, ma'am." Billy grinned, looked at Flynn, then bowed his head. "For food and health and happy days . . . receive our gratitude and our praise. In serving others Lord may we . . . repay our debt of love to thee." His head bounced and lowered again. "And thank thee too for Aunt Flynn and Ford. Amen."

Jackson passed the casserole dish to Ford, then followed with salad and the garlic bread. Once everyone had their plates full, Ford took a mouthful of baked spaghetti. "This is great."

"Thanks, Ford. It's super easy to make. Billy's favorite."

"I know how to help make it," Billy said.

"You're going to make the best husband ever," Flynn teased.

"Yes ma'am." Billy shoveled another bite into his mouth, slurping the length of a long noodle with a squeak. "Plus now I'm in Cub Scouts, so I'll be able to do even more stuff."

Ford looked over at Jackson. "We had some good times in Boy Scouts back in the day."

"Sure did. That and football."

"We should get out and toss some while I'm here," Ford said.

"Cool. Can we, Daddy Jack?"

"Sure, buddy."

Angie piped up. "I don't think I'm ready for Billy and football."

"Mo-om." Billy looked toward Jackson with pleading eyes.

Ford remembered his own mother pacing on game day mornings. "My mom was like yours, Billy. She was always a nervous wreck when I played sports."

"Well, dang," Jackson said. "Maybe my mom didn't love me as much as I thought. She never seemed worried about me at all."

"You were kind of a wild kid. She probably had to pick her battles with you. You're lucky the poor woman didn't take up drinking with all the crazy stuff you used to do."

"Sounds like there are some stories I might not have heard yet," Angie said.

"Don't know if we have that much time," Ford said. Jackson seemed to agree by the way he laughed.

"How long are you going to be in town teaching?" Flynn asked Ford.

"A month."

"I've heard those are hard positions to get. Your work is amazing though, so I'm not surprised."

Her smile made his heart race. She'd been interested enough to Google him. That was something. The corner of his mouth tugged into a smile. "You've seen my work?"

"On the Internet. You mentioned that award on Facebook, remember?"

"I do." He'd messaged her quite a bit those first few months after they'd met.

"I was curious," she said with a shrug.

Great. He'd made her feel awkward. "I figured I'd come out early and grab a few vacation days before I get started. We should do something while I'm in town." He leveled his gaze on Flynn, who just smiled politely until she realized he was referring to her.

She looked like she double-swallowed her spaghetti. "Me?"

"Sure. Why not? We could go dancing. We had fun at the wedding."

She lifted her napkin and wiped her mouth, but Ford wasn't entirely sure she wasn't just stalling. She cleared her throat. "Yes. We did. We had a lot of fun at the wedding. Everyone did."

"So how about this weekend?"

She shrugged, then glanced over at Angie. "Sure. Yes. That would be great."

"Are you going to get a chance to visit with your parents while you're down this way?" Angie asked, as if to give Flynn some cover.

"I'm planning to see them on my way home. It's Pop-pop's ninety-second birthday at the end of the month. My sisters will even be in town. I'm hoping to make it for Thanksgiving and his party."

"That's so neat," Flynn said, her composure restored.

"How are your grandparents doing?" he asked.

"Great. I was just telling Angie that they're staying in one of those golf cart communities. Rumor has it my grandfather is like Richard Petty behind the wheel of that thing, and I think Gran really likes that. I feel like they might need a curfew."

"Nothing wrong with going a little wild at any age."

"Can we get a golf cart?" Billy said, his eyes full of hope.

"Yeah, can we, Mom?" Jackson nodded eagerly.

"I can't catch a break with these two boys," Angie said, wagging her fork in their direction.

"When we get married, I'll buy you one, Billy," Flynn said.

"Those kinds of promises, I'll get in line to marry you," Ford teased.

Her head snapped back in his direction. "Careful. I'll have you fixing toilets and doing chores."

"Not exactly what I'd consider a wild time, but I am good at that kind of stuff. We could work out a trade."

She draped her hands over Billy's ears. "Not in front of my future husband."

Jackson and Angie laughed. "Not that kind of trade," Ford said.

"I'm not buying you a golf cart either," Flynn teased.

"I meant bartering my handyman skills for room and board at your place while I'm in town."

"Handymen are not at the top of my list lately," Flynn said.

He'd hit a nerve. Her smile had faded as quickly as a politician's promises. Scrambling to recapture the playful mood before, he said, "I just thought it would be a little more professional than dorming with the students. Plus, I loved your cooking when I stayed last year."

Angie leaned forward. "We might need to interview you first, Ford."

"I come with good references," he said. "Jackson. Help a brother out, man."

"Oh no, I'm not getting in the middle of this." Jackson pushed back from the table.

Flynn glanced over at Angie and then folded her arms on the table. "I do have all of the materials on-site. The way I figure it, all three bathrooms could be back in working order in just a few days. A week tops."

"I doubt it would take that long if you have everything we need." Ford held her gaze. She looked doubtful.

"If you could do that, I could rent out the other rooms while you're still in town. I had an email request for two couples to come the week after next."

He leaned back in his chair. "Then how can you say no?" *Please don't say no.*

"I guess I can't."

He reached across the table and shook her hand. "Deal." Her grip was tight. Professional. And her skin just as soft as he'd remembered.

Jackson passed the breadbasket around. "I can help you on Tuesday night. That's Angie and Billy's night working the concession stand at the basketball game."

"Sounds like we have a plan." Ford wished there was a reason to hold on to her hand.

"Thank goodness," Angie said. "I'm so glad that worked out. This crazy girl has been talking about possibly selling the B&B and taking her old job back. And she hated that job."

"*Shhh.*" Flynn glared at Angie.

Ford's mood lifted. It just might mean Flynn wasn't as tied to Boot Creek as he'd feared, and that was a plus. For him anyway. "How about after dinner you show me what I've just gotten myself into."

Chapter Seven

Heat flushed Flynn's cheeks. Had she just let Ford invite himself to stay in her house? Would she never learn? He'd barely been there an hour.

She watched him put away a second helping of dinner.

Then again, this would be a good test.

Ford Morton would only be in North Carolina a month. There was no possible chance of a relationship, so she should be able to just accept his help and stay friends.

The friend zone.

Safe.

It might be her first time ever entertaining that concept with a guy as good looking as Ford. Then again, he was an artist, and hadn't she just said she wasn't going to be dating anyone that didn't have a real job? No more freelancers. Brandon had proven to her that that type was the wrong one.

"I'm stuffed," Ford announced. "That was a great meal, Angie. Thank you so much. I hope you don't mind, but I brought a little something for Billy."

"You did!"

Flynn smiled at Billy's delight. Ford really was good with him.

"It's in the top of my blue suitcase," Ford called out over his shoulder as Billy's feet stamped into the adjoining room.

Billy unzipped the bag and pulled out a box wrapped in brown paper. "Is this it?" He ran back to the table, dropping to the floor to open the box.

"You didn't have to do that, Ford," Angie said. Billy slung bits of the kraft paper into the air trying to get to the prize inside.

"That was sweet," Flynn said.

"I've been known to be a softy." Ford gave her a wink. "But if I was real sweet, I'd have brought you something too."

She liked the way his eyes sparkled when he laughed, and when he interacted with Billy, he melted her resolve. "Oh, you're going to be doing much more than that for me. Believe me, I'm satisfied with our arrangement. You, on the other hand, may have some regrets."

Ford held her gaze a little too long. "I don't think so."

His stare made her squirm in her seat. She shifted her focus to Billy who had just pulled out a blown-glass totem pole. "That is so cool, Billy," Flynn said, happy for the distraction.

"It's for good luck," Ford explained.

"That's good because my new soccer team has done nothing but lose."

"Oh no. That's no fun," Ford said. "Well, this should help."

"It's the worst." Billy gave a play-by-play of his day at school and soccer practice. "And I got the number seven jersey. I thought that was going to be lucky," he said. "Like lucky number seven. And I've been lucky. I even scored a goal, but our team stinks."

Ford's expression grew serious. "Did your Daddy Jack tell you about the time we won sixteen games in a row?"

Billy's eyes bulged. "No way!"

"True. We kept wearing our lucky socks, game after game, afraid to jinx the winning streak. Whew! Did our feet stink by the end of that season."

Billy's laughter rolled through the room.

"Hope you saved room for dessert," Angie said.

"That's not going to happen tonight," Ford said, rubbing his stomach.

"Too bad. Flynn made her famous chocolate pecan pie."

Ford glanced over toward Flynn. "Really? Didn't know you could bake."

"If I remember correctly you raved about my breakfast just moments ago."

"That I did, but that's not baking."

"I have a few hidden talents." Quit flirting, Flynn. Friend zone. Just friends.

His smile was a little crooked, and her insides gnawed at her.

"I bet you do." His voice had a roughness to it that made her itch all over.

Was *he* flirting with *her*? They'd chatted a couple of times in random Facebook posts over the past year, but really there hadn't been much more than a quick exchange of hellos and likes.

She looked over at Angie, but she hadn't seemed to notice. It was probably just Flynn's imagination after the talking-to she'd just received from Angie.

Right now she needed to focus on herself, and she wasn't even sure what that meant. With the offer to come back to work at her old job, and the long list of to-dos for the B&B still hanging over her like an overweight albatross, she didn't have time for distractions of the male persuasion.

Angie and Flynn cleared the table. While Angie wrapped up the leftovers, Flynn rinsed the dishes and loaded the dishwasher.

Ford carried the last of the dishes from the table to the sink. "I appreciate you renting a room to the guy who came all the way from Alaska without a reservation."

She laughed. "No big deal. We're friends."

"I'm being serious."

"Don't be too appreciative yet. You're going to be working that debt off. You know that, right?"

"I'm ready."

A pang of anxiety swept through her. "I haven't cleaned. There's stuff in disrepair all over the place." He didn't need to know it was because she'd been wallowing in her own little pity party.

"I remember how organized you were from last year. I'm sure it will be fine."

"Oh, no," Angie teased. "The toothpaste might be to the left of the toilet paper in the hall closet. Can you imagine if that happened?"

"Shut up. I'm not that bad." Only most of the time she really was kind of that bad. Not OCD, but definitely organized to a fault.

"Yes, you are," Jackson and Angie said at the same time.

"You're doing me a big favor," Ford said. "I'd be ruined for a regular bed for the rest of my life if I slept in Billy's truck bed."

"He's not kidding," Angie laughed out the words. "I still think Jackson only naps with Billy because he loves that bed so much. You know they never grow up."

"Guilty," Jackson said as he walked back in the room.

"I have to warn you," Flynn said. "The electrician just got the power back on today after a little incident. The furnace is still on the fritz and there's not even a faucet on the bathroom sink right now. You're going to have to use my bathroom downstairs to brush your teeth."

"That's an easy fix," Ford said.

"Says you. I'm giving you one last chance to bail out."

Ford patted his chest. "Do I look scared?"

Flynn arched her brow and gave Angie a pleading look. Was this some kind of test or something? "One last time—Billy will be sad if you didn't stay here."

"He can come and stay at your house with us one night." Ford turned to Billy. "We could camp over at Flynn's. What do you say, Billy? I won't even make you take a shower."

"Can I, Mom? Tonight?"

"Fine by me. Jackson, are you okay with it? You'd have to pick him up and take him to school."

"Yeah. I can do that."

"We have a deal," Ford said. "Go pack your school stuff, Billy."

And just like that Flynn suddenly had her first guest in months checking into the Crane Creek Bed and Breakfast.

"Sounds like a plan." Things would stay aboveboard with Billy around. This wasn't going to be a rerun from her last stint with a handyman in the house. Friend zone. No problem.

Flynn grabbed her purse, wishing she hadn't given in as quickly as she had, because her house was not fit for guests right now. Even just friends. At the very least she'd like to give the guest room a once-over to make sure none of Brandon's stuff had been left behind. But there was no turning back now.

"I'm going to head on home," she said.

"Billy and I will be over in about an hour," Ford said. "Will that work?"

"An hour would be perfect. Come on over whenever y'all are ready." Flynn headed toward the door with Angie at her heels. The guys were already talking about sports.

"You were no help at all," Flynn said to Angie under her breath.

"What?"

"We were just talking about me getting my focus back on myself and off of men, and you let Ford talk his way right into the house." She looked back to make sure the guys were still occupied.

"Ford is different. He'll only be in town for a month, and you need the free labor. Don't knock it."

That was true. Ford was a great guy. Good looking too. Of course, he'd be going back to Alaska. She might consider leaving Boot Creek to go back to work in Charlotte for a while, but Alaska was a whole other story.

Chapter Eight

Ford parked Jackson's old pickup truck at the curb in front of Crane Creek Bed and Breakfast. Flynn had made the place available to Jackson and Angie for their out-of-town guests last summer, so he'd just kind of landed here. He hadn't spent much time in the place, with the crazy pace of things leading up to the wedding, but it had been a comfortable place to stay.

One thing he wouldn't forget about the house was the smell of that home-cooked southern breakfast Flynn had served up each morning. Or the way she'd looked standing at the island in her kitchen.

A rush of anticipation coursed through him as he got out of the truck, minus Billy tonight, poor sleepy kid. He reached over the side and pulled his luggage out of the bed. The porch light across the street went on. Probably because he'd slammed the truck door. Living in Alaska had desensitized him to having neighbors. He'd have to watch that.

The front porch of the B&B was well lit. White rocking chairs moved in the gentle breeze tonight, like old souls reminiscing. The blue painted boards on the ceiling of the porch cast a soft hue over the space.

It had been August a year ago when he'd been here. The hottest August on record, and just walking outside had felt like someone had draped a wet wool blanket over him—heavy and nearly impossible to move.

Tonight was the kind of night that he longed for. Perfect football game weather. A slight nip in the air that made you break out the jacket, just in case. A light breeze, and more stars in the sky than a man could count or a kid could wish on. Maybe it was a blessing Billy had zonked out. A night under the stars with Flynn seemed like the perfect way to end his first evening back in Boot Creek.

He stepped onto the porch, his boots clicking off a beat that sounded as loud as his heart at the moment. He'd been daydreaming about this moment all day, and yet, walking to the door right now, he felt awkwardly unsure of himself. Not something he was used to.

The screen door squeaked as he opened it.

Add WD-40 to the shopping list.

He knocked on the heavy wooden door and entered. "Hey, Flynn. It's Ford."

She came down the stairs, half out of breath. "Hey, I was just making up your bed."

"Hi. Thanks." He stood there for a moment.

"Where's Billy?" She fidgeted with the ends of her hair.

"He fell asleep before I left. We'll make the campout another night."

"Aww. That's fine. He's such a sweet boy."

"He's great. He sure loves you."

"You're really great with him too. I love kids. I hope one day I have one just like him."

"I've always wanted children too." And there it was again, that awkward silence. And one more piece of information that made him feel a push toward her. "So," he said, breaking the silence that hung between them, "am I staying in the room I stayed in before?"

"I thought that would be most comfortable for you."

"Fine by me. Whatever's easy for you." He hoped this awkwardness would pass quickly.

"I'll show you. Come on."

He followed her, unable to take his eyes off the smooth swish of her hips as she climbed the stairs. Her jeans hugged her curves. Her tooled belt—decorated with little turquoise-colored flowers inlaid between scrolling leather leaves and small silver studs—settled just below her waist. Her long blonde hair teased the bottom of her shirt with each step.

"Right in here." She waved her hand toward the room to the left of the stairs. The placard next to the door was new since his last visit. The small wooden oval looked to have been hand carved. The detailed leaves enveloped the edges of the oval. The name of the room, Blue Ridge Retreat, was in raised serif letters. A nice touch. He appreciated good craftsmanship no matter the medium.

A soft alluring scent, not quite floral and maybe even fruity in a gentle way, caught his attention as he stepped by Flynn. Perfume? Or maybe it was her hair?

He dropped his bags just inside the door. The room was freshly made up, and she'd even brought up an ice-cold metal pitcher of water that sat on the dresser, damp droplets dotting the sides. A mason jar held trail mix, and a tiny white dish of lime and orange slices sat next to a heavy drinking glass.

Maybe one day he'd make her a set of special glasses for each of her rooms. Those were the kinds of projects that were quick and fun and the type of gifts he enjoyed giving.

"As I said there's not a working bathroom up here, but there's a half bath off of the main hall downstairs, and I'll show you where my bathroom is so you can shower."

"That would be great. I always feel nasty after flying all day."

"I know what you mean," she said. "Come on. I'll show you where the shower is now, so you can freshen up and relax. This stuff can wait."

"Before we go downstairs, why don't you walk me through all of the things that need to be done in these bathrooms to get you back in business first."

Her face tinged pink. "I feel so funny about this. I don't want to take advantage of you."

"You're not. I offered."

"Right." She bit down on her lip and sucked in a breath. "Here we go." She pointed to the door in front of him that led to the en suite bathroom for that room. "Take a look at that first. I can give you a copy of my project list when we go downstairs, so you can see what things you're up to tackling."

"Project list, huh? I like that you're organized." He poked his head in the bathroom to take a quick look. A new vanity in an old style replaced the old pedestal sink that had been there before. Really high quality too, only there wasn't a fixture in the entire room. A new toilet, still in the box, sat in the corner of the room. The faucet hadn't been installed and the shower was nothing but pipes sticking out of the wall. It looked worse than it was. "What's the stuff in the bags in the bathtub?"

"New towel bars and stuff. That's not a priority," she quickly added. "I can just store those in the linen closet until I have time to get that done."

If he was going to put things in working order, it wouldn't take more than an hour to add those little niceties.

"All three bathrooms are pretty much in the same situation," she said.

"The cabinets are really nice. Perfect for the period of the house."

"Thanks. They were custom. I wanted more of a furniture look."

"It works," he said. "And picks up the wood in the furniture in the adjacent rooms too."

"That was the plan. If you want to grab a change of clothes, I'll show you the downstairs so you can get that shower."

"That would be great." He went back into his room and tossed his duffel bag on the bed. It only took him a moment to grab a change of clothes and meet her back in the hallway. "Let's go."

She led the way, stopping only to point out where the half bath was. "Make yourself at home to anything in the kitchen too. What time do you want to eat breakfast in the morning?"

"You don't have to do that. I'm not a paying guest. I can just grab something from the pantry."

"If you're going to help me get those bathrooms back in shape, you're better than a paying customer. Please, let me cook for you. It'll make me feel better about you helping me out. Besides, I really enjoy that part."

He could hardly argue with that. "Well, I can't have you unhappy now, can I?"

"You could lose your southern card."

She was quick-witted. He liked that. "Living in Alaska has me on probation already."

"Then you can't risk it, can you?"

"Guess not, but you'll have to let me cook my famous fried pork tenderloin for you one night."

"I can do that."

Ford glanced at his watch. "With the time change, why don't we say nine o'clock for breakfast? Is that too late for you?"

"Not at all. Nine it is." She steered him through a set of double doors off the dining room that led to a short hallway and three rooms. A sitting room, bedroom, and master bath.

"This is big. I didn't realize there was this much house back here."

"It's deceptive from the street," she agreed. "There's a carriage house out back too. It's a double lot. Not side by side, but back-to-back."

"That's different. Do you rent out the carriage house too?" Maybe that's where the boyfriend had stayed.

"No. It used to be my grandfather's workshop. Kind of a man cave before man caves were cool. Back in the day it was actually a real carriage house with stalls for the hitch team and everything."

"Really? That's pretty cool. No room for horses in the middle of town now. Even a small town like this."

"That whole area behind this house was once pastureland. There are some old pictures of what the property used to look like hanging in the library. I'll have to show you those sometime."

"Do you ride?"

"Not since I was a kid, and then it wasn't really riding. My grandfather would sit me up on one of the horses and just lead me around in circles. I thought I was queen of the rodeo."

"We should go riding sometime." Where the heck had that come from? He hadn't ridden since he lived back home in Nashville.

"That might be fun."

He was half surprised that she sounded game. He'd have to practice before he took her. Nothing cool about pretending to be a cowboy. Then again, she was probably being polite. "If I don't get a shower and some rest I'm not going to be good for much of anything."

She scooted out of the way. "Bathroom is all yours. Take your time." She walked out of the room and closed the door behind her.

Her bedroom was neat. Not a lot of frills or knickknacks. He liked that. The furniture was old. Good heavy furniture that appeared to have been from the early 1920s. They didn't make stuff like that anymore. He wondered if it had been hers or if it came with the inn when she'd taken it over. On the dresser there was a picture of her with her parents and one from the wedding last summer with her and Angie standing near the creek.

She'd looked so elegant that day, but in blue jeans and a rock and roll T-shirt tonight, she looked even prettier. He set the frame back on the dresser, then went into the bathroom.

He turned on the water, thankful for the hot spray. His muscles eased against the pressure of the water. He washed his hair and immediately recognized the smell from upstairs. A little too girly for him, but beggars couldn't be choosers. He rinsed his hair extra long, hoping to wash a bit of that fragrance down the drain. It had smelled sexy as hell on her, but that was a whole other story.

Twisting the old handles to shut off the shower, he stepped out of the tub. The thick blue towel felt good against his skin. He got dressed, then wiped down the shower and made sure he left the room just as he'd found it except for some steam on the mirror.

He'd never lived with a woman. Maybe when the right one came along would be the time for cohabitation. He hung the damp towel over the hook on the wall.

When he opened the door to her bedroom, something sweet filled the air. He backtracked the way she'd taken him. In the kitchen he found Flynn gracefully running a spatula under warm cookies and transferring them to a metal cooling rack.

"What are you up to now?"

"Thought you might want a snack."

"I didn't, but now I do." He reached for the rack. "May I?"

"Sure. Help yourself."

He grabbed a cookie and took a bite. "These are great. I take the baking comment back. What'd you do before you took this place over?"

"I was a consultant. I managed million-dollar projects. Herded cats basically."

"I can't picture you in a blue suit and heels every day."

"Believe it. Well, not always blue, but I was definitely a suit-wearing girl and my shoes outpriced my rent most months."

She seemed so low maintenance and fresh. "What changed? I mean you sure don't seem like one of those uptight business types now. No offense."

"Well, I was never uptight," she said with a laugh. "I was really good at my job, but I was in the wrong position at the wrong time and got laid off. Not uncommon in that business."

"Ouch."

"It stung. I can't lie. I never saw that coming. I always figured if I did a good job, exceeded expectations, I'd never be one of those people that got pink-slipped."

"Doesn't always work that way, does it?"

"No. I found myself out of a job and kind of angry. When my grand-parents made me the offer to take this place over, it felt serendipitous."

"I bet."

"Just wait, the story gets better. I was cocky about it. Way too cocky. I thought running this place would be so easy compared to running multimillion-dollar projects."

"And?"

"I was so wrong. Running a B&B is a lot harder than I imagined. There's the housekeeping, cooking, and guest services, and on top of that I have to be sure to keep up the maintenance of the place. I'd rented a condo before I moved in here. Suddenly there was no super to call to fix stuff when things went wrong. But I love this old house—being part of its story now. How about you? Why did you leave practicing law to blow glass? That seems like such an unlikely combo."

"I guess you could say that, like yours, it was the right decision. I love where I landed even if it's not as easy a life in some ways. I finished building my house this past year."

"As in hammering the nails and everything?"

"Pretty much. I did barter a lot of the materials and some of the help, but I had my hand in everything every step of the way."

"Wow. I'd be hard-pressed to put up a tent, much less build a whole house. I haven't even cleaned out the carriage house yet. Right now I'd just be happy to be able to flush a toilet upstairs."

"We'll tackle these projects. Don't worry about that, and maybe next time I need room and board, we'll tackle the carriage house together."

She thrust her hand in his direction. "Deal, if you shake on it right now before you see it."

"I'm not scared." Her delicate hand warmed his skin, and her blue eyes danced with mischief. He could only imagine what he'd just signed up for, but he didn't even care.

Chapter Nine

Worry filled Flynn. Had Ford just been polite last night as she'd walked him through the house pointing out all of the unfinished projects? He acted like all of those to-do's added up to nothing, but it sure looked overwhelming when you considered them all at once.

She'd gone to bed wondering if she might wake up in the morning to an empty guest room. And then she'd mentioned the carriage house. What a dope. If he was gone, it would serve her right.

As she padded down the hall to the kitchen, she wanted coffee so badly she could almost smell it.

I can. Ford stood at the French doors at the back of the kitchen sipping a cup of coffee.

A man who knew his way around the kitchen was sexier than she'd imagined. "I didn't think you'd be up so early," she said.

He turned and treated her to a smile. "Time change never seems to bother me. I just shift with the timeline."

"Lucky you. I used to hate traveling coast to coast on business." She shuffled over to the coffeepot. "Thanks so much for making the coffee."

With a cup of coffee beginning to caffeinate Flynn back to life, Ford went over a list of things he was going to pick up from the hardware store this morning.

"I swear I thought I had everything we needed." His list took up dang near a half sheet of legal paper. The long kind. She went over to her purse and pulled out her credit card. "Here. You can use this."

Ford folded the paper and tucked it into his pocket along with the card. "I hope you'll be pleased to know that as of about thirty minutes ago, you have one fully functioning bathroom upstairs."

"Shut up."

"Or not pleased?"

"No. Really? You can't be serious."

He hooked a finger in her direction and marched her right upstairs to show her.

She stood at the door, half in disbelief at how her luck had changed in just one night.

"I might be the happiest girl in the world right this minute."

"Well, then hold on to your hat, because things are about to get better."

She followed him downstairs and watched as he got behind the wheel of Jackson's old pickup truck and pulled away from the curb.

Just how big of an idiot had she been for having been out of business for so long when at least some things could've been put back together in less than a couple of hours?

She shut the door, and it slammed behind her—symbolic in a way. Like she was removing every mess Brandon had left behind. She only hoped her heart would be as easily fixed as the rest of the stuff that needed repair around here.

Her phone rang and she grabbed it from the hall table. She glanced at the display. It was Angie. "Hey, Angie. How are you this morning?"

"Great. How did you and Ford do last night?"

"He already has one bathroom working. If he delivers on even half of the things he said he could fix, then I'll be back in business next week."

"No way. That's awesome!"

"I know. I'm shocked too. He didn't look the least bit irritated as I walked him through and showed him everything. And Angie, it was almost embarrassing. At every turn there was something. And things he pointed out I hadn't even noticed."

"Jackson said Ford can fix anything."

"Being able to do it and doing it are two different issues. I'll be honest. I half expected him to be gone when I woke up this morning."

"He wouldn't do that."

"We barely know him. How can you say that?"

"I'm a good judge of character. Besides, Jackson would've kicked his butt."

"True." Flynn loved how Jackson took care of not just Angie but all of her friends too.

"Keep me posted."

"I will." Flynn hung up the phone and tucked it into the rear pocket of her jeans. She went upstairs to put everything back in the vanity in the bathroom.

Brandon may not have been organized but she was, and she'd taken everything out of there when they'd started that project. She'd carefully packed each drawer and cabinet in its own basket. Now it was just an exercise of unloading each one into its original spot.

A half hour later she had a stack of three empty woven baskets—made from thin strips of willow—next to her. She closed the vanity doors, then rearranged the guest-sized soaps and shampoos in the large antique apothecary jar that she'd purchased on a girls weekend in Virginia. It was the perfect touch with the new old-fashioned vanity. Mixing old and new always gave such a warm, homey feeling.

She climbed to her feet and carried the baskets to the corner cupboard Brandon had built. She'd designed this cabinet to fit these baskets perfectly, and as she set each one on its own shelf, she was happy with how it was finally coming together.

Flynn went back out to the hall linen closet and grabbed the stack of antique white towels she used in this bathroom and cradled them in her left arm. She carefully rolled each towel and arranged it in the baskets. She grabbed a rag and gave the brand-new faucet one last wipe that left a shine that she could see her reflection in.

"Perfect." She stepped back, admiring what one good morning of work had accomplished. From chaos into order, and now there was no reason she couldn't open reservations to at least a few customers. That income flow would quickly replenish her savings. Why couldn't she be this organized when it came to handling men?

The front door opened, and the screen door slammed behind it. "That was quick," she said taking the stairs two at a time.

"It's just me," Angie said.

"Oh, hey. I wasn't expecting you."

"As soon as I hung up from you I realized that when Jackson took Billy to school this morning, they left his lunch on the counter. I just ran it by the school for him and thought I'd check to see the progress around here for myself."

"Come look."

Angie followed Flynn upstairs. "Looks great. Brandon did do professional work on the cabinetry. At least you got something good out of the deal. It looks nice all finished."

"He did, but I can't believe how quickly Ford was able to put all that plumbing stuff together. I could have been renting rooms all summer." Flynn walked over and showed Angie the other bathroom. "Ford went to get the rest of the stuff he needs to finish this one. He said it won't take but a couple of hours. He's a whirlwind."

"He's motivated to get it done. Brandon just liked being here."

"I can see that now." She pulled the door closed behind her. The unfinished work made her crazy. She'd barely come upstairs lately it bothered her so much, but that was about to change for the better.

"It's not entirely awful. At least it's getting finished now. Ford coming to town seems to be working out pretty well," Angie said. "Billy was a little pouty that he fell asleep and missed the sleepover with you and Ford last night, but he'll get over that."

"Why don't you let Billy come stay with me one night this week instead? He can hang out with me, and if Ford is here, they can do something together. You and Jackson need a night out. It's been a long while since you left Billy with me so y'all could have some time alone."

"We were just talking about going to town for a nice dinner out. We might take you up on that."

"Please do. It would be fun for me."

"Might not be fun for Ford."

He said he liked kids, and he and Billy had hit it off, Flynn thought. "This isn't about him. He's just a guest in my house. If he doesn't want to hang with us, he's welcome to do something else. How about Thursday night?"

"I'll talk to Jackson tonight and let you know."

"Sounds good." It felt good to be number one in her own life.

Angie nodded toward the front of the house. "Ford's back. I'd know the sound of Jackson's truck a mile away."

Ford walked in just as they got to the bottom of the stairs.

Flynn felt her bank account squeeze at the sight of the three bags he was carrying. "Looks like even more stuff when you carry it in like that."

He grinned that million-dollar smile. Perfect teeth and just enough stubble to give him that rough-and-ready look. "I might have picked up a couple of extra little things."

She eyed him, wondering what he had put on her card. Not that she should complain. What she'd make back in rented rooms the rest of this month alone would pretty much pay for anything he could fit in those plastic bags.

He handed her back her credit card, and a receipt.

"I was just admiring your handiwork," Angie said. "You're fast. You're going to work yourself out of a job in a day."

He pulled his lips into a tight line. "You don't think Flynn is going to kick me out when I'm done, do you?"

Angie and Flynn locked eyes. Great. Was he just another Brandon in disguise? He had no idea how sore that point was. "A deal is a deal," Flynn said, swallowing back the bad taste in her mouth.

"Then I'm going to knock this stuff out. You girls have a good day."

"You need my help?" Flynn asked.

Ford stopped halfway up the stairs. "No, ma'am. That would cost you extra." He gave her a wink and tugged on his ball cap. "I'm kind of used to working alone."

"Like I said," Angie whispered with a quick look behind them. "He'll be gone in a month."

And good thing too. Not only was he handsome, but he was handy, and she'd already fallen for that combo in one disastrous way. She had no intention of repeating that mistake. "I feel like the Emergency Alert System test emblem should be tattooed on my forehead."

"It's not that bad."

"I'm a train wreck when it comes to men."

"You're not. You're just . . ." Angie stood there for a minute without a word. "I don't know why you've had such bad luck. I was going to say you're too trusting, but there's nothing wrong with that. There's nothing wrong with you. Just do your thing and keep your heart open. It's going to work itself out. I know it will."

They walked out onto the front porch. "I sure hope you're right."

"And when you do start dating, quit spoiling these men. That's why they take advantage of you. Be nice, but not too nice. Make them work for it a little. You're the prize, Flynn."

"I know you're right, but it's way easier to say than to do. I like doting on people. It's why the B&B has been such a good fit."

"Keep the spoiling to your customers. They love you, and the right guy will earn that himself."

Hopefully. "I'm going to open up the schedule online for reservations this afternoon, and get things back up and running around here. I've got to get my life back on track."

"You're not still thinking about taking that job, are you?" Angie rocked back with a look of worry etched on her face.

"I'd be lying if I didn't admit it's very tempting. This place does keep me tied to this town, and that's not necessarily a good thing."

"You could probably get someone to host while you're away. Don't they have like internships for innkeepers or something? I swear I read about that somewhere. Besides, you might meet Mr. Right while you're out and about."

"Certainly something I could consider. I'm going to start writing a bucket list."

Angie shook her head. "Not me. That's what people in their fifties do."

"You're never too young for a bucket list. It's just a list of things you want to do, and an organized approach to getting them done."

"Leave it to you to overorganize anything."

"I didn't hear you complaining when I came over and helped you get Jackson's kitchen in order after the honeymoon."

"True, and I might need to get you to come over and help me organize the attic too. Combining two households you end up with duplicates, so there's still a whole household of stuff upstairs that needs to be sold or given away."

"My specialty. Just say when." The buzzer went off on the washer. "That's my laundry. I need to start another load."

"All right, I'd better get on out of here. I'll talk to Jackson and see what night he wants to go out and let you know."

Angie trotted out to her car, and Flynn went inside. It was comforting to hear Ford tinkering upstairs. This place always felt better with people in it.

She started a load of laundry, then went into her office. Sitting at her desk, she opened the desk drawer to pull out her little booklet that held all of her passwords so she could log into her website. Could anyone really remember all of them?

In less than two minutes she'd opened up bookings for one of the rooms. Wouldn't it be nice if there was a point and click fix for everything?

Chapter Ten

Flynn settled into the old leather chair at the desk. She felt a renewed interest in getting Crane Creek Bed and Breakfast back on track this morning. A few website tweaks would keep her busy and out of Ford's way. It was so tempting to see how things were going.

It had been a while since she'd messed with the website, but these new online tools made it quick work. She'd typed up some of her favorite inn recipes to add to the website months ago, but had never gotten around to posting them. *Sidetracked* was about the best word she could come up with for what she'd been the past few months.

She added the recipe page, and a slide show to the main page along with some new pictures.

Her calendar caught her eye. It was time to take advantage of being in business for herself.

The weeks that coincided with town events were always busy, so she made sure she marked those dates as open for business, and then took into consideration those times that were slower to use for her own little getaways. She could even offer those dates to her grandparents to come back and stay so they could visit with friends and relax here for a change. A win-win for both of them. Why hadn't she thought of that before?

Time away would also give her more to share with her guests, and that was one of the best parts of owning a bed and breakfast—sharing stories.

She went to her social media accounts and posted an update that she had vacancies. Hopefully, that would translate into a few new reservations too.

Still wouldn't hurt to take on that job, she thought as she looked at her budget, especially since the job was temporary. If she could finish that project in just six months, she'd get the bonus too, and that would put her right back where she needed to be. Six months wasn't that long to sacrifice, but she'd promised Angie she'd sit on that decision for a while . . .

The bright colors from one of the drawings she'd done for her grandparents years ago caught her eye.

Looking at it now, she found it amusing.

Most children probably drew pictures of their own family. Not Flynn—she'd always drawn the family she'd wished she'd have someday. She was the mom. Bright yellow curlicues for hair and a red dress with a black belt and high heels made her look a little like one of those moms out of the fifties shows she'd seen in reruns with her grandparents.

Would she ever have her own children running these halls?

A sandy-haired husband and four children completed the picture. Two boys and two girls, stair-stepped in age. Being an only child she'd always wished for brothers and sisters. Four was perfect. No middle child. And what family was complete without a dog? A bearded collie, of course. Just like the one she'd grown up with. Dad had taken Gus with him when he left. At the time she hadn't even realized that neither Dad or Gus would be coming back. She wondered now if her grandparents had known. They'd never let on if they had. Too bad Granpa was so allergic. At least that was the reason they'd said Dad took Gus with him.

The muscles on the husband in the drawing made him look like a lumberjack without the plaid shirt. Even in grade school she'd been drawn to well-toned big guys. Standing between her and her make-believe husband, the children held hands and wore big toothy grins.

The two boys had blond hair like her, but one of the girls had red hair and the other, brown like the dad. There were little sweeping arcs on each side of the dog's tail, showing he was a happy tail wagger that day.

I may not have that husband or children, but I could get a dog. A little unconditional love never hurt anyone.

Gus had been her best friend when she was a little girl. That dog had filled the role of brother or sister for her. As an only child, you had to get creative, and an imaginary friend just seemed weird. Pretending Gus was a sibling seemed quite natural. The scruffy gray-blue dog had tolerated daylong tea parties and dramatic Nancy Drew readings in her bedroom along with a bed full of stuffed animals. She'd dressed him in her clothes complete with ribbons and barrettes too. Poor Gus had been such a trooper. Much better than Daddy had been about it. Daddy had lost his sense of humor when Mom got sick, and he never smiled again. He seemed to take it quite personally when she dolled up Gus as an imaginary sister. She could still hear Daddy muttering under his breath when she proudly marched Gus out in drag.

And as fun as the short daydream of having a dog was, she knew she couldn't do that now, even though she was settled in Boot Creek. When she'd been working in Charlotte, she couldn't have a dog in her condo, and now with the recent thought of doing some traveling . . . having a pet would mess up the whole plan.

She itched to get her life in order. There wasn't one thing that felt like it was locked in. Not her job, her home, or her love life. Her dwindling finances made her nervous. She wasn't in trouble, by a long shot, but she liked knowing she could weather any financial storm.

She ambled through the house trying to burn off the antsy feeling.

The one thing that always calmed her was cooking.

She went to the kitchen and looked through the contents of the well-stocked pantry. Pulling out all of the ingredients to make stuffed pork chops, she turned the kitchen island into something out of an episode of *Hell's Kitchen*.

She wondered if Ford liked pork chops. For half a second, she considered running upstairs and asking him, but Angie's advice rang in her mind. This wasn't about Ford. Or anyone else, for that matter.

I'm the leading lady of this story.

If Ford didn't like pork chops, her friends Derek and Katy would happily accept some leftovers. Derek loved her stuffed pork chops. Not that she wished a failure on Katy, but it was kind of cool to have a specialty dish that, even with the recipe, no one else seemed to be able to duplicate.

She chopped onions and celery, then sautéed them on the stovetop. In another pan she scrambled fresh sausage. It was always a good day when the sausage man was at the farmers' market. Using a spatula, she broke up the lean meat into small bite-sized pieces. Everyone loved her homemade sausage stuffing. It had been Gran's recipe, but Flynn had upped the savory spices and made it her own. Even her grandfather boasted about it.

With the rest of the ingredients mixed in one of Gran's turquoise and white, butterprint-pattern Pyrex bowls and set to the side, she gave the sauté pan a good stir.

Ford walked into the kitchen. "I could smell that all the way upstairs."

She jumped, sloshing grease in the air.

"Sorry, didn't mean to scare you." He stepped closer to the stove, inhaling the simmering scents. "I don't know how you expect me to get anything done with that smell wafting through the house. I swear I almost drooled on your hardwood floors up there."

"Don't you go slipping and sue me."

"I wouldn't, but if your buddy Megan made one of her candles smell like that she'd be a millionaire."

"You'd just go around hungry all the time."

He scratched his head. "Good point. What are you making?"

"Dinner. Do you like stuffed pork chops?"

"If that's going in the stuffing? I like it already."

She pulled out the drawer next to the stove and took out a dessert fork. Stabbing a piece of sausage, she handed him the fork. "Local sausage. Doesn't get any better than this."

He took the fork and raised it to his lips. He nodded as he chewed. "Man, that's good."

"I know."

"What time is dinner?"

"Figured we already missed lunch so we'd do an early dinner. Around five thirty work for you?"

He glanced down at his watch.

She hadn't noticed the expensive watch before. A nice Rolex.

"I have to go pick up some things, but I'll be back in plenty of time for that."

"Great. I'll set a place for you."

"Are those pork chops going to be baked or fried?"

She could do it either way he liked, but instead she answered with her favorite, "Fried."

"Oh, girl." He clutched his heart. "Careful. I might never leave." He walked out of the kitchen, and she heard him holler out a whoop as he went out the front door.

She put together the stuffing and set it aside. Ford still wasn't back when she'd finished making the salad, so she folded the load of towels she'd washed in preparation for the completion of the other two bathrooms and went upstairs to put them away.

It felt good to have someone back in the house. Maybe having no guests was part of what was making her so unhappy lately. She'd thought she was missing Brandon, but what if that was only part of it. It might be old-fashioned, but fussing over people brought her joy. She came by it honestly from her grandparents, she guessed. It must've skipped a generation.

She set the large stack of towels on the chair in the hall and went into Ford's room to make his bed and freshen his room before he got back. A portfolio sat on the desk near the window.

Hesitating for a moment, curiosity forced her to open the leather-bound book and start thumbing through the pictures. Photographs of brightly colored glasswork filled every single page. Different techniques were explained on some of the facing pages, others held awards or accolades from trade magazines. One clipping even heralded having been featured in an episode of a show on HGTV.

She tidied the room, noticing the way he'd folded his jeans and shirt on the chair in the corner of the room. Unexpected for a man who seemed so rugged.

The pillows with the shams on them had been tucked in the nook next to the nightstand. She picked them up and placed them on the freshly made bed, and then smoothed out the quilt.

"I'm back." His voice carried upstairs, and her breath caught in her throat. She felt like a teenager getting caught skipping school. "Up here," she called and stepped quickly to the handrail with a little wave. "I was just tidying up."

He climbed the stairs. "You didn't have to clean my room. I do know how to make a bed."

"Habit," she said, moving away from the door to his room.

"Thank you." Ford grabbed her hand. "Now quit treating me like a guest and come see what I bought. I think you're going to like it."

"I feel so bad that you had to go back to the store again."

"It's fine. I just wanted to do the job right." He led her to the second bathroom.

She stepped inside and stopped. "I thought you went to get parts. You already finished? What did you go get?"

"Everything on the list *is* done." He raised a finger and handed her one of the bags he'd carried in. "I bought you a present."

A gift? He looked proud of the find. Like a young boy producing the frog he'd just caught in the ditch. That was so thoughtful.

But why? Did he use my credit card to buy me a present like Brandon had? Stop it. This is not Brandon. Let it go. Just be gracious, and quit pre-judging the poor guy.

As casually as she could manage, she accepted the plastic shopping bag and took out the box inside.

A light fixture?

The picture on the box showed a vintage light fixture made of oil-rubbed bronze with a seeded glass shade. The lightbulbs even had carbon filaments. She glanced up at the original sconces that still graced the wide glass mirror. "But . . ."

"I know. If you don't like them we don't have to swap them out. What you've got works perfectly and they are right for the time period of the house, but when I was putting everything back together I remembered seeing these fixtures when I was at the store last time."

"They would look awesome." She hesitated, knowing she needed to be careful with her budget. "How expensive were they?" She had a lot of things to take care of before she started splurging on nice-to-haves, and she wasn't going to make that mistake again. Especially not so soon. And someone else spending her money felt a little too familiar to her recent mistakes.

"Doesn't matter. My gift to you."

"I can't let you—"

"You can't *not* let me. You already said you liked them." He picked up a screwdriver from the counter and started dismantling the original sconce. "Plus the new fixtures point down. Much better light. You'll be happy with them."

The gesture touched her, and he seemed to be getting as much out of giving these to her as she was excited to receive them. "Thank you. This is so thoughtful of you. I love them. They are absolutely my style."

"I thought so, and I'll enjoy them while I'm here."

"I'm glad your bathroom is done. You can give it a good practical test-drive."

"Exactly," he said. His grin was boyish sometimes, making her smile. "Can you turn off the circuit breaker to this room?"

"Sure thing." She ran downstairs and flipped off the switch. At least that was one good thing Brandon had done. It had taken them the better part of a day of yelling back and forth to get this whole panel marked, but that was work well worth the time. "Is that it?"

"That's the one."

She heard the shade slide up in the bathroom. "Need my help?"

"You know the rule."

"Fine. Call me when you have something to show off." She heard him snicker. She could get used to that rule.

The mailman dropped her mail through the front door slot, which meant it was getting close to four o'clock. She carried the mail into her office. Pitching the junk mail, she opened her water bill. Another big one. It was going to be nice to have all the leaky faucets and toilets repaired. Those leaks had really started costing her over the past few months. It had been one of the reasons she'd wanted to get those repairs done. They'd only turned the water off at the source of the problem a few days before she gave Brandon the boot. She wished she'd thought of that a lot sooner while no customers were booked. She could have saved a few bucks.

But that was behind her. Nothing she could do to change that now. Just keep moving forward. Tomorrow would be a better day.

"Flynn?" Ford yelled from upstairs.

She stepped into the hall. "Need me?"

"Are you busy? I'm done up here."

"Not too busy to see." She grabbed the handrail and took the stairs two at a time. She swept back her bangs, wishing she'd thought to put on a little makeup while he was gone. Those thoughts were like bad habits. This was not that kind of visit. She and Ford were friends. No strings. That was all it would ever be. And that was safe.

In a month he'd be gone. Back in Alaska. No pressure, whatsoever.

She moved quickly, excited to see the results, but stopped short of the bathroom when he stepped in her path.

"Close your eyes," he said, placing himself in the doorway to block her view.

"Seriously?"

"Yep."

She closed her eyes. He edged behind her and placed his hands gently over her eyes. She could feel the heat from his body. He led her into the room, strong but gentle, like the night they'd danced at Angie and Jackson's wedding. He was a good dancer. A strong lead. Why hadn't she remembered that until just now?

"Are you ready?" he whispered at her neck.

His breath tickled her skin. "Yes."

He lowered his hand. She opened her eyes, taking in every detail. The bathroom looked even prettier than she'd ever imagined. "Those lights are perfect. They make the room." She turned around. "It looks great. Even ties in with the other fixtures. Oh, my gosh. You put the towel rack up too?"

"I did." He grabbed her hand and squeezed it. "You like it?"

"Like it? No." She turned and smiled. "I love it. This is spectacular."

"No." He shook his head. "Not spectacular." He dropped her hand. "The Northern Lights, now those are spectacular." He leaned against the bathroom vanity and crossed one boot over the other.

"You've seen them? I've always wanted to see them." The thought tumbled from her mouth.

"Pictures don't do them justice. I'm still completely in awe every time I see them." His voice softened. "You feel part of them when you stand beneath their brilliance. The magic created by nature is hard to match. Alaska is full of moments like that."

When he spoke of Alaska she felt drawn into his excitement about it. "You really love it there."

"You have to experience Alaska to understand it. You should come visit some time."

She yearned to see the Northern Lights. To share them with him. "Maybe I will." *Don't get caught up in him. He lives like four thousand miles away, and there's no time for those shenanigans right now anyway.* "As friends I mean."

"Right. Yeah," he said. "You're welcome to come visit anytime. I've got plenty of room. All you need is a plane ticket."

"Alaska is one of those bucket-list kinds of trips." She'd planned to start that bucket list. *A* for *Alaska* seemed like the perfect thing to start it off. Did she just invite herself to his house? "I was getting ready to cook dinner. Do you want to come down and keep me company while I cook? You can tell me some of those stories about Alaska."

"No."

Well, that was honest. "Oh, okay."

"No, no, I meant I won't keep you company, but how about I help out? I can tell stories and help at the same time."

"Are you serious?" He wanted to help? Had Angie put him up to being extra nice to her? That had to be it. Probably some kind of test. Well, Angie was in for a surprise, because she had no intention of failing this test.

"Sure. It'll be fun. I do know my way around a kitchen."

She started down the stairs with him at her heels. "You're on. Is there anything you can't do?"

"I'll have to get back to you on that."

In the kitchen, she took the pork chops from the refrigerator.

He looked impressed. "Now those are some chops."

"I know. No wimpy, skinny chops around here. The butcher cuts them and then slices them down the center for me so I can stuff them."

"Sounds good."

"The butcher is related to the hog farmer. I think they're in cahoots to spoil us with thick cuts to up their bottom dollar."

"Works for me. Where are your seasonings?" Ford asked.

"Pantry."

Ford walked over and opened the frosted glass door. "I thought *I* was organized. Looks like a library in here."

"Does not."

She could hear him shifting things as he spoke. "A grocery store, then. Where are the spices?"

She almost hated to say it. "It's in alphabetical order. All of the spices are together in *S*."

He poked his head out of the door. "You're shittin' me."

"No." She slumped forward, feeling like a dope. "Okay, I'm a little over the top in pantry organization. If they gave degrees for that, I'd have a master's."

"I'll say." He came out with his arms full. "But it's convenient. Can't knock that."

"Thank you." At least he didn't think she was a complete nutcase.

"I might even be a little jealous of your pantry."

"If I come visit, I'll help you with yours." Flynn dumped flour in a shallow pan and set it aside. She generously stuffed each of the chops and then placed them in the pan too. "Can you season and dredge these for me?"

"Do you have specific seasoning you want on them?"

She started to tell him exactly how she made hers, then paused. "You know what. You just go wild."

"I can do that."

And he did. He shook and flipped those chops, humming the whole while. He seemed to be having so much fun that she couldn't help but sneak peeks at what he was doing.

She moved the cast-iron skillet to the stove and added some oil, then turned on the burner. "Whatever landed you in Alaska? Had you always wanted to live there?"

"Heck, no. I was happy in Tennessee. Never really thought I'd leave there."

"Now I'm more curious than ever."

"My parents lived near Nashville. That's where my dad practices law, but I had family out in Franklin and beyond. I spent a lot of time with my dad's dad. We're really close. It's grown up quite a bit since, but there are still working farms out that way too. It's beautiful. I always felt at home in the country. I loved the quiet. And nature."

"And you and Jackson and Noah all went to college together in Tennessee, right?"

"Yep. Best friends since middle school. Played sports together. Fixed up our first cars together. Noah was the man on that stuff. Bagged our first deer together. Got drunk together."

"But none of them ended up in Alaska. Did you follow a girl or something?"

"No. Nothing as romantic as that," he said. "I think girls usually follow guys to new towns, don't they?"

"Really?" She thought about the people she knew that had moved from their hometowns. "Maybe you're right."

"I'd graduated from college and was working at my dad's law practice. Well, not his, but he's a partner there. Huge firm. They have a very impressive client list. Lots of famous country-music-industry types and big companies."

"So contracts and stuff."

"All disciplines of law. Kind of a one-stop shop. No matter what a client needs, they can get it. Cutthroat, right or wrong, they play to win."

"Even if the client is guilty?"

"Pretty much. Or undeserving in the case of divorces and settlements, but the money was great and I moved up very quickly. Probably mostly because of my relation to my father."

"Sounds like a sweet spot to land, if you ask me."

"I was good at it. I just wasn't happy, to Dad's dismay."

"Because he wanted you to follow in his footsteps."

"Yes, and I tried. I worked in his firm for nearly two miserable years. I didn't like that cutthroat mentality. It was exhausting, and it just didn't feel right. Also made me see a side of my father I didn't really like. Maybe I'm just too nice a guy to be a lawyer."

"So you quit?"

"Not exactly. When I handed in my resignation, my dad wouldn't take it. Dad thought a much-needed break and some high-dollar R&R would get my head right."

"Did it?"

"Not the way he'd hoped."

"Because you decided you didn't want to be a lawyer?"

"Exactly. I had no idea what I wanted; I just knew what I didn't want. I traveled across country, and one night while I was in Vancouver I met these folks who worked on a cruise ship. We partied all weekend and they talked me into filling a temporary opening, bartending on a ship bound for Alaska. I was a kick-ass bartender in college. What's your favorite drink?"

"I don't drink much. I did have champagne at the wedding last year, but that's about it."

"Well, then I guess I won't impress you with my bartending skills."

"No, but I'm delighted by your handyman skills. And you're pretty good with a spice jar."

He threw a pinch of salt over his shoulder.

"For good luck?"

"Can never have too much of that," he said playfully. "The cruise went all the way up the coast of Alaska. I saw glaciers and things that I'd only seen on the National Geographic Channel before. I fell in love with Alaska on that trip."

"You never went back?"

"Had to go back. I still had a job and clients who were waiting for me, but after that trip I knew where I was meant to be. I finished out the year, spending all of my extra time learning about Alaska and watching for prime property to go on sale. By that Christmas I'd bought a piece of land, had a temporary place to live, a job, and a plan to move."

"You were brave."

"I was following a dream."

"Sounds exciting."

"It was." He crossed one leg over the other as she placed the pork chops one by one into the fry pan. They sizzled and spattered. "My dad was furious."

"He didn't understand?"

"Not at all. That first year I lived in Alaska things were pretty rustic. I'll have to show you pictures sometime."

She picked up the tongs and turned the chops in the hot oil. Spices filled the air. "I'd love to see them." She wondered if she'd ever be able to do something so brave. To just up and move to somewhere that you'd never lived. Not having a support system of family and friends nearby. It was hard to imagine.

He pointed to the pan. "I'm going to like that."

"I know you will. I'm kind of famous for these." She picked up a dishtowel and draped it over her shoulder. "Can you get the salad out of the refrigerator?"

"I'm on it."

"You're a great help. No, a miracle worker is what you are. I had a handyman living here for six months and he couldn't seem to get my bathrooms finished. Not even one of them."

Ford cut his gaze her way. "He either wasn't as handy as he wanted you to think, or he just liked hanging around you."

She felt the flush on her cheeks. There it was again, that feeling that he was flirting with her. But that was just silly. Or wishful thinking. "I'm not sure which, but I won't be hiring him for any other work."

"Can't say that I blame you, but then I can't blame him either. You are fun to be around."

So was Ford, but she kept that to herself.

Chapter Eleven

The next morning scents from the kitchen roused Ford from a good night's sleep. Savory sage and that sweet and spicy greasy smell that made his mouth water. Sausage.

I could get used to this.

He rolled over onto his back and picked up his phone to check the time. Just after seven.

He got out of bed and pulled on a pair of jeans. The aroma only got better as he headed downstairs. "Does this house seriously smell this amazing every single morning?"

"Please don't leave a one-star review on the website."

"No, ma'am. Not as long as you're sharing."

"I was kind of counting on that. No fun to eat alone. It's a beautiful morning. I thought we'd eat out on the breakfast porch."

"I'm still full from dinner last night."

"You have to eat something, and it's lighter than it smells."

"I didn't say I'd turn it down. What can I do?"

"Stay out of the way, else I'll charge you double," she teased.

"I knew a guy with a rule like that."

"I'm a quick study." She opened the refrigerator and took out a pitcher of orange juice. "You can carry this out for me. I'll be there in just a second."

"I can do that." He meandered out through the back French doors. In the summer it would likely be a sauna out here, but this morning the air was crisp, and the sun warm.

The table was set for two. Cloth napkins and china with a simple blue line around the edge. A little fancy for his style. His mind wandered to plates he might make for her in colors that picked up the vibrancy of the flowers. Glass plates in geranium red, chrysanthemum gold, and the soft, vivid green of new shoots and evergreens.

He sat down and flipped through the email on his phone. There was a message from Gary Graves over at the PRIZM Glass Art Institute. He'd responded to Ford's email asking for early access to the facility this week.

Flynn walked out with a tray of fresh fruit and plates with biscuits and sausage gravy.

"That looks so good."

"Dig in." She sat across from him and placed her napkin in her lap.

"I'm headed out to PRIZM today to check on things before my start date. Have you ever been there?"

"To the glass studio?"

"Yeah. It's open to the public."

"Nope." She took a bite of her breakfast. "I've never been."

"Are you interested in going? If you're not too busy, I thought maybe you might enjoy riding out there with me."

"Might be fun."

"I want to make sure I've got everything I need there. It won't be an all-day thing. There should be some students working. Thought you might like to see that. It's kind of cool."

She hesitated, and for a minute he thought she might say no, and he felt a twinge of disappointment.

"I've never seen anything like that. I mean I've been to art galleries, but not a gallery that also had in-house artists and education on-site like they do. I'm not sure I really understand what you even do."

"Then you have to come. Plus, Gary, one of the owners, said in one of his emails that they opened up a cafe there last month. I'll treat you to lunch."

"I heard about that place. It's called Kaleidoscope or something like that, right?"

"Yes. That's it. Everything is organic. Kind of farm to table, but they only serve breakfast and lunch. I wanted to leave around nine. Think you can be ready by then?"

"Absolutely." They finished breakfast and then she scooted her chair back from the table and picked up the plates. "That's the nice thing about this business. I can pretty much set my own schedule. Let me just get my stuff together."

An hour later they were driving down the back route that connected Boot Creek to Heron Cove, where the PRIZM Glass Art Institute was located. The rattle of Jackson's old pickup truck made it difficult to have a conversation, so they rode in silence.

Thank goodness it wasn't too hot this time of year, because the air-conditioning in the old truck was barely sputtering cool air. It didn't take long for them to give up and just roll down the windows. Flynn sat with one long leg folded up on the seat of the truck and her arm hanging out the window. As they drove she dipped her hand up and down in the wind, chasing the current. He spread his fingers against the wind too. One of those little unspoken synchronicities that made him feel close to her, but if he ever tried to explain it to someone else he'd sound half crazy.

They drove past a white clapboard church. Flynn clicked her fingers, pointing toward the sign.

He read it out loud as they sped past. "'Things are only impossible until they are not.'"

"Isn't that the truth?"

"I suppose it is." He cocked his head, not even sure if he wanted to know the answer. "What do you think is impossible?"

She tossed her head back and laughed. "What's possible would be an easier question."

"I think pretty much everything is possible. I mean, you might have to make some sacrifices, but you can make things work if you really want them to."

"Easy for you to say. You're living your dream."

"You are too."

"Not really. The B&B is great. I love it, but there's more to my dream than owning a business."

"Fair enough. Mine's not just about work either. That's just what I do. Not who I am."

"See. You get it."

He understood that very well. Well enough to have alienated his father. Not an easy thing to do, especially since that had strained his relationship with his mom too. "I do. What more do you want?"

She stared out the window for a moment. "The fairy tale. A family. Annual vacations that we save up all year for. Picnics. Simple stuff, really, but things people don't much think about anymore."

"I want to own my own glass shop, but not like the one I worked in back in Alaska."

"What didn't you like about that place?"

"The facility was great, but it's a tourist shop. We taught people with too much money and time on their hands how to blow glass balls. Seriously boring. And about as creative as counting quarters from a jukebox." So why had he done it for so long? For the few quiet months out of the year that he had time to really create, but he sure longed for the days when that balance would shift. More him, less them.

"You don't think having the business side would increase your enthusiasm for the art?"

He hadn't really thought about that before.

She went on before he could even answer. "I'd think it would be fun to share your love of glassblowing with others. You have a special gift and a skill that most people will never get the chance to experience any other way."

"True, but not like that. It's fun to share the art I make, but taking them by the hand and baby stepping them through the most basic elements of glassblowing is no picnic. I'd rather allow the tourists to watch artists at work making real art. Not glass balls. Even place orders for custom work. And I think I've come up with a way to set up a simulator that would give visitors the chance to experience the process without the risk and without them having to wear smocks and get sweaty. Trust me, it gets old listening to people complain about that."

"You sound a little grumpy."

"I'm not grumpy. I'm just passionate about my work."

"Is that what you call it?" she joked.

"Passion is one of my best qualities." He held her gaze. She had a way of tempting his passion without even trying.

"Oh, well . . ." She tripped over her words, then said, "I was kind of thinking marking chores off of a list was at the top."

"That too." He spontaneously patted her leg, then quickly withdrew it. He hadn't meant to respond with the overfamiliar gesture. It had just happened. "I do like having a plan. That way I get what I want." And he was pretty sure what he wanted was more time with Flynn.

"I have to admit something." She looked away. "I saw your portfolio when I was making up your room. It's really impressive."

He wasn't sure whether to feel like she'd invaded his privacy or proud, but pride was winning out. Snooping did bug him, but he'd left that sitting out, and she had every right to be in the room. It was her house, and business, after all. "Thank you." Plus he liked that she appreciated his talent.

"I'm sure I'd never be able to afford one of your pieces, but I could see one backlit on one of those built-ins downstairs. Wouldn't that be beautiful?"

Wouldn't she die if she knew he'd done that very thing in his own house? "It would." He wanted to make things for her. To surprise her. To delight her in a way only he could.

He pulled into the parking lot in front of the gallery. Ziegler had sent a collection of Ford's work to PRIZM a few months back. They'd planned to display it to get people interested in the special workshops he was leading this month.

At the time Ford hadn't even cared what got sent. Now he hoped it was an impressive lot. He'd be seeing it for the first time with Flynn today, and he wanted her to be impressed.

The long glass window in front of the gallery sparkled with color, but he didn't notice any of his pieces there.

They got out of the truck and Ford stepped ahead of Flynn to open the front door for her.

She took two steps, then stopped like she'd stepped into cement boots. The storefront was filled with fine glasswork of all sizes. Some for display, others for sale. The sparkle and depth of the colors in glass always felt alive to him. Maybe because in a way it was when he worked with it still in a hot liquid form.

"Wow. This is beautiful and kind of overwhelming," she said.

Gary spotted them and walked over. "I'm so glad you could make it out today. Welcome." He cuffed Ford on the shoulder. "Great to meet you in person."

"You too." Ford shook his hand. "This is my friend Flynn Crane. She owns the bed and breakfast over in Boot Creek."

"Nice to meet you, Ms. Crane."

"Flynn."

"Welcome to PRIZM, Flynn. We are so excited to have Ford here. This is a big deal for us."

"I bet," she said.

Her smile made Ford's mood soar. He placed his hand on the small of her back.

"Your work is displayed over here." Gary led them across the space, looking excited to show off what they'd done for him.

Ford watched how cautious Flynn was walking through the crowded room of glass. She clung to her purse—afraid she might knock something over.

He got a rush as they passed lots of really nice work, but there was a drastic uptick in style and color when they moved into the gallery room where his own pieces were displayed this month. He'd forgotten about a couple of these. The huge jellyfish with long tentacles had never been one of his own favorites, but Ford wasn't surprised it was among what Ziegler had sent, because it had always been one of his. They'd hung it from the ceiling at an angle. It looked as if it were pushing itself through the water. In this light and setting, he could understand more why Ziegler had always been so gaga over it.

Flynn's eyes widened and she broke away from him, heading over to the left side of the room.

"This one . . ." She pointed to a tall sculpture. "You did this?"

He'd worked on that sculpture one whole winter. A luxury that selling cases of one of his original designs—a paperweight to one of those home shopping channels had afforded him. Sometimes you just had to pay your dues.

"It's amazing. And delicate. And so real. It's like the vibrant color bands are swirling, even though I know they aren't."

"That was the idea. Layers upon layers." The flame-worked borosilicate glass sculpture reached a full forty inches base to tip.

She crossed the room with the grace of a dancer. "I swear that glass seaweed looks like it's moving too." She swayed to the left and to the right. "How do you do that?"

"Hours of patient work, but I like that kind of intricacy. It's a challenge."

"It looks so fragile like it might break if I even touched it ever so carefully."

"It's stronger than you'd think, but the individual stems and leaves of the seaweed are pretty delicate." He'd repaired and reworked it for weeks. When he'd finally finished the glass seaweed and started working on the individual sea life, it had been like a much-needed vacation. The fish were detailed and involved study and research to get them anatomically and color correct, but it had all been so worth it.

"How'd you get this one?" Ford asked Gary. He knew this piece had been loaned to a museum.

Gary's eyebrows wiggled. "Can you believe the Monterrey Museum of Glass let us get it on loan when they heard we had you on exhibit, and that you'd be here with us?"

"Cool."

"It was in a museum?" Flynn took a step back and turned, staring at him. "You really *are* something."

And so are you, Ford thought. He loved her enthusiasm. It sent his own emotions zinging.

"Oh, yes, ma'am. Has he been modest with you?" Gary pulled his hands to his hips. "Ford Morton has won more awards and accolades than men who've been working glass three times as long as he has."

She wrapped her hand around Ford's bicep. "There's a lot more to you than I thought when I met you last summer."

"More to come," he said. And when she looked up at him with interest in her eyes, he'd never been so tempted to kiss a woman right then and there as he was right now.

Chapter Twelve

She had a rule about dating guests, and for a brief moment when Ford had asked her to come with him to PRIZM this morning, she'd thought about saying no. Thank goodness she'd fought that crazy feeling.

Jackson had bragged on Ford like he was some kind of a celebrity, but he and Noah had also given Ford one heckuva a hard time about giving up his *real job* to play for a living. She'd be lying if she said she hadn't had her own questions about his carefree lifestyle. Fun was one thing. Flexibility was great too, but he seemed to have taken it to the extreme.

How many people gave up a career, a successful career in law, to do art? That couldn't be very common. She'd said it was brave, but was it? Or was it just downright crazy and reckless to drop everything to live in the wilderness?

She'd been accused of crossing the crazy line for leaving her lucrative career to run the B&B plenty of times. Not by her friends but by old coworkers. They didn't understand the appeal or the satisfaction she got from making a special occasion a truly memorable moment for someone. She was part of a lot of people's very favorite memories.

That was something you couldn't study to do. But she'd also done it to be close to friends and family. He'd left everyone he cared for behind.

Gary flipped his wrist to check his watch and then snapped his fingers in the air. "Why don't y'all come with me? We've got some of our advanced students putting on a demonstration. They just got started. You can come and watch from the catwalk."

Catwalk? Who was she to question? She was just here for the ride, so she fell into step alongside Ford.

Leading them through a long corridor of rooms with glass doors, Gary escorted them to the hub of activity. Artists worked alone in a couple of them, and in others groups of people huddled together. They walked so quickly she couldn't really see anything. They climbed a set of metal stairs, then walked out across a space where at least a dozen people wearing blue lab coats and goggles engaged a group of onlookers in a set of bleachers.

"This is the best seat in the house." A wave of heat whooshed by Flynn as an artist dipped a long pipe into a furnace to get hot glass. Bright orange and yellow flames danced in the hole in front of the furnace, leaving spots in her vision as she watched.

The dark-haired man spun the long metal pole into the fiery mass and came out with a wad of what looked like a fireball to her. Alive and liquid.

An hour later the team had each dipped hot glass, then rolled and manipulated, twisted and created what was now a uniform set of glass ornaments. Except for the colors, they looked to be exactly the same size. The student informed the audience that these would go into the cooling process but later boxed into a twelve-piece set of ornaments that they sold in the gift shop and online.

"That would make an awesome gift," Flynn said nudging Ford.

He simply smiled, clearly not as impressed as she'd been, but this was her first time seeing any of this.

"They did a good job," Ford said.

Gary looked on proudly. "This is one of my best classes. I swear they get better and better every year. I can't wait to see what your influence will inspire with this group," he said to Ford, making it sound almost like a challenge.

Flynn wondered what this kind of teaching arrangement paid.

Ford didn't look worried. "I'm looking forward to it."

Gary walked them down the stairs. "Your lab will be over here, Ford."

Ford stepped in front of her and went into the long room. This room didn't have bleachers in it, but it had a lot more equipment.

She hung back, letting him take care of business. He and Gary talked, and she stepped back into the hallway and watched one of the artists work on a glass ball, similar to what the group had just done for the visitors, only this artist wasn't as experienced. He was blowing and reworking the glass, then gave up and started over. It must be a lot harder to do than it looked.

When she stepped back into Ford's lab, she found him and Gary walking toward her.

"You ready for lunch?" Ford asked.

"Starved," she said.

"Our cafe has the best food around. I don't know what they have on special today, but my wife tells everyone she knows not to even bother with the menu. Whatever they have on special is what you need to order," Gary said.

"I'll take that recommendation." Flynn was looking forward to trying it out. If it was good she'd add it to her list of local fare for her guests to try. The gift shop and gallery had already impressed her enough to make the list.

"We get all of our meat and vegetables locally. I think you'll like it. You'll have to tell your guests about us," Gary said.

"I was just thinking the same thing." Flynn reached into the front pocket of her purse and handed him a card. "If you ever need special rates for visiting artists, let me know."

"I'll do that. Thanks."

Ford said, "Thanks for letting me stop by today. I'm looking forward to getting started this Friday."

"We're ready for you." Gary pulled out his phone and checked something. "I've got to run. Y'all enjoy your lunch."

"We will," Flynn said. "Thank you."

Ford led her down the hall back to the gallery. "What do you think?"

"I think you're a big deal."

He laughed. "Tell my dad that, would you?"

"Gladly." She hadn't told him about her relationship with her own father, but it seemed that they had one more thing in common there. Not that her dad wanted her to follow in his footsteps, but he'd been so selfish that after Mom died he never even made the time to find out what she wanted to do. He'd left her with Gran and Granpa and took off. Mourning was one thing, but abandoning your daughter . . . she didn't know if she could ever forgive him for that. It wasn't like she was a child—even a teenager needs her parents. She had been mourning too. She wasn't even sure where he was right now, and most of the time she didn't even care.

Kaleidoscope's intimate room, painted in deep jewel tones, was welcoming. They were seated at a large table in the corner, with one of Ford's glassworks displayed just behind them. It was obvious Gary had given the folks a heads-up that she and Ford were going to be dining there by the way the waitress was fawning over them.

"It's so nice to meet you, Mr. Morton. I'm Beth. I own Kaleidoscope."

"Nice to meet you." He reached for Beth's hand. "This is a good friend of mine, Flynn Crane. She runs a beautiful bed and breakfast over in Boot Creek. One of the best cooks I've ever known," he said.

A good friend? And a compliment. Flynn felt a warm glow flow through her. "Thanks," she said to Ford.

"That's wonderful," Beth said. "We'll have to swap recipes sometime."

"Sounds great."

Beth grinned. "We do all of our own baking right here on-site. I have to tell you that we're kind of known for our muffins."

"Then you're going to want to talk to this gal about giving up her family recipe for Pumpkin Pecan Crunch Muffins. I don't even like pumpkin, or I thought I didn't, and I swear I could eat my weight in them," Ford said.

He hadn't even said anything to her about that. "I wondered where those last two went," Flynn teased.

"Guilty," Ford said with a laugh. "Midnight snack."

Beth said, "My grandmother used to make those. I've never been able to perfect her recipe. I swear she left something out. Man, it's been way too many years since I've had them. We've got to talk."

"I'll make some and send them over with Ford while he's here."

"I'd be happy to pay you for them," Beth said.

"Don't be silly. You can just tell folks about my B&B when they need a place to stay. I'm just over in Boot Creek. Neighbors helping neighbors."

"Fair enough." Beth turned to Ford. "Will you be using the dorm or staying in Boot Creek while you're in town."

He hesitated.

"He's staying at the B&B," Flynn said, unwilling to let him get away so soon. If for no other reason than that she owed him for all he'd done, or maybe Beth's interest bothered her more than she'd care to admit.

He didn't seem to mind her interruption.

"Great," Beth said, but Flynn could see a little disappointment in the edge of that girl's smile. "What can I get y'all today?"

Ford ordered the burger with pimento cheese and bacon, and she went with the flatbread of the day with hand-pulled organic chicken and fresh veggies and herbs. The food was as tasty as it was nicely plated.

"This might be almost as good as your cooking," Ford said.

"I'll take that as a compliment." She took a sip of her sweet tea. "So good. Your burger looks good too."

"It is. Sure beats a drive-through."

"Do they have fast food at all up there?"

"Sure. It's not like I live in the wilderness. I live in a small town not unlike Boot Creek. We have shops on Main Street that stay open year round and several tourist shops specifically catering to the cruise ships that dock in the harbor nearby. We even have a McDonald's and banks and churches."

"I guess when I think of Alaska, what comes to mind are polar bears, ice fishing, igloos, and Inuit. Oh, and mush dogs."

"The Iditarod."

"Yes," she said with a snap of her fingers. "The Iditarod. Saw that on television."

"You'll have to come visit me. I'll show you *real* Alaska. It's huge. Makes Texas look like a map dot."

"Really? Don't tell the Texans. You know how proud they are of their land mass."

"We have T-shirts poking fun at them. 'Ain't Texas cute.'"

"That's just wrong."

"Pretty much. But it's funny. My property is midway up the coast-line. It's a nice piece of land on good high ground. A view to write home about."

"I still can't believe you did most of the work on your house by yourself."

"My dad's dad could build anything. I learned so much from him without even realizing it. Just hanging out and helping them. An education that you can't buy. He and my dad are so different."

"Did he come help you?"

"Pop-pop? No, I wish he'd been able to be a part of it. It's just too long of a flight for him to make. I did buy him a smartphone and taught him how to video call. We shared things that way. He'd have loved

Alaska and he'd have been right there to help me. I think we could've built that whole place in one summer together."

"Do you have brothers and sisters?" she asked.

"Just sisters. Three of them. I was the baby, so they took good care of me. Also taught me all the ins and outs of how to behave around women. I got more thumps on the head as a teenager than I care to admit. Those girls were ruthless." He chuckled. "Still kind of are."

"You'll probably make a great husband someday."

"I hope so."

That was a first. Usually guys seemed to run when you even mentioned the word marriage or even relationship. Too bad he didn't still have that real job. And too bad he didn't live closer.

Chapter Thirteen

Flynn stood on the front porch watering the bright purple and orange pansies. They'd taken off, overflowing the planter boxes that hung from the white porch railing. She pinched back a few to put in a vase in Ford's room.

The rusty wheelbarrow in the front yard still held pumpkins and mums that looked like they'd been on a steroid regimen, the way they overflowed from the sides. They'd looked pitiful when she'd bought them for just ninety-nine cents a pot at the Piggly Wiggly, but boy did they perk up after just a week of loving care and fresh air. The purple, maroon, and gold blooms practically covered the pumpkins now, but it would be perfect for Thanksgiving too.

Ford stepped out onto the front porch. "There you are. Wondered where you were off to so early."

"Just out here doing my morning chores."

"Thanks for leaving breakfast for me."

"I didn't want to wake you."

"I think the time change is finally catching up with me. I never sleep this late."

"No worries. It's an Indian summer day today. Perfect day for a little laziness."

"I've never been one to be lazy." He propped a foot against the bottom rail of the porch. "I was wondering if I could take you out to dinner tonight. Jackson said there's a nice place up the road."

"He's probably talking about Bella's. It's really good."

"Interested?"

She was. Very. In fact, if the beating of her heart was any indication, she was more interested than she should be. She tipped the watering can up and set it down. "I can't. Sorry." But she wasn't, in a way. She knew better than to get interested in him. He'd be gone soon. Thankful for the safety net of an honest excuse, she pasted a smile on her face. "I told Angie I'd watch Billy. He's going to spend the night. I try to do that once a month. Gives them a chance for a date night. Plus, I love having Billy here. We always have fun. Keeps my 'favorite aunt' title intact."

"That's nice of you." He put on his sunglasses.

She liked the way he looked in them, even if she couldn't see his eyes through the reflective lenses.

"Mind if I hang out with y'all?"

"Not at all," she said. "It'll be a far cry from Bella's, though. If that's the kind of dinner you had your mouth set on, you're going to be disappointed. I'm making chicken tenders and mac 'n' cheese."

"Sounds good to me. How about I pick up dessert? I mean if you're sure I won't be intruding on your time together? I did kind of just invite myself, didn't I?"

"Not at all. You're welcome to join us. It'll be low-key, whatever we do."

"I like it." A mischievous grin swept across Ford's face. "Sounds right up my alley." He headed down the steps, then spun around, walking backward as he spoke. "I'll see you later."

"I'll be here." She watched as he drove off, realizing she was still smiling. He charmed her like a boy, but there wasn't anything boyish about his build or the way his arms felt when he was close.

She went inside and took chicken out of the freezer for dinner. Then she went into the living room and rummaged through the bottom drawer of the built-in bookcase for the goodies she'd picked up at a yard sale a few weeks ago—three toy trucks and a Yahtzee game. She'd almost forgotten about the math flash cards and oversized United States map puzzle she'd also bought.

Last time Billy had stayed, it had been right before school started. He'd been so excited that he'd insisted Angie let him pack his lunchbox and bring it over. They'd had a peanut butter and jelly sandwich dinner on the patio, and then played H-O-R-S-E at the basketball court in the park behind the Baptist church. He'd beat her fair and square too.

After finishing up her chores for the day, she sat down at her desk, delighted to see that she'd received three new reservations in December for the B&B. She'd been worried that after having no vacancies for so long, some of her regulars might have found new favorite places to stay. That didn't appear to be the case.

She confirmed the dates for each of the guests and then transferred the information to the paper planner she still used as a backup to the online system. There was something about those clouds of data that always left her wary that something might go wrong.

Angie's voice rang out down the hall. "We're here!" And then a flurry of running footsteps followed. Billy appeared in the doorway of her office—out of breath and grinning.

"Hey, buddy!" Flynn rose from her chair.

Billy raced across the room and flung himself around her waist before she stood up. "Hi, Aunt Flynn. Are you fixing me macaroni and cheese for dinner tonight?"

"Of course I am. How else does a girl get to be the favorite aunt?"

"Yay!" Billy dropped to the floor and turned to face his mom. "I told you she'd make it for me."

Angie shrugged. "You've got to quit spoiling him."

"No I don't. That's what good aunts and grandparents were made for. To spoil wonderful children."

"Great," Angie said.

The front door slammed shut and Billy jerked to a halt. "Who's that?"

"Oh, no!" Flynn pretended to be afraid, but only for a half beat. "It's probably Ford."

Billy's eyes popped open wide, and then he skedaddled from the room.

Angie leaned back and peeked out into the hall. "Did I just hear Ford tell Billy that he's hanging out with y'all tonight?"

"Probably. He asked me out to dinner, but I told him I had plans. So he sort of invited himself. He's bringing dessert. It'll be fine."

"Really now?" Her lips pursed. "So tell me. Would you have gone out with him?"

"I guess." Flynn felt like it was a trick question. "It's not like it would have been a *date* date. He said he wanted to take me to Bella's."

"Really?" That smirk of hers spread across her face. "Only nice place in town. I think he likes you."

"Stop it. He's just grateful he doesn't have to stay at the dorm at the gallery."

Angie didn't look convinced. "He's super sweet."

"I know, but remember it was you who gave me the advice to just cool it for a while."

"Hey, what are you two girls whispering about in here?" Ford asked.

"We're talking about you," Angie said.

Flynn swatted her arm.

"I know better than to ask more." Ford chuckled. "I'm going to run upstairs and jump in the shower and change. Can I help you with dinner?"

"Nope. I've got that under control. We'll be in the kitchen or out back on the patio when you're done."

"Sounds good. You and Jackson have a fun night, Angie." He vanished up the stairs.

"Thanks, Ford."

Flynn waited until she heard the door close upstairs. "See. Just friends." Flynn hoped that would appease Angie. "What are you and Jackson going to do tonight?"

"I wanted to just stay home and order pizza, but he wants to go bowling."

"You'll have a good time." It didn't sound exactly like the kind of date you needed a sitter to have. Not like you can't take your kid bowling with you. "Maybe he's just trying to surprise you."

"Maybe. He seemed pretty excited about it." Angie let out a sigh. "I'll have fun once we get there. It'll be nice to have an adult night no matter what."

"Yeah. That's the way to look at it."

They went into the kitchen.

Billy sat with the flash cards spread out in front of him. "I see you found one of the surprises I got for you," Flynn said.

"I can do some of these," he said with pride.

"Show me."

He held up the card that showed 5 + 1. "This is six."

"Great, Billy," Angie said. "He's been working really hard on his numbers."

"That's impressive," Flynn said. "Now, you'd better get out of here so you can look pretty for your big date tonight."

"I'm out of here." Angie turned to Billy and held her arms open wide. "Give Momma some hugs, and you be good for your Aunt Flynn."

"I will," he said.

Shortly thereafter, Ford walked into the kitchen wearing a pair of cargo shorts and a T-shirt, hair still damp. "Hey, Billy! What's up, bud? Mind if I hang with y'all tonight?"

Billy ran over and high-fived Ford. "Cool!"

"Y'all have fun," Angie said. "I'll pick Billy up at seven thirty in the morning to drive him to school."

"Sounds like a plan," Flynn said.

Billy sat down at the table. "Love you, Mom."

"Love you too, kiddo."

Flynn sprinkled shredded cheese over the macaroni and cheese she'd just made, and then slid the whole casserole dish into the oven to brown the top. She turned up the burner under the cast-iron skillet and started cooking the chicken tenders.

"I could get used to this southern cooking, but I'm afraid I'm not going to fit into any of my pants by the time I get back home." Ford pushed out his stomach and rubbed it, making Billy burst into a fit of giggles. "Didn't stop me from bringing dessert home, though."

"What's for dessert?" Billy asked.

"It's a surprise. And no one gets any unless all of our dinner plates are cleared."

"No problem there. I love Aunt Flynn's dinners," Billy said. "I'll have room for dessert."

Flynn flipped the chicken in the hot grease. "While I'm cooking, go check out the living room. There are a few other toys I picked out for you, Billy."

Billy got out of his chair. "Come on, Ford." He swung his arm in a big circle and ran out of the room.

She got a kick out of the loud hoot and holler she heard when Billy saw the trucks. If there was one sure way to make that kid happy it was with trucks.

Billy came back in the kitchen schlepping all three of the trucks in his arms, one hanging at an odd angle as if it might fall.

"He wouldn't let me carry one." Ford had his lip hanging in an exaggerated pout.

"Are you pouting?"

"Maybe," he said, poking his lip out even further.

"You have to share with Ford, Billy," Flynn said, flashing Ford a teasing grin.

"Can we play out on the patio until dinnertime?"

"You can play out there and I'll bring dinner out as soon as it's done. We can have a picnic. Does that sound like a good plan?"

"Yes!" Billy wobbled off, trying to hold the third truck up off the ground, then stopped. "You can carry one, Ford." His lips pulled into a straight line as he looked down at all three of the trucks. "You can play with the Ford truck, since it's named after you."

"Thanks, man." Ford reached for the blue truck and followed Billy outside.

The sound of Billy and Ford sputtering like diesel engines outside made her laugh. One of them made a crashing sound. And darn if that hadn't sounded like a cow mooing. Boys.

She turned off the stove and filled a basket with chicken tenders, then stacked three paper plates on top of the basket to carry out. The mac 'n' cheese emerged browned to perfection when she slid it on the counter. While it cooled a bit, she went upstairs and got a king-sized sheet out of the linen closet to use as a picnic cloth.

She went out on the patio and opened the sheet, giving it a parachute lift and then straightened it out on the ground. The guys never even noticed her. "Looks like y'all are having fun."

"Monster truck races," Billy said. "I'm winning."

"I went off the track," Ford confessed. "But I didn't know the patio was out of bounds."

Billy pushed his lips together and made a skidding noise as he pushed his truck past Ford's. "I just lapped you!"

"I thought we were on a time-out," Ford argued.

"No way," Billy said.

"You're going down," Flynn teased. "Dinner's ready. Give me a minute and I'll get everything out here."

"Need any help?"

"No, you two play. I've got this." It took her three trips to get everything out to the porch, but as soon as the picnic was ready, Billy ordered Ford to "park the trucks."

"This is my favorite dinner." Billy picked up a chicken tender and bit into it.

Ford made a plate, heaping a spoonful of macaroni and cheese on his plate and snagging two chicken tenders. "I think this just became my favorite dinner too, Billy."

That kid had an appetite. She never had any trouble getting him to eat when he stayed with her. There were only a couple of chicken strips left when they were done. Ford had enjoyed seconds and thirds.

"You're the best cook in the world, not counting Mom."

"Thank you. That's the best compliment in the world." Flynn gathered the leftovers and Billy carried in the tray with the plates and plasticware on it. "Thank you for helping clean up."

"You're welcome, Aunt Flynn."

She ruffled his hair. That ticking clock always went crazy when she got to spend time with Billy. She ached for one of her own.

When she went back outside, it was just starting to get dark, and the first thing she noticed was that the guys hadn't folded up the sheet like she'd expected they would. Instead, they'd draped it over the clothesline to make an A-frame tent, anchoring it to the ground with some rocks.

Ford had taken the portable fire pit from the patio out to the yard and built a small fire about six feet away from the tent.

"What are y'all up to?"

"Camping," Billy announced. He flung himself on the ground with his head sticking out one end of the makeshift tent. "I'm going to watch for stars."

"I'm not much of a camper," Flynn said. "The ground is hard. Why don't we get the big cushion off of the double chaise lounge from the screened-in porch. We can lie on that."

"Can we?" Billy jumped to his feet.

"Sure."

Ford followed Billy to the porch and carried the cushion while Billy trailed him carrying a couple of the smaller chair pillows.

"We're going to be comfy cozy," Billy said, a million-dollar smile on his face tonight.

Ford pushed the cushion into place under the big sheet, scooting the rocks. The breadth of the cushion helped push the tent sides wider and hold its shape. "You gonna sleep over with us, Flynn?" He gave her an exaggerated wink. "Pretty please with cherries on top?"

Billy crawled inside. "This is so cool. It's like a tree house on the ground." He lay on his back, crossing his feet and putting his hands behind his head. "This is the life."

Ford sprawled out next to the tent and laid his head on the soft mattress. "It is pretty comfortable. Only thing that would make it better is if you'd start belly dancing and waving palm leaves over me," he teased Flynn.

"Don't get any bright ideas. I'm not feeding you grapes, no matter what you say."

"I knew I should have gotten fruit for dessert."

Billy scrambled to the edge of the tent, peeking out the end toward Flynn. "Flynn usually makes cookies for our treat."

"I was in charge of dessert tonight," Ford said. "Tonight we're doing manly stuff."

"Excuse me," Flynn said. "Cookies are manly."

"Okay, they are, but this will be just as good. Maybe even better." He got to his feet. "You'll see," he said. "My dessert is going to be great."

Billy folded his arms. "I don't know. Guess we'll see."

"Can I get just a little bro-code faith from my amigo here? I'm try-ing to impress this girl," he said to Billy.

Billy slapped his hands over his mouth, holding back a swirl of laughter, but Flynn wasn't laughing. Her insides tumbled. She let the comment hang, not wanting to read too much into it.

Ford went inside and came out with a brown paper sack and three wire hangers.

"Store-bought." Billy rolled his eyes.

"How old are you?" Ford dropped the bag on the ground and started untwisting the hangers, straightening them into three long wires.

"Seven."

"I don't think I knew the difference between store-bought and homemade when I was seven." He pulled a bag of marshmallows out of the sack and threaded three on each wire hanger. "I might not be able to tell the difference now."

He handed the bag to Flynn. "Will you divvy up the graham crackers?"

"Sure."

"And that guy," he said pointing to Billy, "can unwrap the choco-late bars."

"Yes!" Billy fist pumped and did a little two-step. "I'll do quality control."

"You've been around Jackson too long." Ford pointed his two fin-gers toward Billy and then to his own eyes and back again. "I'm watch-ing you."

Billy unwrapped the candy bars and set them on the plate next to the graham crackers Flynn was breaking in half. "I'm watching you back," Billy said.

Ford armed them each with a wire hanger. "Have you done this before?"

The boy shook his head. "No. Mom makes s'mores in the microwave."

"That's just so wrong. Okay, come stand right here next to me." He clicked his fingers toward Flynn. "You too, pretty girl."

Pretty girl? She felt as gooey inside as one of those marshmallows. She shuffled up next to him and held her hanger out like a fishing pole in front of her.

"Nice technique," he teased.

"I've melted a marshmallow or two over the years."

Billy mimicked them, hovering his marshmallows over the fire a safe distance.

Flynn's marshmallows caught on fire.

"Yours are ruined," Billy yelled out.

"No way. This is how they get the gooiest." She pulled her wire in—the marshmallows black and crispy.

Ford wrapped his arm around her waist and helped her blow out the flame. "Good job," he said squeezing her.

"Thanks." When he stood that close, it was all she could do to keep her own gooey center in control.

"I'm not eating those ones." Billy pulled his lips into a Billy Idol sneer.

"More for me." She took a graham cracker and stacked a piece of chocolate on it, then slid a marshmallow on top of it. The chocolate immediately softened under the heat of the toasted marshmallow. "This is going to be so good."

Billy bounced on his toes. "Mine next."

Ford helped Billy finish his marshmallow and stack his s'more, then made one for himself.

"Ready?"

Billy lifted his and bit into it. "Tastes even better than Mom's."

"We will never tell her that," Flynn said.

There were enough leftovers to make s'mores for the neighborhood, but it had been fun. The night sky glittered with a smattering of sparkling stars. Billy wiped his hands on a paper towel and then lay in the tent with his head hanging out on a pillow.

"Are you tired?" Flynn repacked the leftovers back in Ford's paper sack.

"No, ma'am. I'm looking for shooting stars again."

"The last time he was here there was a meteor shower. We came out at one o'clock in the morning to watch for them," Flynn explained to Ford.

"We saw a ton. I made wishes all night." Billy stared into the sky.

She didn't have the heart to tell him that there weren't any meteor showers tonight. It would be a miracle if he caught a glimpse of even one shooting star.

"Let's all watch." Ford knelt down and climbed into the tent. "Come on, Flynn."

Who was she to argue? Billy lay right smack-dab in the middle, with Ford on the right, so she slid into the empty spot on the left.

"There's one!" Billy pointed to the sky.

"Are you sure?"

"Yes! Look. Another one."

Wishful thinking was a powerful image in the mind of a seven-year-old. "Make a wish," she said quietly.

"I did."

A few minutes later Billy was asleep.

"Do you think he really saw a falling star?" Ford asked. "I didn't see anything."

"No. Probably not, but it made him happy, and there's never anything wrong with making a wish."

"I made a couple, just in case," Ford said.

"It's a beautiful night. Thanks for hanging out with us."

"I wouldn't have missed it." He reached his arm across Billy and touched her cheek. "If this little munchkin wasn't sleeping so soundly between us, I'd lean over and kiss you right now."

She didn't even know what to say. She'd had the very same feeling.

"Don't say anything." He winked and closed his eyes with a slight grin playing on his lips.

A few moments later, Flynn heard Ford suck in a deep breath. She rolled over onto her belly, watching both Billy and Ford sleep under the starry night. Billy looked so tiny lying beneath the sheet next to Ford.

This was a perfect night. Nothing fancy, just simple fun. Sharing time with people who made her feel special.

She slipped her phone out of her pocket and set the alarm. There was no need to disturb them. They had everything they needed for a good night's rest. She'd make sure that Ford got up in time to get ready for his first class tomorrow and Billy had time to get up and brush his teeth and hair before Angie came by to take him to school.

The only thing missing from this picture was three more children and a dog. She turned back over and watched the sky.

A star soared across the southeastern arch. She squeezed her eyes shut and made a wish.

Chapter Fourteen

Ford jerked awake. It hadn't been much more than a whisper, but the sound had pulled him out of the middle of a dream involving a weird paintball war at a demolition derby—no place for a lady, and it had definitely been a woman's voice.

His inability to lift his arm to rub the sleep from his eyes woke him in a panic. Last night quickly came back into focus when he saw the top of Billy's head nestled beside him.

"Sorry," Flynn said.

He twisted his neck toward the sound of her voice. She was standing outside the makeshift tent. "When did you get up?"

"A little while ago. I'm an early riser. I thought you might need to get up so you'd have time to shower and eat before you go to the gallery today."

Ford eased Billy to the side without waking him. "Thanks," he whispered. "What time is it?"

"It's still pretty early. It's only six."

"Oh, good." Ford gave an extra wide stretch.

Billy stirred when Ford yawned.

"Good morning, sleepyhead." Ford ruffled Billy's hair.

Billy giggled. "Good morning. I forgot we camped."

"I did too. Must mean we slept pretty good," Ford said.

"It was a fun night, and yummy dessert. Can we have s'mores for breakfast too?"

"Better than cookies, wasn't it?" Ford flashed a grin toward Flynn, who was already pursing her lips. He liked her competitive nature. "And way more fun with me here, right?"

"No way," Flynn shot back. "Just different fun, right?"

"It's always fun here," said Billy.

"A tie," Ford said. But he wasn't really competing with her. In fact, the three of them being together is what had felt so right about the whole situation.

"Oh, no you don't. You better go get ready for work. Billy and I are going to make breakfast. He's a great helper." She started toward the kitchen. "A really wonderful blue-ribbon breakfast."

"I'll crack the eggs."

"Hope you're good at that, young man. I don't like my eggs crunchy," Ford said as he climbed to his feet and headed inside.

"He had a good teacher."

"I'll be the judge of that." He climbed the stairs, a little stiff. It had been a while since he'd camped. Last night was worth a few aches and pains though.

The hot water in the shower felt good against his tight shoulder muscles. He could stand there forever under the pounding water pressure thinking about Flynn lying under the stars. What her lips would have felt like against his. His hands on her body, but there was no time for that this morning. He dressed in a pair of heavy jeans and a stream-blue Carhartt three-button Henley. He tucked his shirt in and then pulled his leather belt through the loops. He tucked his wallet and keys into his pockets, then grabbed his phone and went downstairs.

Billy's and Flynn's voices floated up the stairwell as he walked downstairs. He'd taken a little too long in the shower. Too bad he wouldn't have time to eat breakfast with Flynn and Billy, because whatever it was they were fixing smelled delicious.

"Aunt Flynn said you have to go to school today too," Billy said when Ford walked into the kitchen.

"I hadn't really thought about it like that, but I guess you're right. Except I'm the teacher."

"That's cool," Billy said. "You can talk in class and not get in trouble."

Ford and Flynn exchanged a smile. "True. Hope you stay out of trouble today, Billy. And Flynn, I'll see you tonight."

"We made you breakfast." Billy grabbed a bundle off the kitchen island and took it to Ford. "She said you might need it to go. It's a sammich."

"That was really nice of you. Thanks." Ford took the sandwich.

"It was her idea," Billy said. "She's nice like that."

Yes, she was. Almost perfect and, even though he'd come here with her on his mind, being here now almost scared him. She loved this place.

Flynn leaned against the island. "Have a great day."

"It's off to a really good start."

"I know. I am the number one aunt after all."

He leaned in and whispered, "You look so fine, even after sleeping outside under the stars, I hate to leave." Easing back, he glanced down at Billy. If the little guy hadn't been standing there staring at them, he'd have pulled her up close and shown her exactly how good she looked.

Her mouth dropped open, but she didn't respond. Instead, she just smiled and waved her fingers as he turned to leave. His glance caught the slight blush rising in her cheeks.

Ford got into the old truck. Feeling unusually mellow, maybe content, he didn't bother to turn on the radio. He'd thought he'd be more excited about today. He'd been planning this session for a while, but in contrast to last night it didn't seem quite as big a deal.

Being with Flynn had felt more real than anything he'd imagined. He could see them together, with children, enjoying the simple things in life. Laughing and working on things together.

The residency was going to pay the bills for a while, and with the gallery closing down, he needed that. After last night he felt inspired to create something extra special just for her, but that would just have to wait until after class. However, after class he was pretty sure the only thing on his mind was going to be hurrying back to her.

He pulled into a parking spot around back near his studio entrance and went inside to set up. They'd supplied a nice selection of tools for his use, but he'd brought along a few of his favorites. He put all of them where he wanted them, adjusted some of the racks and rods, and then inventoried the glass supplies and colors.

He'd start the group off with something easy, but cool, to build their confidence and inspire innovation. Push them out of their comfort zone a little, while helping them form partnerships with other students.

Making art could be solitary, yet the collision of two different thought processes inspired innovation, and that's when really great art happened. One thing about some of the really big pieces he was so well known for was that sometimes you had to have a partner to help you transition the pieces and stack the glass. It just wasn't something you could pull off alone if you wanted to really push the science of hot glass techniques. The right partner could make such a big difference on big pieces. He'd been lucky to have worked with some great artists back in Alaska. Too bad most of them didn't stick around for long.

A pretty redhead came into the studio, her hair up with a pencil stuck through it. "Ford Morton?" She thrust her hand out and headed toward him like a jouster. "We're so glad to have you. Our artists are chomping at the bit to learn from you."

His hand became sweaty. He shook her hand and mumbled, "Thank you." Ford never had been good at taking a compliment.

She glanced at the clipboard in her hand. "I hope it's okay that we increased the size of today's session slightly. We had the museum reps from the Norfolk Botanical Gardens in town, and they were so excited when they heard you were here."

"I've got a couple of pieces displayed there."

"That's what they said." She clung to the clipboard, pulling it to her chest like a life preserver saving her from rough seas. "We've been dying to do some cross sharing of pieces with them, so that's why I thought to slip them in. They won't be active participants, just observers."

"That's fine." Could be a win-win. He might be able to sell them a few new pieces rather than just have the museums swap.

Attendees started entering the room and chatting. Ford took his time, meeting each one individually and listening to their inspirations and aspirations. He'd have plenty of time to give them information, mentor them, but listening was the best way to be sure he helped each of them meet their individual goals.

The pretty redhead tapped one of the punty rods against the concrete floor to get everyone's attention.

"Good morning, everyone. We're excited here at PRIZM Glass Art Institute to have one of the top glassblowers in the nation with us. He's come all the way from Alaska. So when you're not here in class learning, I bet you'll hear some pretty interesting stories." She went on to recite his bio and accolades. This part always made Ford feel weird. It was like bragging.

Ford stepped forward. "Thank you. I'm honored to be here and to share and learn with you. Glassblowing isn't for the lazy. It's a fast medium. The spontaneous nature requires us to respond quickly and I think that's where the real magic of our artistry is. I rarely go into a piece, unless it's contracted specifically, with an end product in mind. Like in dance, or in music, you have to go with the flow, the rhythm, and the colors as you progress. Letting yourself experiment and remaining unafraid of failure, you'll come up with something that brings harmony and interest to not only you but the observer."

Heads nodded. If he took one thing from all those years in law school it was the ability to draw in a group of people and hold their interest. Wasn't every group a jury, in a way?

Four hours later he'd lectured and helped the artists with some simple techniques that would allow them advance no matter what level they currently were.

They broke for lunch and Ford checked his phone. He had a text from Flynn that a package had arrived for him, asking if he'd like her to bring it over. He started to message her back, but called instead.

"Hello?"

Her soft voice felt welcome. "Hey, Flynn. Thanks for the text."

"Ford? I didn't mean to disturb you. The box is from Alaska so I wasn't sure if it was something you needed for your class today."

"I wasn't expecting anything." The only people that knew exactly where he was were Chet and Missy. He hadn't left an address with anyone else.

"I have an appointment just east of Heron Cove today. I'm happy to drop the package by for you this afternoon when I get done."

It could wait, but seeing her here held a certain appeal that he'd rather not let pass. "Yeah, that would be great."

"Okay, well I'll see you in a little while. I'll text when I get there, if that's okay. Or I could leave it at the front desk."

Knowing she was coming by made him stir. He'd just left her a few hours ago, yet he was anxious to see her now. "Come on back to my studio."

"Are you sure?"

"Positive. I'll see you in a little while." He hung up the phone and checked his watch. For someone who'd just been put out of a job and was thousands of miles from home, he sure felt on top of the world.

The students were working on their projects—a takeoff on those standard Christmas ornaments that they sold by the dozens. Things were starting to get real. Each student had been challenged to come up with their own design based on the new techniques Ford had taught them this morning.

A couple of creations were already looking very promising—one student's in particular, which integrated feathers of all types and colors. While the rest of the class worked on the assignment, this young lady had tried to find a way to incorporate the task into her feather-focused body of work. Once she'd made the simple glass globe, she'd blown a bright peacock feather, tiny in size but big on design. Even for a seasoned artist it was an impressive piece, and she'd laid it right into the glasswork, layering another and another until the beautiful feathers joined tip to tail around the ornament.

Ford connected two of the beginners who'd really impressed him with two of the seasoned students. The competitive nature of the new glassblowers pushed the boundaries and innovation of the seasoned artists. Always good to see.

Half the benefit of this type of instruction was that each of the students also contributed to the learning experience with their own styles and ideas.

He caught a glimpse of bright turquoise to his left. Flynn stood in the doorway watching, looking fresh and pretty.

He waved her in, then walked over to greet her.

She handed him the package. "It's really impressive to see people working all at once."

Ford turned and tried to observe as a first-timer. He'd forgotten the feeling he'd gotten the first time he'd observed hot glass in progress. It had been awe inspiring. Now it was just another day. "You're getting a treat. These artists are a good bunch. I'm impressed."

"I don't know what I expected, but in my mind I pictured you demonstrating. This is so interactive."

"Instruction won't get you too far in this kind of stuff. You have to get in there and do it. Feel it for yourself. And everyone brings their own little intricacies to the process."

"It's hot in here."

"Well, we are melting glass."

"Good point. I'd have to blow glass in my bathing suit." She plucked the blouse from her arm. "I can't even imagine how hot it is in the summer."

Flynn in a bathing suit was something he didn't mind imagining. Just the thought was making him bust out in a sweat himself. "You get used to it, and you have to wear the right clothes. None of that man-made stuff. If that stuff gets hot, it'll burn and melt into your skin, and that hurts like the dickens. Can't risk that."

"Don't you worry that you'll get burned?"

"I'm careful." He opened the package as he spoke. "Son of a gun."

"What is it?"

"These are some ornaments I'd made the first year I was with Glory Glassworks. I haven't seen them in years. Kind of forgot about them actually."

"Let me see." She leaned in to look at the foam-wrapped box of four ornaments. "They are gorgeous. You made those?"

"I did." He lifted a note card out of the box.

"Everything okay?"

He nodded as he finished reading. "Yeah. I'm good. I told you about Glory Glassworks going out of business right before I left. I thought this was from Ziegler, the owner of the place. He had these."

"Who is it from?"

"Friend of mine owns a bar in town. He said he bought the whole set for a hundred bucks. Ziegler had to have been mortified. If they'd let him sell the assets himself he'd have brought more than ten times that for this collection." Ford reread the note. Ziegler had made him promise not to call Ford. "Looks like they are putting the building up for auction next."

"Is that good?"

"Could be. I'd love to buy it. I had plans for that place. I just never knew Ziegler was at risk of losing it. I could've helped him."

"People are so funny about asking for help."

"Like you?"

"Guilty as charged," she said. "Thanks for all of your help. I really do appreciate it."

"I really do like doing those fixer-upper kind of things." He couldn't really say anything about not asking for help, though. He wasn't one to ask for help either, but now he needed to figure out a way to bid on the Glory Glassworks building. Thank goodness Chet had found a way to avoid breaking his promise to Ziegler to keep the auction quiet by writing about it instead of calling. Chet was wily that way. "Thanks for bringing this by. I appreciate it. It'll be fun to show these folks something I did back when I was still green too."

"That doesn't look like rookie work to me."

He held one of the delicate ornaments by the fourteen karat gold hook. "Sometimes it's not about how *long* you've invested yourself, but how much of yourself you've invested that makes the difference."

That comment could apply to him and Flynn. They hadn't spent much time together, but the time they'd spent was more precious than anything he'd experienced in his life. He wanted more.

Chapter Fifteen

A week later, Ford had fallen into an East Coast rhythm and, as much as Alaska was tugging at him in hopes that an auction date would be announced soon for the Glory Glassworks Gallery building, he also felt anxious as the days ticked away to the time he'd be leaving this place behind. And not only this place but Flynn.

Waking up to the smell of fresh coffee and home cooking each morning could spoil a man. And if that wasn't enough, her smile was.

He'd never been much of a morning person, but maybe that was just because he'd never started his days off quite right. Like with fluffy towels and their soft flowery scent. He was dying to know how Flynn looked stepping out of the shower and wrapping herself in one of those. So far he'd remained a gentleman. But she was tempting—he needed to make a move soon, or else he'd be leaving here with no romance in his future.

He drove to work with her on his mind. The radio still set to the station Flynn had dialed in last night when they'd ridden over to Criss Cross Farm for a cookout with Jackson and that gang. He smiled when he recognized Flynn's favorite song on the radio. She'd mentioned it last night as she belted out the lyrics like she was on the Grand Ole Opry stage with no microphone. She wasn't a very good singer, but she didn't seem to care.

Great. Now that would be in his head all day.

He turned down the road to PRIZM Glass Art Institute.

The sign out front still bore the announcement of his arrival and the special sessions he was leading, even though they'd been sold out for over a month. The way things were going he'd be tempted to say yes if they asked him to extend his stay for a week or two to accommodate those on the waiting list.

He parked and went inside. It was still early, and he liked it when it was quiet like this. Inside, he gathered his materials for this morning's work session.

"Good morning, Ford. Before you get started, I want you to meet someone," Gary said.

"Sure." Ford wiped his hands on a rag and walked over to meet the man.

"This is William Barron. He runs the museum shop down in Norfolk, Virginia. They are interested in talking to you about a showing."

Ford extended his hand to the older gentleman. Everything about him looked put together. His suit probably cost as much as Ford earned last month. "Thank you. Nice to meet you, Mr. Barron."

"You can call me William. Nice to meet you too. We have three of your latest collection that Winston over at Glory Glassworks Gallery shipped us last month. I tried to contact him last week, but I got an auto-responder reply that said the gallery wasn't going to be shipping to the lower forty-eight any longer. What's going on?"

"Not my story to tell," Ford said. "But you've got it right. I've got what he had in inventory at my place in Alaska. I'd be happy to help you. In fact, I'll be looking to get those pieces placed quickly."

"Are you moving here?"

"No," he said without hesitation. "My home is in Alaska, but I can get you an updated catalog of the pieces I have available."

"That would be great."

Ford pulled out his wallet—a leather one that had once been Pop-pop's. It had seen better days, but he had no desire to carry anything else. He and his dad might not be able to see eye to eye but his grandfather had always understood him. He'd been the only one supportive of his decision to move to Alaska. Ford plucked out a business card and handed it to him. "I have some new things no one has seen yet. I'd love for you to have a look."

Gary perked up. "Now wait a second. Count me in too."

"If you want to give me some extra comped time in the studio, I'll do a special one-of-a-kind piece for you while I'm here."

"I think I might get the better half of that deal," Gary said.

"You just might, but I like to keep those new techniques sharp. As much as I enjoy teaching, it doesn't give me the creative outlet I need. I'm chomping at the bit for some time of my own."

"You just let me know when you want time and I'll make it happen. Stay longer if you like," Gary said.

"If you decide to stay a bit longer, I hope you'll come visit our gallery in Norfolk," William said. "I think you'll be really pleased with how we've got you displayed. We look forward to growing that collection."

"Great. I'd be happy to help you with that. Any other questions I can answer? I've got twelve creative minds waiting on me in there."

"No. Thanks for giving us a bit of your time this morning." William stepped to the side. "I may stay and watch for a bit."

"Sounds good. I'll get the updated catalog emailed over to you tonight when I get done here, and I can ship out whatever you like as soon as I get back to Alaska."

"Ford's residency with us is for a month." Gary raised his eyebrow. "Unless I can talk him into staying longer."

William paused. "I hope you can talk him into staying for the benefit of the institute, but part of me wants him to get back to Alaska so I can get my order filled. I've kept you long enough. Thank you for your time, Ford."

"Pleasure was all mine." Ford walked into the studio feeling like things were starting to go his way. This trip was paying for itself in ways he hadn't expected. Gaining new collectors, an offer to come out to another gallery in the spring, and Flynn.

He was in such a good mood that he picked two students out of the class to stay and do a thirty-minute session on advanced techniques, since tonight Flynn and Angie were meeting up with girlfriends.

When Ford got to the Blue Skies Cafe, Jackson had already staked out a table. He walked inside and slid into the booth across from him. "Where's Billy? I figured you'd have him tonight."

"He's at a Cub Scout meeting. By the way, Billy's still talking about that tent you made out of a sheet last week. You're a bigger deal than Santa Claus."

"We had a blast doing that," Ford said. It had been the night he knew exactly what he wanted his future to look like.

"He is the coolest kid, isn't he?" Jackson's expression said it all. "From what Angie says, Flynn seems to think you're a pretty cool kid too." Jackson punched Ford in the shoulder. "You dog. Don't you break her heart, or I'll never hear the end of it. They're best friends. This is right up there with dating sisters."

"Flynn said something?" He balled his hand in a fist and opened it, trying to release some of the nervous energy. Ford had planned to mention his feelings to Jackson, but now he was way more interested in hearing what she had said about him.

"You *are* interested in her, aren't you?" Jackson looked at him, waiting for an answer. "Your lack of answer is answer enough." His friend dropped back laughing.

Ford leaned forward. "How crazy would you think I was if I admitted I'd been thinking about her for a while? Like since your wedding?"

"No way." Jackson pushed his hand through his hair. "Do you know how much crap I'm going to have to listen to from Angie? She swore y'all would be a perfect match at the wedding. I told her she was crazy."

The waitress stopped by the table and took their order.

"Well, at least now I understand why you've been so busy over there at her house."

"It was part of the deal. You know that. I stayed for free and helped her with her to-do list."

"Whatever you say, man. Sounds like you may have had your own agenda all along, but don't worry. No one else will hear that from me. I like seeing you like this."

"Like what?"

"All googly-eyed like a teenager over Flynn."

"Who says?"

"I was your wingman in college. I know how you act when you're not serious. And the way you're acting today is not like that."

Couldn't hide things from a best friend. They'd call bullshit on you so fast it would sting. "It's been fast, but yeah. I like her. A lot."

"If there's even a maybe, you're an idiot if you don't at least give it a chance. Flynn is a nice gal."

"I know that, and I've really liked spending time with her, but I don't think she'd ever leave Boot Creek."

"Have you asked her?"

"No, but she loves that house."

"That's not your decision to make. Just be honest with her, and let things move from there."

"I don't want to look like I'm moving too fast."

"Right now you're not moving at all. You may as well be a taxidermy moose head."

"I've made a couple of subtle moves." Were they too subtle? He did only have three weeks left before he headed back home.

"What do you have to lose?"

"Nothing or everything." And he didn't want to lose her before he even had her.

"I always thought you'd be the first one of us to get married and here you are the last one of us."

"Thanks for the reminder. It's not for lack of trying."

"You must be one dud of a roommate."

"I'm a great roommate. I pull my weight." But he'd never lived with a woman. That wasn't his style.

"Then just think about what I said. I don't care one way or the other, but I'd hate for you to miss out on the kind of life I'm living now. I've never been happier. Don't say anything to Flynn, but Angie and I have been trying to get pregnant."

"That's great, man." Ford felt a twinge of jealousy. Even from the outside looking in, Jackson's life looked pretty good.

~

Flynn pulled into the driveway. Just as she got out of the car, Ford parked at the curb in front of the house.

She walked up the sidewalk, then waited for him on the porch. "How was your night with Jackson?"

"Good." His long stride put him at her side in just a few steps. "Did you girls have fun?"

"Always do." She pulled her keys from her purse and unlocked the door. "I wonder sometimes why we don't do it more often."

"Easy to get caught up in the day-to-day. We should all prioritize the things that make us happy."

She twisted the key in the lock and opened the door.

"I wish it was that easy." She put her purse down on the table inside, but paused for a moment. *He* made her happy. Being with him made her feel uniquely like herself. Unaware of anything else. It was comfortable, like they'd been together for a long time, even though they'd only spent days . . . not months together. And perfect. And so not perfect. He was exactly what she said she didn't want. Why was it always that way?

"It can be that easy. Should be, really."

She shrugged. What could she even say to all of that? He was right after all. It should be easy. But her relationships never had been. "I'm going to try to schedule more time to get out and do things over the next year."

"Like what?"

"I don't know. Maybe some weekend trips. A class here and there. Work on that bucket list I plan to start." She walked into the living room with him following along.

"The one with Alaska on it?"

"Maybe." She glanced around the room. It wasn't her style, didn't even really represent her. *But.* "I love this place. Maybe it's the memories that this house holds. My mom grew up here. My grandparents spent the best years of their lives here. I spent the best days of my childhood here. Maybe I kind of hoped being here would make that happen for me." She took in a deep breath. "Is that so bad to wish for?"

"Not at all. Everyone dreams of finding that right person to complete their life."

She hadn't said anything about finding someone; he'd kind of read that into what she'd said. But he was right.

"And taking some classes," he said. "We should always keep learning. What kind of class are you going to take?"

She was glad for the topic shift. "Maybe I'll take a glassblowing class. Watching your students was really interesting."

"I could make that happen for you."

She shook her head. "I'm pretty sure I wouldn't be worthy of an instructor of your caliber. I was thinking maybe a beginner class or something."

They sat down across from each other, and Ford leaned his elbows forward, resting them on his knees. "I'd really like to teach you. I'm a good teacher. I told you I teach tourists. I'm very patient."

"Why would you want to do that when you're teaching all day long?"

"I'd much rather teach you . . . a friend . . . a very beautiful friend . . . than a stranger, any day of the week."

A smile tugged at the corner of her mouth. He thought she was beautiful. She tried to hide the smile with a funny face. "I'll probably be your worst student ever."

"Let's find out."

"You're serious, aren't you?"

"Completely." Ford sat back. "And if you're really that bad, we'll probably still have fun. What are you doing tomorrow afternoon around four?"

"Nothing that can't wait."

"Meet me at PRIZM. You and I have a glassblowing date."

The word *date* made her ears tickle. Don't get your hopes up, she thought to herself. Things were going so well since she'd made the decision to just take things a day at a time and learn to love her life without someone else in it. Stay the course. At least until tomorrow.

"I'll come on one condition," she said.

"What's that?"

"That you let me reciprocate by helping you with something one day."

"Done."

"Excellent." She clapped her hands, then raised them in the air like a gymnast who'd just stuck a perfect landing. "This is going to be fun."

"It's going to be great." He stood and tucked his shirt tighter into the back of his jeans. "I've got an early morning tomorrow, so I'm going to get to bed. Don't make breakfast for me. I won't have time for it."

"Okay," she said. "Good night."

He reached down and gave her shoulder a squeeze.

"That feels nice." She laid her head over to his hand still on her shoulder.

He placed both hands on top of her shoulders and started kneading her muscles, slow and deep. She closed her eyes and breathed in. "Did you take a class in massage?"

"No, but I have been told I give the best back massages around."

"You'd get my endorsement." She tipped her head to the right. His warm hand grazed her cheek as he continued to rub. She wished he'd take her into his arms.

He stopped. "Sleep well, pretty girl."

"Good night, Ford."

She sat with her back to the doorway, listening to his footsteps as he walked through the room toward the stairs.

Disappointed.

She closed her eyes, promising herself that she wouldn't let herself get carried away. Ford's friendship had become extra special, and his timing was perfect.

She was thankful for his help with the B&B and how he'd helped her remember to prioritize her own things. That would have to be enough.

Chapter Sixteen

A heavy storm had rolled through Boot Creek around five, and when the thunder woke her, she'd been unable to fall back to sleep. The morning that greeted her was gray and gloomy. She'd given in and pulled on a pair of yoga pants and an NC State T-shirt that had seen better days. She started the coffee and then went to check the porch for the newspaper.

When she opened the door, mist blew inside. The rain pounded the roof like a herd of wild ponies. Loud and powerful.

The sweet smell of the rain drew her outside. Nothing better than a storm.

She picked up the paper, tossing it inside. Water dripped down her arm. She swept at it, then leaned against the porch column, letting herself get lost in the melody of the pounding rain. Lightning danced in the distance and the thunder rolled.

"It's coffee o'clock," Ford said through the screen door. He pushed the door open with his foot and stepped next to her. "I brought you a cup. One sugar and one cream, right?"

His voice sent a welcome feeling through her. "Thank you. Yes." *He noticed how I take my coffee.*

He sucked in a deep breath. "It's nice out here." He handed her the cup of coffee, the mere touch of his hand sending warmth through her.

"I love storms," she said. "Kind of ruins my hair, though." She had to look like Medusa after standing out here in the rain for no telling how long. He looked refreshed and smelled of soap like he'd just gotten out of the shower.

He edged closer to her. "You look good to me."

A bashful rush of heat flooded her cheeks. "Thank you. That's sweet." She pulled her hair back, twisting it into what she hoped was at least a passable ponytail.

"Flynn, I've got something I need to say."

"Is something wrong?"

"No." He set his coffee cup on the porch rail, then took her hand in his. "Something's right. So right. I've enjoyed spending time with you."

"I've had fun too." What was he getting at? Did he think she was expecting something from him?

"The truth is I've been thinking about you since last summer. When I came back for the residency, I wanted to find a way to spend time with you."

"You did?" She was flattered, but a part of her felt a little duped too. He'd planned this?

"Yeah. Is it just me?" He looked so hopeful. "I think we have something kind of special going on here."

"Oh." She let her hand rest in his, because if she moved it, she was afraid he'd see her shaking. It wasn't just him. She'd felt it, but she'd resisted. He was everything that she'd promised herself she wouldn't fall for again. She looked into his eyes, and she couldn't lie. "It's not just you."

The way his eyes crinkled at the corners made her insides dance.

He grasped both of her hands in his and leaned in and kissed her softly. Rain blew against them. Was it the kiss or the cold rain that had just sent that shiver up her spine?

He rubbed his hands up and down her arms and then swept her against him, giving her a squeeze that made her heart thunder.

"I'm scared." She hadn't meant to say it out loud. "I'm not good with relationships. I don't want to make another mistake."

"Why not see where this goes?"

"You'll be gone soon. Thousands of miles away."

He leaned back looking into her eyes for a moment. His eyes begged for her trust, and her heart wanted to so badly.

But part of her wanted to run inside and lock him out of the house to keep him from stealing her heart. She was rebounding. That's what it had to be. She knew better.

He placed a kiss on her forehead. "Think about it. It could be fun."

"I like fun." But what she really wanted was so much more. Saying she would concentrate on herself was one thing, but her heart seemed to always be on the lookout for that one who would complete her. She lifted her coffee to her lips. "Ugh. That got cold fast."

"Let's go in and get a warm-up." He held the door for her and she ducked under his arm and went to the kitchen. "Want breakfast?"

"I don't have time," he said.

"I have just the thing." She held up a finger for him to hold on a second, then went into the pantry and sorted through a basket on the left top row. She walked back over to the counter holding three vacuum-sealed, candy-bar-sized packages. "Homemade biscotti. Almond, double chocolate pecan, or white chocolate cranberry?"

"You're kidding me."

"Or all three?"

"No ma'am. You're going to make me fat." Ford took the darkest one of the trio. "No contest. Double chocolate pecan all the way. I'll leave some for tomorrow."

"There's more."

"They've been in there the whole time?"

"I make big batches of them. The vacuum sealer rocks. They'll keep for like six months, longer without the chocolate." She laid the other two on the counter.

"I'll take this with me for an afternoon snack." He slid a hand over and snagged the almond one. "Maybe I need this one with my coffee now."

"I'm sure you do." She opened the other one and took a bite before pouring coffee for them both. "We're in for a couple days of rain. We need it, though. It's been dry for a long while."

"You okay driving out to the studio this afternoon?"

"I'm not afraid of a little rain. Four o'clock, right? I mean, unless you've changed your mind," Flynn said.

"No, no way am I changing my mind. I can't wait to share glass art with you. It's an experience you'll never forget."

"Good. The furnace guy is coming back this morning to give me an estimate, but I'm all yours this afternoon," Flynn said. "What are we going to make?"

"Memories," he said putting his hand on top of hers.

She bit down on her lip. His touch sent waves through her. "I'm ready."

"Ah, well, I better set your expectations low right now. There are so many things that can go wrong. You need to enjoy the process of it first. When you finish, we'll still have to bring it down to room temperature. Until you get through that, there's no guarantee you'll have anything at the end."

"Well, that doesn't sound fun at all."

"I'll help you—I'm pretty sure I can get you to make at least something small. We'll just do either a glass or an ornament. I can help you make whatever you want, but those are good starter projects."

"I'm in your hands."

"A good place to be."

She didn't doubt that for one minute. Were they still talking about glassblowing? "I'm really excited about it." Him *and* the outing.

He raised his coffee cup. "I've got to be there early. Do you mind if I take this coffee with me? I'll bring the cup back. I promise."

"I think I can spare a coffee mug if anything happens."

"I could make you a new one."

"Even better."

"Thanks, cutie." He dropped a peck on her cheek, then headed out of the room. Coffee in one hand and that chocolate biscotti in the other.

She spun around and leaned against the counter. *Figures guys like him don't live around here. How am I supposed to "see where this goes"? It's a waste of time.* But denying her feelings wasn't something she was about to try.

She'd just be careful to not let her heart get ahead of her brain this time.

Am I falling for him?

She shook her head. "I'm not," she said out loud. "I can't." Ford was sweet and fun. And tonight she was going to experience something new. But she was in control of her feelings this time.

Proud of herself for realizing things were okay, better than okay, she cleaned the house and even dusted the panel molding in the living room. Whoever invented that stuff should've invented a finish that resisted dust. It was a full-time job.

An hour later the electrician and the HVAC guys had come and assessed the situation. Turned out the electrical work was the culprit for the furnace failure too. She should be able to get another year or two out of the furnace—a relief. The electrician promised to have everything done no later than next Friday.

Things were coming back together.

Yet despite that strong start, the day seemed to be dragging by, like Christmas Eve when she was a kid.

To fill the time, she took a long leisurely bath and then picked out something to wear. Standing there in her panties and bra she dressed and undressed three times before she reminded herself that this was not about trying to impress him or anyone else. It was about being herself, and not setting her clothes on fire, of course. If something came out of this little get-together and it worked, it worked. If not, then it wasn't meant to be.

I'm the prize.

Finally, she slipped on her favorite pair of faded jeans, western boots, and a T-shirt with "blessed" in script across the front. The soft peach T-shirt gave her skin a nice glow. She slipped on a button-down denim shirt like a jacket and rolled up the sleeves.

She opened the old jewelry box on her dresser. It had been her mother's—the one thing that she would never get rid of, aside from the wedding rings Mom had once worn that still lay nestled in the first drawer. Considering she'd be using her hands, she slipped on a long necklace that had a pendant with a watch on the back of it, forgoing the wristwatch today. She layered a silver necklace—with simple turquoise and silver beads every six inches—on top of the other necklace, then decided that was probably not the best idea either. She took off the jewelry and pulled her hair into a ponytail.

The rain had slowed by the time she had to leave. Nerves danced inside her as she drove. Those few words between them this morning had changed things. If they let things go any further, there might be no turning back.

At four o'clock on the nose, she stepped up to the observation glass that ran the length of the studio where Ford was working.

She'd expected him to be wrapping up a session with students, but instead he was working a large piece of glass that looked like a plate. Bright blue and green lines crisscrossed a pattern that looked like flowers and leaves. Very pretty.

He must have caught her in his peripheral vision, because he smiled and gave her a nod. He spun the rod, running what looked like a heavy cloth under the glass, causing it to steam.

She took that as an invitation to come on in. "Hey. That looks a little scary," she said stepping into the room. The temperature in here was at least ten degrees warmer than out in the hallway.

"What's scary about it?"

"Aren't you afraid you'll accidentally touch the glass and burn yourself?"

"Not anymore." His confident smile was charming. "Don't worry. We're going to keep things simple, and I'll keep you safe."

She bit down on the left side of her lip. "Hope so."

"Let me just finish this up." He continued working the plate. Smoothing it into a perfectly polished disc. His muscles flexed with each move, forming and molding the soft glass.

He worked quickly. Spinning, shaping, and snipping. "What do you think?"

"It's pretty."

"Good. I'm glad you like it, because I made you a set of four." He carried the plate over to what looked like a big box.

She followed him and watched as he placed it carefully inside.

"This is the annealer," he said. "It will bring everything slowly to room temperature."

She peered inside. He had made her a whole set of them. "They're beautiful. You really made these for me?"

He nodded. "Now let's introduce you to my world."

A few minutes later she was wearing a frumpy blue lab coat that looked more like one of those housecoats her grandmother used to tidy in on Saturday mornings. That and a pair of oversized goggles made her feel like an oversized bug.

He pulled out his phone. "Selfie."

"You have got to be kidding. Look at me."

"You're adorable." He leaned in and wrapped his arm around her shoulder. "Give a thumbs-up and look like you're having fun."

She did as he asked, with a big openmouthed smile. After the flash, she tossed back her head laughing. "You're a goober."

"You'll be glad we have this picture one day."

"Somehow I doubt that."

"Trust me."

"You know those two words never lead to anything good."

"I'm going to let that go." He grabbed a punty rod. "Come here."

She stepped closer, unsure if the sweat she felt beading at the back of her neck was from the equipment or from being so close to him.

He leaned in. "You know you can trust me."

She took in a quick breath. Could she? The problem was she wasn't sure she could trust herself.

"Couple quick tips," he said. "Everything is hot. If something starts to fall, let it. Resist the urge to catch things. Just follow my lead." He shifted his weight to his right leg as he picked up a hollow tube about four feet long. "This is the blowpipe. We're going to use this to get the blob of glass out of the crucible. I'll do that part, and then I'll get you to work the rest of it with me."

"I'm ready." But her hammering heart had her worried she might pass right out onto a glob of the hot glass.

"What's your favorite color?"

"Red."

He poured a scoop of red broken glass pieces on a table. "Silver or gold?"

"Gold."

"This is fourteen karat gold leaf." He laid the thin sheeting on the other end of the table.

"Real gold?"

"The real thing." He tapped the pipe on the floor, bouncing it up into his hand. "You ready?"

"I think so. Am I actually going to blow on that thing?"

"Yes. That's kind of how it works."

"Is it going to be hot?"

"Not unless you inhale, but I can do the actual blowing if you like. When you're ready, just tell me and you can try it to get the feel for it."

"I think I like the idea of you doing most of the work." She hoped he didn't notice the blush that was rising up her neck. She wasn't thinking about the glass right now. She couldn't keep her mind off him. There was something raw and sexy about being around all this hot equipment. She brushed the sweat from her lip and tried to concentrate on what he was doing.

He dipped the pipe into the fiery furnace and withdrew it. A ball of bright glowing glass danced at the end of the metal.

Anticipation zipped through her veins. There was something beautiful and frightening about the glass in this state.

"Okay, now we have to keep spinning the pipe to prevent the glass from dropping. Come here and turn it with me."

She stepped closer and placed her hands next to his. "Like this?"

"Not so fast. It's not speed that's keeping the glass on the pipe. A steady turn is all you need to keep the glass in balance. Good. See how it's retaining that shape?"

"Yes." They moved slowly. In a steady rhythm—together—as one.

"Now watch as we slow down. See how we lose the shape." He picked up speed and the glass steadied. "I'll dip it back in the glory hole to keep it pliable so we can work some magic."

She giggled. "That sounds a little nasty." And that was about the most high school thing she could've said right now.

He snickered. "Kind of, but it's innocent. Help me."

She wished her eyebrow hadn't quirked up like that just then. He'd noticed it. She read it in his face, but he didn't say anything.

This was his life's work. Why was she making jokes? Nerves. She always giggled at the most inappropriate times. It had gotten her in trouble all the time as a kid.

She followed Ford's lead, holding the pipe in the fire. The heat made her skin tighten, and she felt panic rise as the shape of the glass drooped when he lifted his hands, letting her turn the pipe alone. "I need your help."

"You've got it. Slow down. Nice and steady. There you go. You're doing great."

"What are we making?"

"Right now it's not about what we're making as much as the process of doing it. Just relax."

She nodded and tried to match his movements.

Her eyes glazed over a bit. Maybe from the heat. Maybe from the magic of controlling something that seemed so uncontrollable.

"We're going to start with making snowmen or caterpillars."

"Those are two completely different things."

"Not really. Watch." He turned and slowly went through the process of making the caterpillars. "You'll get used to using the jacks, how to constrict and pinch the glass in liquid form. You'll get used to turning the pipe. It's a lot of moving parts with both hands. That's not easy for some people."

"You make it look simple."

"Give it a try."

She tried to re-create the moves he'd just made. "Not quite as good as yours, but close."

"Very good. You're a natural. Keeping the glass centered is one of the toughest things for students to get down. You're doing great." He stepped back. "Are you having fun?"

"Yes. It's cool." She laughed, almost a little giddy. "Well, hot, but in a cool way." And he was hot . . . in a hot way.

"All right, let's make a glass globe. You ready?"

"Yes."

He pulled her in front of him, wrapped his arms around her, and helped her over to the crucible to dip out a hunk of glass.

They spun the rod, and each time the shape began to go cattywampus, he got the rhythm back.

"Now we're going to keep turning the rod on this table." He led her over to the table with his arms still around hers. "See how we're shaping the glass?"

Her arms moved with his, spinning and rolling the shape against the table. "Yes. This is amazing."

There was something primitively intimate about sharing art with an artist that she couldn't quite wrap her head around. She'd admired his collection, but to stand side-by-side and work the hot glass together deepened the intensity.

"Okay, now we're going to pick up the colored glass." He helped her raise the pipe and set it in the colored glass, then rolled the shape again.

The hot glass seemed to swallow the tiny bits of glass, changing its color along the way.

As the pieces became one with the hot ball of glass, her heart raced. Was it the effort of the continuous turns, or being so close to Ford? His arms were strong.

She leaned against him, feeling the strength of his arms.

His sweat.

His breath felt cool against her hot neck.

He moved with the ease that could only come from years of practice, and she imagined his hands on her as a skilled lover.

She had a feeling she'd melt in his hands, much like this glass.

Ford spoke close to her ear. "Just nice and easy. Find a rhythm and keep the movement steady and smooth."

"This is sexier than that pottery scene in the movie *Ghost*," she said. His arms flexed slightly, sending a shiver through her.

"Really?" He lowered his mouth closer to her neck. "That sounds promising."

I sure hope so. She giggled and the soft stubble of his chin tickled as it grazed the bare skin of her neck.

"Hope you won't be disappointed."

She swallowed hard. They worked together well. There was no doubt she was in dangerous territory with him now, with the feelings that were stirring inside her.

And by the time they'd laid the gold leaf into the red glass ball, she wasn't sure if she was in love with the process or this man that seemed to be shaping her at the same time.

He set their completed globe on a little stand, dropping a little kiss on her nose. "See. Not half bad."

No, not bad at all.

~

Ford sat across from Flynn at the Blue Skies Cafe.

"I still can't believe how much fun that was," she said, spinning her straw like one of the rods.

"It's addictive. If you think you liked what we just did, you'll have to do it again. I'm telling you. It's pretty amazing." He watched her expression. Would she want to do it again? Her eyes danced, making his insides do a little tango of their own. "Wait until you make something all by yourself."

"I'm not sure I could ever do it alone. You were doing a different thing with each hand."

"I'd be there to help, of course. You'd be surprised; you become ambidextrous. That's for sure. But a lot of the work is easier as a pair. One person spinning, the other laying on new pieces of glass. That kind of thing. It can be done alone, but it's even better with a good partner."

She touched her mouth. He wasn't sure what she was about to say, but she'd stopped herself.

"Did you try the beefalo when you were here for the wedding?" she asked.

"Isn't it just a fancy hamburger?"

"So much better than a burger. It's the specialty here, and they buy the meat fresh from Criss Cross Farm where Jackson works. You'll love it. Everyone does."

He closed the menu and set it to the side. "You haven't steered me wrong on anything yet."

The waitress took their order and dashed off.

"I won't steer you wrong," she said to Ford, her glance turning into a gaze.

She felt it too. Ford reached across and laid his hand on top of hers. She jumped, but didn't move otherwise.

"I believe that," he said. He liked the way the corner of her nose wrinkled when she smiled like that. The way she did when he said something nice to her. Bashful in a sexy-as-heck kind of way.

His phone vibrated across the table and a raucous chime broke the intimacy of the moment. Probably just as well, because he was getting ready to say something that he'd probably regret, since he'd be gone in a couple of weeks.

"Ford, here."

Across the line Chet sounded like he was hollering into a tin can. "Heard from your buddy at the glass shop yet?"

"Hey, Chet. No. Why?"

"Word is they are going to let him try to sell the place outright after all. Well, not all of the property, but where the glass shop was. One last chance to lower the debt before they swoop in and auction it off for a bargain basement price."

Ford's mood soured. "Why hasn't he called me? I told him I was interested."

"Probably overmortgaged the place. He would never try to sell it to you for more than it's worth."

"What that place is worth to me is for me to decide." His jaw pulsed.

"My thoughts exactly, which is why I'm calling you."

"Thanks, man. I got the package, by the way. How's everything else going out there?"

It was good to hear Chet's voice. "Weather's been mild as hell, so business is good. People are getting out. No complaints here."

"Good. Glad to hear that."

"Things going good there inland?"

"Yes. Even got a couple of new potential contracts. It's paying for itself in ways I hadn't expected." His gaze caught Flynn's. She was the best part of it all. "Do you have a new number for Ziegler?"

"Yeah. Hang on. He gave it to Missy yesterday. She's helping him eBay some stuff." There was shuffling and Ford could picture Chet rummaging through a stack of papers on top of the desk right off the bar. "Here it is. You got a crayon?"

He pulled a pen from his shirt pocket and grabbed a paper napkin from the dispenser against the wall. "Go."

Ford wrote down the number and then got off the phone.

"Everything okay?" Flynn asked.

He brought her up-to-date, filling in the blanks from the other side of the conversation that she hadn't been privy to.

". . . and I want that place. I could turn it into so much more than a tourist trap. We could do year-round work and really market the pieces. I even thought of doing student camps. A chance for artists to see Alaska and experience the nature while refining their craft. I think it could make money."

"Is this your dream?"

He pursed his lips, running a hand under his beard. "I guess it kind of is."

"You're not sure?"

"Well, the dream used to be building my house. The house is done." Did he dare say his dream included a wife and children? "I guess this would be the natural next step."

"Then I guess you need to go to Alaska."

He'd have to call and let Benson know if he was coming back early. That guy took watchdogging the property seriously. If they showed up at the house and Benson rolled up to check on things, he'd likely shoot them and then ask questions. He let out a long, slow breath. "I wonder how PRIZM would feel about me splitting up my time?"

"People around here are pretty laid back. Won't know until you ask, but I'd think you could sell it right if you spin it as giving the students time to put some of the new techniques into practice while you're gone, and then pick up where you left off when you get back."

"I like the way you think," Ford said.

"You should talk to them in the morning. They might have flexibility in the course schedule to break up your sessions with the students."

"I will definitely do that." She had a point. It would buy the students some practice time before tackling the more difficult techniques. They could even finish an extra project. "Thank you for that suggestion. I think it could work." It felt good to have someone on his side.

"You're welcome. And I'll do you one better. I'll make you some muffins to take in. They're my secret weapon," she said with a flirty wink. "No one can resist them. You're almost guaranteed to get your way."

"Remind me to be careful if you ever offer me a muffin." But he was pretty sure he'd be happy to give in to anything she wanted. The only regret he had about Flynn was not giving that little itch of attraction a chance when he'd first met her last year. Where would they be today if he had explored it back then?

She wrinkled her nose. "I only use them for good."

"Sure you do," he teased. "I can help you bake them."

"I might have to charge you extra if you 'help.'"

"I don't even care."

She brought her hand up to stifle her giggles. "Then I say we get this dinner to go, and get busy." She got up and went to the counter to switch their order to takeout. She sidled back up to the table. "They'll bag it up for us."

He pulled his money out of his front pocket and walked up to the register to settle. The waitress handed a large paper bag over to Flynn. "Need utensils?"

"No, thank you, we're taking this home," she said.

Home. That sounded so good.

~

They ate dinner in eleven-minute intervals between muffin rounds. When they were done they had three dozen. Enough for the whole team at PRIZM.

He dried the last bowl as they cleaned up the kitchen and then laid the damp towel flat on the counter to dry. "Thank you for today. It was a really good day. The muffins look as good as they smell." Her can-do attitude made him believe it too. Had he ever met anyone as thoughtful as Flynn? "Thank you."

"You're welcome."

He wished she'd share his bed tonight, but would that push her too far too fast? He put his arms around her and kissed her. She responded immediately, matching his eagerness. Her hands stroking his neck sent pleasant jolts through him, as he explored the soft lines of her waist, her hips. Maybe it wasn't too soon.

She stepped back blinking with a smile. "I think we better get some sleep."

Was she thinking what he was thinking? His heart did a flip and then a flop, and he tried to hide the geeky teenage grin trying to escape.

"You have a big day ahead of you tomorrow," she said.

"But I've got the secret weapon. I'm not worried."

"I'm not either. People around here are flexible. When you tell them what's going on they'll be excited for you to get back there and make the deal."

"Hope you're right." He made himself step away from her, hoping like hell she'd follow him. He reached for her hand.

She placed her hand in his and gave it a squeeze. "Good night." She turned and walked toward her room.

He stood there aching for her. *Say something clever.* She had to be feeling the same way after that kiss, but she was already halfway down the hall. "Good night." He walked away feeling like a dope. Why couldn't he close the deal with her? She'd seemed interested. He thought the feeling was mutual. He'd be going back to Alaska soon. Was that more of a reason to make a move fast? Or was he just looking for any excuse to have his way with this beautiful woman?

~

He slept deeply and woke up anxious.

The smell of bacon filled the warm kitchen. "All my favorites?"

"It's the only way I knew to help you today, and I want to help."

And he wanted to kiss her again. If she kept this up, he might never want to leave. But he would. There wasn't anything here in North Carolina that he needed. Unlike Jackson, Ford's ties were in Tennessee. If he wasn't in Alaska, then that's where he'd be. If they were going to be together, it would have to be in Alaska.

"We made your secret-weapon muffins. Are you telling me now that you're worried that they may not work?" he asked.

"Oh, they'll work. No doubt there." She hesitated. "I guess I just want to feel like part of things."

"Then come with me." There. He'd said it, and man did he hope she'd say yes.

"To work?"

"To Alaska."

Chapter Seventeen

Flynn tried to get comfortable in the spa chair next to Angie, but the truth was, her stomach was swirling as fast as that bubbling water that she'd just stuck her feet into. Angie was going to have a cow when she heard that Flynn had agreed to go to Alaska with Ford. And maybe she should. Was she crazy?

"Can I get you ladies something to drink?" the spa owner, Miss Kelly, asked. She was a short woman with hair teased up as big as a beehive, and one of those singsongy voices that sounded like everything she said was a question.

"Wine for me," Angie spoke up.

"Water for me."

Miss Kelly gave Flynn a tilted smile. "Are you pregnant? Wasn't one of you getting married last year when you were here?"

"That was her," Flynn said. "And no. I'm not pregnant." She wiggled her toes in the water. *If only.*

The spa owner hustled to the back while two of her daughters got to work on their pedicures.

Flynn let the young woman lift her foot from the water and remove the polish from her toes. "I was wondering if I could get you to pick up my mail next week and water my plants for me," she said to Angie as casually as she could manage.

"Are you going somewhere?"

She didn't make eye contact. Couldn't. Angie would see right through her. "Yes." *Just tell her. I'm a grown woman. If I want to go on a trip, I can go on a trip.* Just like she'd been thinking before Ford ever walked back into her life. That's one of the benefits of owning her own business. They'd talked about it. Angie had even encouraged it.

Angie sat quiet for a long moment, so long that Flynn was tempted to look to see if she'd even heard her.

"Just yes?" Angie asked. "Where are you going on short notice?"

"Alaska." Flynn could feel the surprise zinging from Angie, even a chair's length away. Without turning her head, she knew that Angie had catapulted to an upright position.

"Alaska? With Ford?"

She tried to look nonchalant. "*Mmmm-hmmm.* It's on my bucket list, and he invited me. It's just for a week. Don't get all crazy acting."

"I'm your best friend. I know you. I had a feeling something good was going to happen between you two."

Could she tell Angie about the kiss? Part of her was afraid that if she talked about it, those feelings might disappear. "He's a great guy. I'm really excited about this trip. Can you believe I might actually see the Northern Lights?"

"Yes. I can believe it. There's a good chance this time of year to see the Northern Lights in Alaska, but this is not just about a trip to Alaska. He likes you, Flynn."

The words made her heart sing. Yet she said, "We barely know each other." And even though that had been meant to back Angie down a notch, it settled like a pocket of worry on her gut. She really didn't know him that well, but her feelings were real. Already. Was that good or bad?

"Jackson swore me to secrecy," Angie said, "but he and Ford talked about you when they went out the other night. He said Ford is really into you."

She couldn't hide the smile that danced over her lips. "You're going to kill me. I know it's soon. But I'm into him too."

"Do you know what you're doing?"

"This is totally different from anything I've ever done or anyone I've done it with."

"You've done it?" Angie sat forward. "You heard her, didn't you?"

Miss Kelly's daughter just smiled.

"I heard it," Miss Kelly said, handing Angie a glass of wine and Flynn a bottle of water. "Who is Mr. Lucky? Hope you have a warm coat. You're going to need one in Alaska."

"Or maybe she won't," Angie teased.

"Nothing happened. I swear. We're friends. We have fun." Good lord, there was no way she could tell Angie about the kiss now. She'd either try to talk her out of going or plan a bachelorette party while she was gone. She and Ford had agreed things were complicated. This just proved it.

"Not one thing wrong with that. Best friends make the best lovers."

"You're the one who told me to quit trying so hard."

"Exactly, and now that you have, you're finally making a good connection; you're not trying at all. So, are you booking separate rooms?"

"It's not like that, Angie. The glass shop where he worked is going up for auction. He's going back to bid on it. I'm staying at his house."

"Couldn't he just phone in a bid from here?"

"Probably, but he wants to be there, and he invited me. It's a once-in-a-lifetime trip."

"A romantic one."

"We're two consenting adults taking a trip together. That's all. He knows the place. It'll be like having my own personal tour guide on a quick, fun trip. It's perfect. Plus I can stay at his house and all it's costing me is the airfare."

"Have you seen pictures of his house?"

Flynn shifted in her chair. "No, but he's told me about it." She hadn't even thought to ask him if he had pictures. Surely, he had some on his phone. Oh well, she'd just see it in person.

"You're going to fall in love with it too."

Too? Was she that transparent? "I did not say I was in love with him." Fine, her feelings were bigger than she was admitting, but she was barely out of her last relationship. It was absolutely crazy to blunder into another one, especially with another craftsman—one that lived far, far away. No. She was not going to fall into that trap.

Flynn's phone rang, but she couldn't reach her purse from the pedicure chair. Miss Kelly swept it up from the hook on the wall and handed it to her. "Maybe it's your lover boy," Miss Kelly teased. Flynn glanced at the display. It was Ford.

"Hello?" She held the phone tight to her ear, hoping Angie and that nosy busybody Miss Kelly couldn't overhear.

"It's set. They were great about rescheduling things here. I just booked two tickets for us to leave the day after tomorrow."

"We're really going?"

"Is that him?" Angie grabbed for the phone, missing. "It is, isn't it? You better treat my best friend right," she shouted at the phone.

Flynn glared at Angie.

"I take it you told her," Ford said.

"I was just telling her when you called. I'm so excited. We're going to have fun."

"You're going to love it. I wish we had more time so that I could take you way up north, but you'll get a good idea of what it's like. And hopefully I'll be the proud owner of a new studio by the time all is said and done. Maybe you'd better bring that muffin recipe."

"I know it by heart, and you're a pretty good helper."

Miss Kelly blew a kiss toward Flynn. "I know it when love's in the air," she said.

Ford's next words tumbled out with excitement. "I'm taking you to dinner tonight to celebrate just in case I do get the glass shop."

"You don't have to do that."

"Sure I do. Eating at the Manic Moose Saloon is pretty good, but it's not a celebration spot. We'll celebrate tonight and head into Alaska feeling confident about the win."

"Who am I to argue?"

Angie was mouthing "What?" from the next chair.

Flynn held up her finger. She couldn't listen to Angie and him at the same time, and Miss Kelly dancing around blowing kisses was a bit distracting too.

"You don't seem the argumentative type."

She smiled. "I'm not." What was there to argue about anyway? She was going to Alaska with an amazing man who sent her insides reeling like a Vegas slot machine. And no one had made her feel this way before.

"Good, then I'll see you at five thirty. I'll make the reservation."

She didn't have the heart to tell him that even for Bella's, the nicest place in town, a person didn't need reservations.

"We're going to dinner," Flynn said, tucking her phone back into the top of her purse.

Miss Kelly took her purse and hung it back on the wall. "In Alaska?"

"No, at Bella's," Flynn said. "Tonight."

Angie looked dumbstruck. "And you're really going to Alaska."

"Yep. He already bought the tickets."

"He's paying for your ticket?"

"I didn't ask him to buy it. I mean, I expected I'd pay my own way. I'll pay him back."

"Clearly he had other things in mind. Sweetie, you are the prize here. If he wants to pay for your ticket . . . let him. Jackson said Ford seemed very interested in catching up with you from the very minute he hit town."

"We're just two friends that were in your wedding. We have something in common. You and Jackson. You shouldn't be surprised that we get along—you and Jackson do. I'm doing so well for once at keeping my distance, don't encourage me."

"I'm not. I'm just observing."

"What am I going to wear tonight?" Flynn mentally raked through her jam-packed closet. "I could wear my black dress with the pink flowers on it."

"And that nail polish will look perfect. I love that dress on you," Angie said.

"Good. We're celebrating to put positive vibes out to the universe to help him get the building. I hope it works out."

Angie just smiled.

"He's really excited."

"And if you didn't care about how he felt, you wouldn't be nearly this excited." Angie settled back in her chair. "What's that saying? When someone else's happiness is your happiness. That is love."

Flynn flopped back in the chair. She couldn't win with Angie these days. That quote replayed in her mind.

~

Ford sat in the living room flipping through channels on the television while he waited for Flynn to finish getting dressed. Jackson had assured him his white dress shirt and blue jeans were adequate attire for Bella's.

Jackson hadn't said anything specific, but the undertones in the conversation let Ford know that Jackson approved if anything happened between him and Flynn. A year ago they'd acted like they were protecting him from her. Talking about her biological clock and her being on the hunt.

He understood the urgency she felt. He had it too. He wanted a family. A life to share. Memories that would fill up his heart and soul for a lifetime. Were there real feelings growing between them? His felt real. Mess-up-his-gut-when-he-laid-eyes-on-her real.

"Are you ready?" Flynn said.

He dropped the remote and turned to see her standing in the doorway in a short black dress with hella high heels that made her legs look longer than summer days in Alaska. Her hair was swept back into a silver barrette, and soft, messy curls peeked out from the back; curls he wanted to run his hands through.

"Wow."

She brushed the bottom of her dress with her palms.

"You look beautiful."

"Thank you."

He stood staring, but he couldn't help himself. He didn't want to break the moment or the feeling that had come over him just now. "Yes. Yes, I'm ready. Jackson said we could walk over from here, but those don't look like take-a-walk shoes."

"Sure they are." She jogged in place. "See."

"Hurts me just thinking about it."

"Lucky for you, you'll never have to find out. Bella's is only two blocks over. It's a pretty night. We can walk."

"Just as well, because there's no way I'm putting you in Jackson's old farm pickup looking like you do."

"Don't be silly. I'm the same girl you just taught to blow glass. The one in the T-shirt and messy bun."

He could only imagine how she might look in his T-shirt and nothing else.

"Let's go." She led him to the front door, only a small black wallet in her hand. They went down the walkway and he took her hand as they crossed the street and walked up the block.

Bella's was humming when they walked in. A waitress stopped at the counter by the door, looking so frazzled he wasn't sure she even noticed them standing right in front of her.

"I made a reservation," Ford said. "Morton."

"You can seat yourself anywhere you like," the waitress said, then pivoted toward the kitchen.

"Have a preference?" he asked Flynn.

"Over there will be good." She pointed to an empty booth in the corner.

He placed his hand on the small of her back as she twisted to walk between two tables of noisy old women. "Looks like someone busted out all the gray hairs from the old folks' home," he whispered into her ear.

She laughed and slid into the booth. "They look like they are having a pretty good time."

"What can I get y'all to drink?" the same waitress asked, slapping down two cocktail napkins on the table.

"What will you have, Flynn?"

"A glass of ice water, and can you make me one of those blackberry slushy drinks? I know it's out of season, but they are so yummy. No alcohol though."

"Sure. We can make that for you. Sir, what can I get you?"

"I'll have a Crown and ginger," Ford said.

The waitress laid two leather menus on the table. "I'll go through the specials with you when I get back."

"Thank you." Ford glanced over at the rowdy table; this wasn't exactly what he'd had in mind for tonight. He'd had his hopes on a quiet, romantic evening. "It seems like a good night for celebrating."

"It sure does. You've got to be so excited about bidding on that building."

Excited didn't begin to describe it. "I've had my money saved for a long time. I've just been waiting for the right opportunity. Now that my house is done, it's good timing. I ran back through all of my projections last night." The universe seemed to be lining everything up—one at a time. The location. The career. The house. The girl. The building.

Does she feel what I'm feeling? There's something there, but he wondered if her feelings were as strong as his.

The waitress dropped off their drinks and ran down the specials. "Do you need more time?"

After they ordered and waited for the waitress to exit, Ford raised his drink. "To a fun trip to Alaska together." *Maybe the first step in the longest journey of our lives.*

"To us."

Us. "And this time you'll stay in my house, and I'll cook breakfast for you every morning." Preferably while she slept in his bed.

"That'll be a first. I can't wait."

When was the last time she'd truly enjoyed herself with a man? Sure, she'd been in relationships and done her share of dating, but time with Ford was different.

She was excited to see what his house looked like. You could tell a lot about a person by their home.

It occurred to her that she'd made an assumption that his home would be rather nice. Mostly from the bits and pieces Angie and Jackson had shared in conversation over the past year. She had no idea what he drove, and who knew how much money a glassblower made for a living. Would his house be a total bachelor pad? Full of taxidermy? Or one of those off-the-grid places she'd seen on the Alaska wilderness shows on cable? No telling, but she could rough it for one week. As long as he had a real bathroom.

"I can't wait to share my Alaska with you. The nature there is so different. Big. Vast. You get a clear sense of how small you are in comparison to this big world we live in. We could even go fly-fishing."

"That looks so hard to do."

"It's not as difficult as it looks. I could teach you."

"If you're as good at teaching fishing as you are at glassblowing, we should be able to fill a freezer. I felt like I did pretty well yesterday, if I do say so myself."

The waitress slid their plates onto the table in front of them.

"You did great," Ford said. "I'd let you partner up with me on a project." He sliced into his prime rib. "Cooked perfectly. So tell me what you want to see in Alaska."

"What do I want to see in Alaska? Gosh . . . whales. A moose." She took a bite of her prime rib, still thinking. "The Northern Lights. Oh, I want some of those cute furry boots, and a real Alaskan Ulu knife. I don't know. Surprise me!"

Ford laughed. "We might need more time."

"No. I'm sure I'll get a good taste of Alaska. The priority is you getting to bid on that building."

"We'll work it out."

For the next half hour they ate and discussed the trip. Ford said, "This place is a lot louder than I expected it to be. If you're done, would you mind if we go ahead and get the check and leave? I could use a quiet evening."

Flynn was puzzled by his abrupt change in mood. "I wouldn't mind at all."

Ford paid the bill and they went outside.

"It's a nice night," she said, hoping it wasn't something she'd said that had made him want to leave so quickly.

"It is. You haven't asked when the auction is."

"Figured you'd tell me soon enough." She hadn't asked, because part of her was still unsure if it was really going to happen. Maybe he was having those same feelings.

He took her hand. "I like the way you think. You're more patient than most of the women I've known."

"I don't know if that's a compliment or not." And why was he suddenly comparing her to other women? That struck her wrong for some reason.

"It's a compliment," he said with a quick squeeze of her hand. "We fly out on Tuesday. Gary was able to reschedule everything at the school for the rest of the week. I have to be registered for the sale by Thursday."

"Even if we get delayed for some reason, we should be there in time," Flynn said.

"That's what I was thinking," Ford said. "Plus it'll give us an extra night to have the chance to see the aurora borealis."

"So, there's a chance we won't see them?" They turned on her block.

"It's not a sure thing, but I've got a friend with a plane if we need to go farther north to see them. There usually is some snow by now, but the temperatures have been milder. Global warming and all. So you'll need warm clothing, but nothing Antarctica-like."

"Are you serious?"

"About the weather? Yeah. People down here may not believe it's an issue, but we see it clear as day up there. The glaciers are shrinking and winters are warmer. Where we used to see snow, we're seeing more rain and ice."

"Won't hear me complaining about that. No snow means we'll be less likely to be snowed in. I'd be lying if I didn't admit that my biggest fear about going to Alaska is getting stuck there."

Visions of hunkering down on a big chunk of ice in a furry jacket in a snowstorm crossed her mind as they stepped onto her porch. She opened the door and he followed her inside.

"We do have airplanes. It's not like time travel."

"Quit teasing me."

"I'm just playing. You're really going to love it."

His own love for Alaska showed in the way his face lit up when he spoke of it—the way his voice softened. "Thank you for letting me tag along," Flynn said.

His smile was gentle.

"How much do I owe you for the plane ticket?" Flynn asked.

"It's my treat. I'm looking forward to your company."

"I can't let you pay for my ticket."

"Sure you can. You let me stay at your place for free."

"You've done more for me over the last week than the guy I paid did in six months. Trust me, you've been a bargain." Why couldn't he just be a normal white-collar guy living in the lower forty-eight? If he'd stayed a lawyer, living in Tennessee, she'd be head over heels right now.

"I enjoy that stuff. I love working with my hands. It's part of who I am. Part of why I couldn't stand being a lawyer."

"And then you moved to Alaska and lived happily ever after."

"You might watch too many of those Hallmark movies. It wasn't exactly that smooth a transition, but I'm happy. I found peace, and by then I'd found that I had a natural talent in glassblowing, and things just all seemed to work out."

"You don't seem to be a starving artist. What would you do if you weren't pursuing your art? Maybe some other part of the law?"

"No. That's behind me. I'd probably build houses or do renovations, remodeling, that kind of stuff. I enjoy working with my hands. I think that's why glassblowing appealed to me so much."

"I never really thought about glass that way."

"It's very physical. You saw some of that today."

"I did. It actually surprised me. Tell me about your house. Or the cabin. That's what you call it, right?" She wondered if the small structure she pictured in her mind was accurate.

"I'd rather show it to you."

"Guess I'll be patient."

"Just until Tuesday," he said.

Well, now that he'd said her patience was so attractive, she could hardly show how anxious she was really feeling about the trip. "Tuesday."

The word had barely gotten out of her mouth when he pressed his lips to hers. Her vow not to become involved dissolved for the moment in the passion that swirled around them.

Chapter Eighteen

Flynn held up two sweaters. A brown cable-knit and one with cute ribbons at the bottom. "Which one?"

"Take them both." Angie started moving underwear, socks, and pajamas from the bed to the suitcase. "At this rate, you won't be done packing until it's time to be back home."

"I don't want to overpack." She took a pair of black pants off a wooden hanger and laid them on the bag. "I told you the binder with all of the information for this place is in the office, right?"

"Four times."

"And the electrician should finish up this week."

"I know, Flynn. It'll be fine. What are you so worried about?"

"Everything. Angie, what if this is a big mistake?"

"Then you will come home with a cool adventure under your belt, and I promise this place will be in even better shape than you left it."

She pushed a hand through her hair, then sat on the edge of the bed. "Ford makes me feel like no one else ever has. I keep telling myself this needs to stay friendly, but then he kisses me, or touches me as I cook, or puts his hand on the small of my back as I step in front of him, and all of that goes tumbling."

"You're overthinking it all." Angie pulled one of the straps across the things in the suitcase. "If it's meant to be, it will be. Just relax. You have nothing to lose."

Except my heart. She sucked in a deep breath. "Relax. Just enjoy it. We're adults."

"Yes. Now what jewelry are you taking to go with these outfits?"

"I have no clue. How do they even dress in Alaska?"

"Just dress like you. But warmer." Angie lifted the lightweight camisole pajama top from the suitcase. "A lot warmer."

"Put that back. I need that. I'll bring a sweatshirt to go over it." She tossed her NC State T-shirt into the bag, and as Angie leaned on the bag to help her get it zipped, it occurred to her that when she came back from the trip her life could be completely different . . . if she wanted it to be.

~

Ford watched Flynn sleep beside him as the plane made its final descent into Juneau. It had been one long day of flights, and it wasn't over. They still had to take the puddle jumper.

He couldn't wait to see Alaska through the eyes of someone who'd never been there before; the idea of watching her delight in the things he loved was alluring. For the first time in his life, he wanted to share what he loved most with someone else. And for the first time in his life, he was with someone he felt he could share his whole life with. Even as anxious as he felt this morning when he stepped into the kitchen and saw her, he knew things were going to be okay.

The plane's landing gear squealed against the tarmac as they finally arrived in Alaska.

"We're here?" She swept her bangs from her face and peered out the window. "That seemed fast."

"It was a shorter flight than the last one, but you did sleep the whole time."

"Thanks for the first-class ticket. I'd have never been able to justify the cost of the upgrade."

"You might not have splurged on the flight out, but I bet after flying coach you'd be willing to pay extra for the room to stretch on the way back." He checked his watch.

Flynn's phone chirped.

Ford glanced over as Flynn looked at her phone and saw that it was a text from Angie.

Angie: Have The Time Of Your Life. Relax. You're Ready. So Is He.

Flynn scrambled, shoving her phone in her pocket without even responding.

He got their bags from the overhead and they headed to baggage claim.

"Why don't they just transfer the bags here, too?"

"We'll be on a small private plane from this point."

"Not sure I like the sound of that," she admitted. They got to baggage claim and the bags were already chugging around the conveyor.

"You must be good luck," he said as their bags came around. "I've never gotten my bags this fast."

"I do what I can," she teased.

"One more little hop, and then my friends Chet and Missy will pick us up to drive us the rest of the way."

A guy in blue jeans and a blue hoodie met them at baggage claim. "Hey Ford. Traveling a little heavier than usual, I see."

"Hi, I'm Flynn."

"Carson Callahan. Hope you don't mind small planes."

She glanced at Ford. "We just got off one."

Ford and Carson laughed.

"That," Ford said, "wasn't a small plane."

Skeptic, she said, "How small are we talking here?"

Carson looked at Ford like he was crazy. "Really? You didn't prepare her?"

"Prepare me? For what?"

Ford hadn't really thought about it, but now that Carson brought it up, it was going to look like he'd withheld the information on purpose no matter how he responded. "It's fine," he said. "It's a small floatplane."

"Six passengers," Carson said.

"Wow." She stood there quiet for a moment. "That is small. Six of us, huh?"

"There will just be the three of us tonight. The good news is everyone always gets the seat they want."

"I've never been on a seaplane. That's kind of cool." Flynn looked over at Ford. "Another first for me."

"I like her attitude." Carson grabbed Ford's bags and they followed him out to a white van parked just outside.

It was a short ride from the airport to an old log-sided lodge on the shore. He drove past the lodge down a gravel road to the water.

"We're here."

Ford watched Flynn's expression, but thankfully she didn't look upset or worried. Excitement filled her face as they drove up to where the three tiny floatplanes bobbed in the water at the dock.

Carson parked and started moving the luggage to the plane, then helped them board. "Let's go."

They were buckled in and in the air in less than ten minutes. "Can't beat these lines," Ford teased. "Are you okay?"

She nodded. "It's a lot louder than I thought it would be."

"Yeah, that's why we have the headphones. So we can talk."

"I like it." She gave him a thumbs-up. The flight wasn't nearly as scary as she'd expected.

When they landed at Carson's dock, Chet and Missy were standing in the small building that wasn't much more than a fancy shed with a big glass window in the front. Chet held a big piece of cardboard that read "Welcome Home, Y'all!" Chet had teased Ford about his southernisms, *y'all* in particular, for as long as they'd known each other.

"Ford didn't mention he was bringing someone so beautiful back to Alaska. Nice to meet you. I'm Chet. That's my wife, Missy, hugging on your friend. Hope you packed a heavy coat, because they're calling for snow this week."

She looked to Ford with a surprised look on her face. "He told me it had been mild out here and layers would be fine."

Ford walked over with Missy at his side. "You'll be fine. If not, I'll find you a jacket to wear."

"If he doesn't, you and I can go shopping in my closet," said Missy. "There are still a couple of the local shops open too."

"Perfect."

Carson carried their bags in. "All set."

Ford paid him and caught up with the rest of them to pile into Chet's huge black four-wheel-drive crew cab pickup truck.

Chet twisted around in his seat. "First trip out here to Alaska?"

"It's my first trip to the West Coast."

"You're in for a treat. There's no place on earth like Alaska, but have to admit I love North Carolina too," Chet said.

"You've been to North Carolina?"

"My sister married a Navy guy. They lived in Virginia Beach for years. We'd do family gatherings down on the Outer Banks in the summer."

"The beaches are lovely all along the coast of North Carolina. Boot Creek is more centrally located, but the nice part about that is that we're just a few hours from the shore or the mountains. Best of both worlds." Flynn turned to Missy. "Ford said that you and Chet own a bar nearby."

"The Manic Moose. I'm the manic. He's the moose."

Flynn laughed out loud.

Ford loved how she seemed so unaware of her laugh. It was pleasantly feminine, but when something tickled her she really belly laughed. "I bet you know everybody in town."

"Just about, but I'm not really sure that's because of the bar. More likely it's because we've lived there nearly our whole lives. I grew up in town, and Chet was born up in Fairbanks. His parents moved here when he was in junior high."

"I get what you mean. I live in a small town too. Someone described it last year as being so small that you could fit every one of our townsfolk in the Grand Ole Opry at one time."

"Sounds like something Ford would say." Chet smiled. "From a head-count perspective we're that small, but in land mass we're very spread out. There are some folks that live off the grid who never come around, but for the most part it's just like any other small town. Everyone knows each other. We know all the gossip, and it's a helpful community. We look out for each other."

"That's the best part of a small town. My grandparents lived in Boot Creek originally, and I spent summers with them there. I grew up down in Charlotte, but when I got laid off they offered to sell me their inn. I leapt at the chance to relocate and give it a try."

"How do you like running an inn?"

"I love it." She filled them in on her experience at the inn. "I love meeting new people, and cooking for them is very satisfying. Food is kind of my love language."

"You can cook for me anytime," Chet said.

"And you'll be lucky if she does," Ford said, "because she is an amazing cook."

"Thanks, Ford."

"You should make your famous muffins for Chet and Missy while we're in town. Y'all will love them. You could probably sell them too."

"What kind of muffins do you make?" Missy asked.

"All kinds, but I make really good Pumpkin Pecan Crunch Muffins."

"And biscotti. Tell them about the biscotti you make," Ford said.

"I don't think the guys from *Katie's Ring* are the biscotti type," Chet said. "And if you're smart, Ford, you won't be talking about froufrou French pastries around those boys. You might get your ass kicked."

Ford shook his head, and whispered to Flynn. "He's full of crap."

Missy spoke up. "I'm sure we could move some muffins. We're doing a big seafood special tomorrow night to help them celebrate their king crab haul. Y'all should come."

"I love crab boils. We do what we call a low-country boil. It has sausage, shrimp, blue crab, potatoes, and corn for an all-in-one-pot, all-you-can-eat buffet. I grew up on blue crabs," Flynn said. "And oysters. We added oysters on the months with *r*'s in them."

"Oh honey, our crabs are four times the size of those little blue crabs you catch out on the East Coast," Missy said.

"And way easier to pick," Ford added.

"I'm ready. And I want to try some fresh Alaskan salmon while I'm up here."

"We can make that happen," Ford said. "What's the special tonight at the Moose?"

Missy leaned forward between the two front bucket seats. "We got fresh halibut in this morning. We're stuffing it with crabmeat and offering it fried or baked."

"I could eat a horse," Flynn said. "Those light snacks didn't hold me over."

"Me either," Ford said. "We'll stop by the Manic Moose with Chet and Missy and eat before we go home." Ford turned to Chet. "You haven't heard anything else about the sale, have you?"

"You'll be able to check out the building tomorrow. See what's left intact. I've heard that Ziegler has moved a lot of stuff out. I'm not even sure how much of the equipment is still there."

Not for the first time, Ford wished Ziegler had spoken to him about what was going on before they'd gotten to this point. If Ziegler had sold off the furnaces and stuff, that would cut into the value of the buildings and lessen Ford's willingness to spend the budget he'd set aside. He sure hoped he hadn't flown back here for nothing.

~

"Flynn. Wake up. We're here."

Flynn opened her eyes. They felt gritty as she blinked, letting the pieces fall back into place. Alaska. She was in Alaska, thousands of miles away from home with a man she barely knew. A blast of music wafted into the truck as someone walked inside a nearby building.

"Sorry," she said. "It's been a long day."

"I know. Come on, let's get some real food, and then we'll head up to my place."

He must've sensed her hesitation, because he quickly added, "You'll feel better after you eat. I've got this coast-to-coast travel thing down to a science."

"Okay." She pushed herself out of the seat and let him help her out of the truck. When her feet hit the ground, her legs ached in resistance. She'd much rather be climbing into a bed right now, and if there'd been a hotel or an inn in sight, she'd be beating feet in that direction.

The area was dark. Shops lined the street in both directions, but the only storefront that appeared open for as far as she could see was the Manic Moose. The overjoyed character on the sign held a sudsy mug of beer in one hand, or hoof, and wore a hunter's hat that was balanced between prominent antlers.

The parking lot was full of pickup trucks and four-wheel-drive vehicles.

They walked into the Manic Moose. The bar was much larger than it looked from outside, but with all the dark wood inside, the light struggled to reflect off anything, making the space feel dark and more closed in than it actually was. Bright neon beer signs peppered the long wall, and the pool balls in play clicked to the rhythm of a popular country song. She wasn't sure why she was so surprised to hear a good ol' George Strait song out here in Alaska, but it had caught her a little off guard.

Missy had already put on an apron and was pushing beer across the bar. "You two want a menu or are you going to do the special?"

Flynn said, "I'll have the halibut special you were talking about."

"Fried?"

"Any other way?"

Missy laughed. "Not for you southern types, I suspect." She looked over at Ford. "She might just fit in around here."

"I'll have what the lady is having and the biggest water you have."

"Easy enough. Next table that opens up is yours," she said.

"We're fine at the bar, Missy. We're not going to be here that long."

"Okay, then let me get this order into the kitchen."

While they waited for their food, Flynn had the strange feeling that people were staring and whispering about her. She must be paranoid. Exhaustion would do that to a person.

Flynn overheard someone behind her say, "She's from North Carolina." She turned to see a brunette woman next to a short guy with a buzz cut and full-sleeve tattoos covering his arms from his short sleeves down. It wasn't snowing and the temperature wasn't too bad, but there was no way Flynn would wear short sleeves in this weather.

"You didn't stay away long," the man muttered to Ford as he walked by, not even giving Ford the opportunity to respond.

Ford shrugged and took a sip of water.

"What do you think of our town, little lady?" A tall man with biceps the size of coconuts stepped up behind her.

Ford recognized the man as one of the crew from the fishing boat *Katie's Ring*. Ford never did like it when people acted too familiar, but it was always news when someone brought a new person into this small town.

"I just got here, but it seems really nice," Flynn said.

"You'll either love it or hate it." He held Flynn's gaze a little too long.

"No middle ground?" She'd rather have told him to skedaddle, but she'd be polite even if he did seem a little drunk.

The guy grunted. "Nope."

"So far I like it. I like the way the terrain is terraced so you can see the rows of buildings and homes. The weather is way better than I thought it would be. Oh, and those seaplanes are cool. I'm sure I'll be just fine."

"You serious about that guy?"

"That's really none of your business, sugar." She smiled as nicely as she could, and it lightened her mood when she saw Ford almost spit his water across the table.

The guy slunk away. "She's no sissy, prissy girl. I'll give her that," she overheard him say to his buddies.

Her backhanded insult had earned her points in a weird sort of way.

Missy brought their dinner out and set it on the bar in front of them. "Rolls are fresh out of the oven too."

"Thanks, Missy." Flynn dove straight in. Now that she'd woken up, she was getting a second wind. Tomorrow would probably be a different story.

She'd just taken a big bite of the stuffed halibut when an older woman wearing a tie-dyed shirt and fringed suede coat that had to be from the sixties walked up and gave Ford a hug. "We didn't expect you back for weeks."

"Just here for a few days, then heading back east. I had some business to tend to here."

"You're back to bid on Ziegler's building, aren't you?" the hippie lady said.

"Yes ma'am. Louisa, meet my friend, Flynn Crane."

Louisa lifted her chin as if she was sizing Flynn up for something then burst into a big grin. "Hello, Flynn. Welcome. Hope you enjoy your stay here. We love Ford, so don't go breaking his heart or anything." She leaned in close, the fringe of her coat tickling Flynn's arm. "Nothing worse than a moping, heartsick man. Especially when the population is four men to every woman in this one-horse town."

"I don't think you have to worry about that." Why did everybody assume she was here to test-drive moving north? It was a visit, and she'd be here less than a week. If anyone needed to worry about a broken heart, she had a strong feeling it was her. The only thing wrong with the package that made up Ford Morton was that it needed airmail delivery.

"Good. You've got yourself a good one here." Louisa patted Ford on the back. "You just holler if there's anything I can do for you. I know everyone around here. I own the drugstore on the corner. Open noon to five, seven days a week."

"Thank you."

Flynn watched as the woman walked away, then turned to Ford, who said, "She's the pharmacist. So she really does know everyone."

She looked like the type to serve up pot brownies and herbal remedies, but that was probably better than modern medicine anyway. Who was she to judge? "Are these people always so eager to fix you up with someone?"

"Is it such a bad thing to maybe be my girl?"

Flynn squirmed, unsure of how to answer that. "I might have thought about it when I met you last summer."

"At the wedding? I thought about it then too."

She snapped her head back so fast that her neck muscle twinged. "You did?"

"Sure. You looked hot, and you're a good dancer, but we didn't get much of a chance to really get to know each other."

"They kept us pretty busy."

"Do you remember me texting you the week after the wedding?"

"I do. You'd accidentally sent me that picture of the glacier. It was so pretty."

"That was no accident."

Where was this conversation going, and why did he wait until he had me halfway across the world to share this?

"I've been thinking about you since the day I left Carolina. I just wasn't sure how to approach that."

"And it took you a year? You're making this up."

He crossed his heart. "I swear."

"Why didn't you say something then or sometime in the last year? Or maybe when you first came to town?"

"Because it was Jackson and Angie's wedding, and I guess I didn't realize how interested I was until I left and couldn't stop thinking about you. When I got the invitation from PRIZM to come for the month, I cleared my calendar. I've been looking forward to the chance to see you. I could've stayed in the dorm, you know."

She thought back to when he'd shown up. Had she invited him, or had he invited himself? Now that she really thought about it, he had jumped right in on the chance to help her. He could've stayed with Jackson and Angie. Billy had been so excited about it.

"We're a good team. I kind of think we could be more," he said taking her hand.

Missy cleared their dishes. "Good?"

Flynn was thankful for the interruption. She rubbed her belly. "So good. I ate way too much, but it was delicious."

"I hope you'll come back and eat here with us while you're in town." Missy tapped the bar in front of Ford. "We're praying things go the way you'd hoped, Ford."

"Thanks, Missy. We're heading out."

"Truck's unlocked."

Flynn followed Ford, wondering what the sleeping arrangement was going to be at his house. It would be so much easier if he only had one bedroom and there were no decisions to make.

When she glanced over at him, he gave her a wink.

She had to find a way to handle the involuntary reactions to his flirtation. She practically felt herself swoon.

A light drizzle had started when they stepped outside, and that helped the swoony heat that had just filled her. The air was cold and damp. Ford walked over to Chet's truck and got their luggage out of the back and set them on the ground. "I'm just parked right over there. Wait here and I'll pull around."

"Okay." She bounced, trying to stay warm. A puff of smoke blew in front of her as she breathed a sigh of relief to put a little distance between her and Ford for just a minute. Long enough to text Angie. She texted as fast as her cold fingers would go, finishing the sentence as she heard the engine of a truck start across the way.

Flynn: Feels So Right!?!? Scary.

She pushed the phone down into her purse and picked up her bags. When Ford pulled his SUV around, she opened the back door and started loading the bags in. By the time he got out of the driver's seat and walked around to help, she'd already closed the door.

"I'd have gotten those." Ford held her door.

"I'm quite capable." She had no intention of ever playing damsel in distress.

He waited for her to get inside, then closed the door and jogged back around to the driver's seat.

"We'll have to come to town and pick up some groceries tomorrow. There's no food in the house since I planned to be gone for a month, but there's nothing open right now."

"I think we can probably make it through one night."

"Fair enough. I might not be as good a cook as you, but I have a few specialty dishes that'll keep us from starving over the next few days."

"I'm not picky," Flynn said, but that wasn't entirely true. She was, but she could always help cook and that way she'd be sure to have something to eat that she liked.

Main Street was quiet. The Manic Moose looked to have been about the only game in town. Several shops had "For Lease" signs in the windows; others looked like they'd be closed through the winter. The roads became dark quickly. The rain and wind picked up, making it hard to see in the darkness.

"I guess rain is better than getting snow," she said quietly.

"We get a lot of rain here."

"I expected at least a little bit of snow." She'd even bought UGG boots, thinking they'd be the perfect footwear for Alaska. That felt like a silly waste of money now. She could've just brought her waterproof hiking boots with her.

"How far is it to your house?"

"About forty minutes."

That felt really far. In the short time they'd driven, things were already looking pretty rugged and rural. Her mind raced, wishing now she'd asked Jackson for details about Ford's house.

Chapter Nineteen

Those jackasses at the Moose had made things awkward, and he'd be damned if he'd lie to Flynn about how he felt when she'd straight-out asked him about it.

She'd been quiet ever since he admitted to being interested. Maybe he'd misread her. He'd thought she was kind of into him, but she had a point. He lived a long way away, and at the end of a twenty-hour period of flights to get here was probably the worst time to mention it.

He hoped she'd fallen asleep but was half afraid to look over there. The last thing he wanted to do was put his foot in his mouth again.

His hands slipped on the steering wheel, sweat pooling in his palms in anticipation of Flynn seeing his house for the first time. He'd worked so hard on it, and he was proud of how it had turned out.

It was a far cry from the teepee he'd lived in that first summer he'd moved here. That had been part of his pay for taking tourist groups down the river looking for wildlife, like the resident bear that he made up stories about, pretending it was a rare sighting. He knew the animal's habits and there wasn't much surprise to the trips after just a few weeks, but the people were a whole different story. His southern flirting skills paid off. And wooing pretty tourist girls into a teepee had turned out to be easy.

With only about eight hundred year-round residents, you learned to make the best of new women hitting town, because everyone knew everyone and most were already spoken for.

The drizzle made the drive even darker than normal. There wouldn't be any Northern Lights watching as long as this weather set in. He'd really hoped they'd get lucky and see them on her first night here.

The more time he spent with Flynn, the more he was convinced that she was the right woman for him. Like the way she'd handled that guy in the bar. She stood up for herself and still kept it ladylike. He liked her sensibilities, her fearless nature, and most of all that she was southern to the core. From her accent to her zeal for fried food.

Plus, he already knew his best friends in Boot Creek liked her, and Missy had whispered her approval too. Louisa would've made her disapproval duly noted had there been any, but she hadn't uttered a peep.

The drive felt so much longer tonight. He was thankful when he took the last turn and came up over the clearing to see that Benson had taken it upon himself to leave the lights on for them.

Anxiety had gnawed at him for the last thirty minutes about her first impression of the house, but the way she'd just sat up in her seat made all of that fall away.

Since he'd chosen to forgo window treatments to let nature color the view, lights set on a timer while he was away poured through the windows, casting a golden hue into the dark night.

"That's gorgeous. It looks like one of those light-up Christmas villages," Flynn said as he slowed down. "So warm and inviting. We're stopping?"

"We're here."

"This is your house? The *cabin*?"

"Yep." He took the key from the ignition. "Home sweet home. *Mi casa es su casa* and all that."

She blinked. "You're not serious." She sat back in the seat. He hoped that look meant she was impressed.

"Yeah. I'm serious. This is it."

She reached for her purse. "This is way bigger than a cabin. It's not what I had pictured at all."

"Come on inside." He carried their bags up to the porch, then touched the keypad with his finger. The door unlocked. He held the door for her to go inside first.

"Thank you." She stepped inside, and a small gasp escaped her pretty lips as she stood, slowly turning around. She walked over to the huge fireplace. The stacked stone ran straight to the top of the second story, and the loft that extended from his bedroom opened up to the living room below, allowing the heat to rise and warm his room. But rather than focusing on the massive stonework, she knelt in front of the hearth and admired the fireplace screen. "You made this?"

He nodded.

"Ford, this is no cabin. Not in size. Not in style."

"Well, it's in the woods. And the style is simple."

"The finishing touches are far from simple. I've never seen a stair railing like that. Did you blow those glass bubbles in the railing yourself?"

"I did." His heart pounded. With pride, yes, but more so at the way her eyes lit as she noticed each little thing.

"Aren't you afraid those blown-glass balls will break?" She walked over and touched a bright cobalt blue one. Bigger than a bead, but smaller than the ornament they'd made. "Are these like caterpillars? Like the ones you were having me make in the shop?"

"Pretty much. Very simple, yet elegant."

"Trying to equate the simplicity of the glass to the comfort of the cabin? Easy. I guess I can buy that." She shrugged like it was no big deal. "Let me know if you break any of these. I'll whip up some more for you. No problem."

"I'll hold you to that."

"Sure. I learned from the best." She walked to the dining room, swiveling to take it all in. "This chandelier is gorgeous."

"I worked for months on that thing. I knew exactly what I wanted it to look like, but it definitely stretched my skills."

"It would cost a fortune to buy something like this."

"I can tell you, with the number of hours I put into it, there would be a very limited audience who could afford it. If I ever leave this place, it's coming with me."

"I don't blame you." She turned and put her finger to her lips. "I hate to even ask this, but you do have indoor plumbing. Right?"

Ford was so tempted to tell her no. But even the look on her face at his brief pause had him laughing.

"Yes," he said. "I'm not off the grid. This was about as far as I could go up the mountain and still have some of those luxuries. I did have a nonnegotiable plumbing requirement. Some things are just not fun in the cold. Even for guys."

"Can I hope for a bathtub?"

"You can. And you won't be disappointed."

"My trip is already perfect. Nothing can ruin it now. I've had fresh halibut and we have indoor plumbing and a tub. I'm set."

And now, imagining her in his tub, his trip had just gotten better too. "Somehow I think you're going to be demanding a few more things."

"I'm not the demanding type."

She wasn't. It was one of his favorite things about her. But bantering with her was so much fun he couldn't help himself.

She picked up a framed picture from an antique table in the corner of the dining area. "Is this your dad?"

"Yeah. That's us when I was practicing law with him."

"You clean up nice, Mr. Morton, but I think I'm kind of partial to the blue jean version of you. You do favor him," she said.

"Only in looks. We're completely different." He felt his mood dip. Even just thinking about Dad made his temper dance like a fighter on the ropes. "Dad is very money driven. If it's not going to benefit his bottom line, he isn't going to do it."

"Well, being money conscious isn't a crime."

"Even on my birthday, he'd plan parties that would incorporate people he wanted to network with. He never made it to a ball game, but you can believe he never missed a golf game with a client. I was starting to act like that and it freaked me out. I didn't want to be like him. I want to have a family, and I will put them first. If I'd stayed at the firm, my life would have been so different." He'd never looked back. Even talking about it now had a way of dampening his mood. He shoved the thoughts to the side. "Let me show you around."

"I'd like that."

He took her through the kitchen first.

Flynn's mouth dropped. "This is a chef's kitchen." She walked through the space, her fingers gliding across the granite countertops. "You are going to have to let me cook for you in here. Please don't make me beg."

"You won't have to beg. I've had your cooking. Remember?"

"I can't wait. I've never seen a range hood made out of rocks before. That is so beautiful against the deep tones of the cabinets."

"Well, figure out what you want to cook or bake and make a list. We'll be going to the store tomorrow." Ford guided her through the rooms downstairs. "You've seen just about everything down here. Kitchen, dining room, living room. There's a guest room and a full bath over here. I thought you'd prefer to sleep on this level. It'd give you some privacy."

"Thank you." She stepped into the room. "Very nice." She poked her head into the bathroom. "Love the tub."

"There's a bunch of girly stuff in the armoire. My sisters sent me a ton of stuff when I got this room done."

"They love you."

"They do. They spoiled me when they weren't torturing me." He opened another door off the hall. "Laundry room—I have a chute that drops here." He opened the door in the wall to show her the basket of clothes. "Pretend you don't know that those have been sitting in there since I left for Carolina two weeks ago."

She raised her fingers. "Girl Scouts' honor."

"That's it down here." Ford climbed the stairs, and she followed him. He flipped the light switch at the top of the stairs. More blown-glass accents were nestled in alcoves all the way down the hall. Each was backlit, like a gallery.

"Did you make each of those pieces specifically for those dimensions?"

"Are you asking me whether the chicken or the egg came first?"

"Or the alcove or the art. Yes."

He picked up one of the pieces. "These are some of my early works. Things that had special meaning to me."

"It's beautiful."

He showed her his bedroom. "I can't wait for you to see the views when it's light tomorrow."

"It'll be daylight? I thought you had six months of darkness in Alaska."

Ford shook his head. "I think a lot of those rumors are started by people who live here to keep the rest of the world from discovering how awesome it is here. We are still south of the Arctic Circle so we do have sunrises and sunsets. And even in the summer we have some nighttime hours. The daylight hours are lopsided but we have them."

"I feel so misinformed."

"The sun will rise around nine thirty. It'll set somewhere around three thirty or four, so it won't be much. And if it's cloudy it'll seem much shorter. I hope we get some clear weather."

"Do you have Wi-Fi here?"

193

"I do. I couldn't be without it. However, it's satellite and can be sluggish, so you'll have to be a little patient with it sometimes." Ford walked through his room, which thank goodness he'd left fairly neat, and showed her his bathroom. "Out here there are two more bedrooms and a bathroom." He started at the far end and worked his way back to the master. "This is the smallest bedroom."

He opened the door, and she walked into the room. Only one piece of furniture was in the room, and that was a white rocking chair. "My grandmother used to rock me in that rocker. Mom said I was a colicky baby and the only person that could keep me quiet was Gran."

"This is a nursery." Her voice softened.

"Yep. That door leads to the master. And I built the dressing table and drawers into the wall to save space. Dressers are always oversized for those tiny clothes."

"Never thought about that, but you're right." She walked over to the outside wall. "Is there a significance to this?" She pointed to the three cutouts in the wall. Not windows, just simple shapes that he had glassed and then blown colored glass to cover. A crescent moon in blue, an orange sun, and a purple shooting star.

"Not really. I'd like to have three children. So I chose three shapes that represented nature and beauty. That kind of inspired me."

"So the three charms represent the three children."

"Never really thought of them as charms, just shapes, but I like that."

"Do you want boys or girls?"

"Doesn't matter. How about you? Do you want children?"

"Four," she said almost automatically. "No middle child that way. Two boys. Two girls."

"Were you a middle child?"

"No. I was an only child, which is probably the only thing worse than being a middle child. I always thought it would be so neat to have brothers and sisters."

"As an adult, I'd agree. As a kid, I once asked Pop-pop if he could slip my sisters in with the cattle at auction so I could get all the attention. Dad worked so much he probably wouldn't have noticed they were gone for a week." Sad thing was it probably wouldn't have gotten him any more attention anyway.

"You would not."

"Oh I would've. My sisters were all older than me. They dressed me up, made me play dolls and tons of other embarrassing stuff."

"I believe you're holding a grudge?"

"No." The memories still brought joy, although there were days that they'd really humiliated him. "I loved my sisters. And being the only boy and the youngest, it was kind of like being everybody's favorite. I never lacked for attention."

Flynn sat in the window seat built in under the only real window in the room.

"From there you'll be able to see the tip of Minton's Peak in the daytime. It's snowcapped year round. Very pretty."

"I can't wait to see it all in the daylight." Flynn stood. "It sounds like you were really close with your family. Well, except for your dad. Isn't it hard to be so far away?"

"Sometimes. I'm planning to spend some time with my family in Tennessee at the tail end of my Carolina trip." He walked to the door and she followed him out of the room. He gently pulled the door closed. He could picture Flynn sitting in that room with a child in her lap in his grandmother's old rocking chair. "But family isn't always about siblings or blood relatives. It's about who we let into our lives. Who makes our lives better."

"I believe that too."

"I still make the effort to get home for special occasions, and I keep in touch with everyone via the Internet and video calling. That helps, but the people in this town have become something like family too. Maybe you'll come with me to Tennessee. I could show you around."

"I've never been. One more place for the bucket list, I guess."

"Come on downstairs." He led the way back downstairs and sat in the recliner. "You get it, right? I mean you and Angie are like sisters. Jackson is just as much family as some of my blood relatives."

"She's like the sister I'd always wished I had."

"You're every bit of an aunt to Billy. He loves you like family too." He'd enjoyed seeing how Flynn and Billy interacted. The night under the stars with the two of them was the closest thing to perfect he'd ever felt.

Chapter Twenty

The unfamiliar surroundings had Flynn grabbing for the quilt when she opened her eyes and could see straight outside. The bare windows hadn't been as daunting in the night. Once she remembered she was in Ford's house in Alaska, her worry subsided. She kicked the covers back and got out of bed.

She and Ford had lain in the living room and talked until nearly four in the morning. She'd taken a bath, and realized that was a pretty bad idea when she'd fallen asleep in the tub. She'd woken up in neck-deep, chilly water, fearing she'd never have gotten warm again.

Even snuggling deep under the covers wasn't enough. She'd finally gotten up and added layers and socks to help retain the heat. If she hadn't been so afraid that she'd wake up Ford by running another bath, she'd have done that to warm up.

She ran her fingers across the shiny finish of the molding that framed the window. It wasn't hard to imagine Ford standing here with a tool belt slung low on his hips, hammering nails—not a bad image to get stuck in her mind.

She had no idea what time it was since her phone was on charge in the living room. She got dressed in a pair of jeans and a long-sleeve T-shirt and went to the kitchen in search of coffee.

"Good morning."

"Hey. I didn't hear you come downstairs."

"I haven't been up long, but I do have coffee ready for you."

She clasped her hands together. "Thank you. I'm desperate for caffeine."

He opened the cabinet and took down a large glass mug.

"Oh good. That's a nice big one. I guess I should have warned you that I get downright wicked if I miss my coffee in the morning." She added a teaspoon of cream and sugar and then took a long sip. The man could brew a perfect cup of coffee. "This hits the spot. Thank you so much. I should order some mugs like these. They're really pretty."

"I can make you some."

"Don't tell me you made these too."

He pulled his lips into a thin line. "Okay."

"You did? Of course you did. What can't you do?"

"A lot of things."

Somehow she doubted that. "I have a feeling I'm going to need a nap this afternoon. I'm still tired."

"A whole day of flying is tiring. Now you know why I wanted just to go to bed on the first night I got into town."

"I'm feeling kind of bad that we made you do dinner with us at Jackson and Angie's now."

"You should. I was a zombie."

"You faked it pretty well. So what's our plan today?"

"I'm going to go see what all the details are at the glass shop. Would you like to come with me? Or I can drop you in town and you can wander through shops while I go and then we can reconnect for lunch or an early dinner."

"I'd love to come with you. If you don't mind. I can't wait to see your plans for the place." She admired how well he knew what he wanted. The B&B was already in her family. His dream was something he'd come up with.

"Mind? I value your business sense. I'd love to get your opinion."

She did have experience that could be valuable if they were talking strategy or return on investment, and just thinking about that made the day seem even more appealing. "Then count me in. Can we grab something on our way to town to hold us over until we get a chance to go to the grocery store?"

"I know it was dark last night when we came in, but there's pretty much nothing from here to town unless you want to stop and borrow breakfast food from a neighbor."

That would get the rumors rolling. "I don't think I'm ready to meet your neighbors under those conditions."

"You already met some of them last night, but if you can make it back down the mountain, I promise to feed you first thing."

"I'm ready when you are."

"Then let's hit the road."

Walking out the front door was Flynn's first chance to really see his property. The landscaping was sparse, but what was done looked neat. As she walked to the truck she noticed the line of wire that ran around three sides of the property up to the road. "Is that your property line?"

"No. Far from it. I've got twenty acres, most of the property is wooded, but there's a nice stream on it."

"Then why the wire?"

"Just to keep the bear and moose from becoming too much of a nuisance."

"Bear?"

"Grizzlies. Some black bear. They ransacked the place before I had the place finished. Tore right through the back door because a guy I had helping me left a lunch bag out. Not sure if I've just been lucky, neater, or helped by the wire, but I haven't had any problems since I installed it."

"There goes my idea of enjoying that front porch at night to watch the stars."

"You'll be safe with me. I've always wanted to be a hero."

"I'm not sure that's how I want to test you."

As they drove, she stared out the window at what was mostly uninterrupted wilderness with an occasional house or shed tucked along the way. Nothing else was anywhere near as impressive as Ford's house though. At least nothing she could see from the road. He was right. Alaska was big. Spread out. And she suddenly felt very tiny in its midst.

Ford pulled his SUV in front of the Glory Glassworks building. "This is where I used to work."

She leaned forward. "It's a bigger building than I had pictured in my head."

"Ziegler owned the whole building, but I'm really only interested in this end of it. I'm glad they've parceled it out." He got out of the truck. "There's a coffee shop just up the block. Good coffee and really good homemade venison sausage or bagels with smoked salmon if some local fare sounds good."

"Sounds Alaskan to me." She skipped to catch up with him on the sidewalk. A few people were walking into the glass building as they walked by. Flynn watched Ford observing them. He looked irritated to see anyone else showing interest. "They could just be looky-loos."

"Yeah. They could." That seemed to right his mood. They grabbed a seat in the coffee shop and had a quick breakfast.

"I don't want to get too much because we'll only be here a few days and then I'll be gone again, but we'll go to the market while we're here."

"I think we can get by with some basics," she said. "And if I buy stuff we don't use, I'll make the promise right now that I'll cook it up and freeze it so it doesn't go bad. Plus, then you'll have some good cooking to come home to." The thought of cooking for him warmed her. The thought of him coming back without her, though . . . bothered her more than she expected.

"Sounds good to me. Maybe I should add more stuff to that list."

She swept the paper off the table and put it into her purse. "Let's get to work, mister."

Ford held the door to Glory Glassworks open, and she slipped under his arm to enter. A woman in a blue blazer manned the front desk. "Are you interested in purchasing the property? I've got the floor plans and some detailed information right here." She patted two stacks of paper.

"Thank you." Flynn grabbed two sets and handed one to Ford. "Have you had a lot of interested parties come through here this morning?"

"Some," the woman said.

Flynn and Ford turned and walked toward the door. She tilted her head toward him and whispered, "That translates to not many."

He gave her a hopeful look and then began touring her through the facility, while she followed along on the paperwork.

"What makes this particular location so appealing to you?"

"You mean besides the fact that it's already pretty much set up, even with the missing equipment? And that it's close to my house?"

"Yes. Besides that."

Ford rubbed his hands on his temples. "That's pretty much it. Well, that's not entirely true. I feel inspiration here. I've done my best work to date right here in this shop."

"But I'm looking at these numbers—his cost per square foot is really high. Do you know how it compares to other buildings in the area? If you could find another location that was maybe not right here on the water, you could probably build out exactly what you need, buy the equipment, and still come out ahead."

Even though he didn't say a word, he didn't look too pleased with her suggestions. "Ziegler had this place overmortgaged. I'm sure the bank is trying to cover the loan. It'll be tight, but I can make it work."

"What's the process for shipping out of here? Have you compared dollar-to-dollar from other locations?"

"I've done that, but it's worth it to me to live here. I love Alaska. It's not necessarily a dollars-and-cents decision."

She knew how that was. She felt the same way about the B&B, despite the difficulty with the renovations. "I understand."

"Do you really?" His head cocked to the side.

"I think I do."

"I'm going to walk through here again. I know they're taking sealed bids, but would you mind checking up front on the specifics of how we need to submit our bids while I have another look around?"

"Sure. I can do that." It seemed like he really just wanted to have some time alone with the building, with the practicality of his dream. She should've kept her mouth shut. Unfortunately, she'd never been good at that.

He caught her hand as she started to walk away. "Don't get me wrong. I understand what you're saying. I asked for the advice. It's just hard to hear when my heart has been so set on it. You have some valid points. Thank you for being here. I'm glad you came."

"I'm glad I'm here." She felt the connection, like a partnership with him. She wanted to help him, and she felt even worse for opening her big mouth now. "I can just meet you out front when you're done."

"Yeah, that'll work," he said.

Flynn usually had a great sense of direction, but somehow backtracking through the building, she made at least one wrong turn, because she ended up on a loading dock. This certainly would make it easy to load freight on a barge from here. Probably not a huge asset to a glass shop but for someone. A good selling point she hadn't seen mentioned on the listing, but then maybe the loading dock wasn't part of the parcel Ford was planning to bid on.

She caught snippets of a conversation downwind from her.

"It's the perfect place to put the cannery. We can also process smoked salmon and ship it all from right here. No more middle man." The voice was gruff, like one wrought from years of smoking, but when she turned around, the man, probably midfifties at best, was dressed in work clothes, standing with three other men, two wearing suits and looking out of place. Probably the money.

Flynn stepped back out of their line of sight. *So, Ford* did *have serious competition for the building.* She turned the ringer off on her phone and pretended to be talking on it just in case anyone did see her hanging around.

"I don't care if they think they can keep the artsy-fartsy stuff going."

Her protective side flared at the dig.

"This is prime real estate and we're a fishing community." The man sounded belligerent . . . drunk, really. "This is what Alaska is meant to be known for."

"Sealed bids, man. It's anyone's game," said one of the suited men. "Unless we bid high."

"Bull. I'm telling you, sealed bids ain't sealed all that tight. They can still get us information just before closing time and let us know where we need to be. That woman with the black hair is going to leave a number on the calendar for me. We're in, man."

They were going to cheat? She hated a cheater, but was it really her place to get involved? Or was she protecting herself? On paper this purchase wasn't really in Ford's best financial interest unless he could get the cost per square foot down to a reasonable number.

Leaning back, as if an inch closer would make a difference, she listened intently, hoping for some discussion that would include a ballpark number that she could feed to Ford to help him, but the men had switched topics.

She lowered her phone and stuffed it into her purse. When she turned around, the four men were walking outside onto the dock.

Of course, if Ford didn't win the bid . . . maybe he'd end up back in North Carolina at PRIZM.

Chapter Twenty-One

Ford checked his watch again. Where had Flynn gotten off to? He texted her again and then turned as the door to the building opened and out walked Flynn.

"I was beginning to think maybe something had happened to you," Ford said, lifting his phone.

Flynn pulled her phone out of her purse. "Oh goodness. I silenced my phone. I forgot. I'm sorry. I got all the information you need for the bids, along with the paperwork."

"Thanks. I'd like to work through some numbers with you tonight if you don't mind."

She sucked in a breath, and for a moment he thought she was going to say no, but she didn't. "Sure. I'll do whatever you need."

"I'm sorry about back there."

"Don't be." She smiled pleasantly and grabbed the arm of his coat. "Let's get this shopping done or you'll be dealing with a cranky roommate in the morning."

He got in the SUV and started the engine. "That's motivation."

She pulled her seat belt across her. "It should be."

When they got to the market, they worked like a well-practiced SWAT team. He drove the cart. She went down the list calling out the items as he plucked them from the shelves.

"Do you want salmon tonight? I make a couple of great salmon dishes and we have five different types of salmon that we can get fresh."

"I'd be crazy to pass that up."

He spoke with the guy at the counter and asked him to select the best pieces. "These look great. And do you have any nice filet mignon back there? I'm thinking surf and turf one night. Good?" He looked to Flynn.

"Sure."

He watched her closely. She was being amicable, but she wasn't herself. Had he pissed her off earlier? He hadn't meant to, but that glass shop was his dream. Her questions were valid. He knew they were, but they were also like a wet blanket on his excitement.

"I'm going to walk over there and get a few breakfast items on the list and then we'll be about done here."

"Okay," he said. "I'll meet you over on the dairy aisle as soon as I get done here."

She stood holding an armful of items by the time he wheeled up next to her. "Perfect timing. I was running out of fingers." She let the groceries slide from her arms into the basket, then she picked out a couple of different types of cheeses. "Wine and cheese one evening?"

"That would be nice, and I have some really good stuff in my wine chiller."

"Perfect."

Her smile seemed genuine. He could tell because of the little wrinkle that formed near the bridge of her nose. A real smile. The quiet nagged at him, though. That wasn't like her and it worried him. He didn't want to screw this up.

She insisted on paying for the groceries, since he'd bought her plane ticket, and he gave in reluctantly.

In the parking lot he hit the button on his key fob to open the hatch of his SUV.

Together, they loaded the groceries into the back. She leaned inside to push one of the bags in farther to make room for more and he couldn't stop himself. As she slid back out he caught her by the shoulder and spun her around, taking her into his arms. He placed a safe, closed-mouth kiss on her lips but sweet and tender. He needed her to know what he was feeling.

"I've been wanting to do that for so long," he said.

Her lips parted, but she didn't say anything, and in that moment his heart felt as if it dropped to the bottom of his gut. She wasn't feeling it?

Then she wrapped her arms around his neck and kissed him, and there was no holding back this time.

"I'm falling in love with you, Flynn. I want you to share this place with me." He pulled her closer. "Please tell me you're feeling the same way. Or even just tell me I'm not crazy. We'll figure it all out later."

"I am definitely feeling something. The last couple of weeks . . . Ford, these have been the best days ever."

He kissed her, and his smile had to be bright enough to make a rainbow somewhere, if only in her heart.

There hadn't been many words on the drive home. Mostly just hand-holding and smiles. Her lips still felt bruised from the kiss. Not because it had been rough, but he'd caught her by surprise. The kiss sent tingles through her body and her heart jumping to conclusions. On one hand she was so excited and on the other, terrified that she'd let something happen in an impossible situation.

They put the groceries away and, while Ford showered, Flynn made a breakfast casserole that they could just slide in the oven in the morning. It didn't take her long to get it put together and into the refrigerator. She walked through the house, looking at it through a new lens. Could she live in Alaska?

His dreams were here. It was beautiful. The people were nice. He was amazing.

She went upstairs, lost in thought. She resisted the temptation to interrupt his shower. Instead, she stepped into the nursery.

The bright moonlight glowed through the cutouts on the back wall—the blue crescent moon, orange sun, and purple shooting star.

She sat in his grandmother's rocking chair. The fresh, glossy white paint stood out against the worn soft edges on the arms. Signs of loving hours spent in it. She picked up the blue cloth box from the small table next to the chair and set it in her lap.

Carefully, she lifted the lid. Inside there were small blown-glass figurines . . . those three shapes again. A folded piece of paper was tucked into the lid of the box. She took it out and unfolded it carefully. It was an article from a magazine that chronicled research about children and the positive effects of the bright colors of a blown-glass mobile.

The mobile pictured in the article was constructed of twisted metal that scrolled into pretty curlicues. Each tiny glass figurine hung from the metal. The mother, a well-known movie star, stood next to a child in her crib with the mobile hanging above it. Ford was quoted in the article as saying, "These are back-to-the-basics mobiles. No fancy music. No motors turning the designs. They hang from the ceiling and are so light that a gentle breeze will move them, or air from a standard fan. There's nothing wrong with keeping things simple."

These pieces must have been set aside to make a mobile for his own children one day. This room felt magical. It was small but well organized.

She'd never met a man so eager to have a family. It wasn't hard to picture him as a father. She'd seen him with Billy.

Her fingers grazed the smooth wooden handrail as she walked down the stairs. She hadn't noticed before that the house was fairly childproof too. Simply decorated. Tasteful. Colorful. His glass art had been housed in niches in the wall or up high, where little hands couldn't accidentally tip them over.

She made herself at home in the kitchen, making a salad to go with dinner, and then she showered while he cooked. After dinner they lay on the couch together, watching television. She must have fallen asleep in his arms, because when she woke up, the television was off and she was on the couch alone with a crocheted afghan over her. She wished she could crawl into bed with him now, and part of her was tempted to climb the stairs and do just that. But there hadn't been any more of those seductive kisses since they'd arrived. Maybe he was cooling to the idea now that he was back home. She walked into the guest room and sprawled out on the bed. *Don't overthink it, Flynn.* It had been a tiring trip. A good one, but tomorrow was another day. She'd just have to trust that the right thing would happen.

The sky was still dark when she awoke. Her phone showed it was six thirty. The sun wouldn't rise for a few hours, but she was finding the shorter daylight hours weren't really a bother.

Coffee brewed as she preheated the oven to cook the casserole. Still in her winter pajamas—black yoga pants with red bows on them and a black T-shirt—she set the timer and went out to the living room. She felt relaxed sitting here in his space enjoying the quiet.

Ford came walking down the stairs, hair all a-muss, in sweatpants and no shirt.

Who knew a glassblower would have a six-pack like that? He raised his arms high above his head, stretching with a loud groan. *Wait a minute.* As the front of his pants dipped slightly she realized there was clearly an eight-pack. And that was making her feel a little drunk.

She wished she hadn't fallen asleep last night. Alaska was looking better by the moment.

Flynn got up and followed him into the kitchen. She took the casserole out of the oven and served it up while he poured a cup of coffee.

At the table there was a comfortable quiet as they enjoyed breakfast together.

"This breakfast casserole is great."

"Good. Eat up else I'll be spending my last day in Alaska stuck in your kitchen."

"That was your deal."

"I know. I should've thought that through better."

"Can't say I'm going to mind getting stuck with some of your cooking in my freezer. It would be nice to come home to."

"And I never mind getting stuck in a kitchen, so it's a win-win."

"Speaking of winning, I was thinking we'd go out today, then swing by and submit my sealed bid at the end of the day."

"I've been thinking about that." Flynn fidgeted—something he'd never seen her do before. "They aren't closing bids until Friday at four o'clock, right?"

"Yeah, but they are accepting bids until six tonight. We'll have time to play and stop by." But her expression didn't change. Maybe she wasn't enjoying spending time with him as much as he'd thought.

"That's not what I was worried about," she said, then shook her head, clearly flustered. "Worried isn't the right word, but what I was thinking is that you should wait until Friday toward the end of the day to place your sealed bid."

"Why? I know what I have to spend, and I know what's fair market for the place. I'm not trying to take advantage of Ziegler's situation. He's a friend. I don't want to capitalize on his misfortune."

"I admire your loyalty to your friend, but you want to win the bid too. If we can find out how many other people are bidding, maybe we can factor in a predictive variance to make a better bid. You said yourself this is a small town. We might even catch wind of the ballpark of those other bids."

"I love the way you think."

"So you'll do it?"

"Sure. I told you I respected your advice." He rubbed his hands together, excited about the possibilities. "So, now that that is settled, I thought I'd take you on that whale-watching trip."

"Really?"

"Yep. Now, I'm going to be honest with you. The best time to see humpbacks or orcas is usually like May through September, so we're out of that window, but my guy said that because the weather has been mild he's still seeing a few. He's going to take us out on a private ride, but don't get your hopes up too high."

"Still. Fun. Thank you."

"He'll take us to see some glaciers and eagle nesting areas too. I haven't been in forever. It'll be fun to go with someone who's never been before."

"This might be the best Thursday of the week." She grinned.

Ford stopped and then laughed. "Yeah, guess that's a safe bet."

Chapter Twenty-Two

Bidding on the Glory Glassworks Gallery building had opened an hour earlier. Ford drummed his fingers on the leather steering wheel. His dream was so darn close he could practically feel it.

He gripped the wheel tightly as he pulled up. Several people milled around the building this morning. He'd hoped not many people would bid on the property, but there was no question it was prime real estate. The reality of his chances made him nervous.

"What's the matter?" Flynn asked.

He'd always thought he'd buy it directly from Winston Ziegler. He'd been certain he could work a fair deal with Ziegler, but a sealed bid was a whole other ballgame.

Ford had looked at other buildings in the area and none seemed as perfect. He'd hate to have to start over. He'd based everything on what he knew about production and revenue at this location, and building out a new space would change his budget dramatically.

Rubbing his hand across his beard, Ford said, "I wonder how many of these people are actually bidding on this property."

She cast her glance away from him, toward the street. "Hard to say. It's waterfront property. It's safe to say you won't be the only one bidding."

"I've never bid on a property before," he said.

"Me neither, but I guess this would be like trying a case that was high profile. It will get a lot of attention just because of what or who is involved. And in those kinds of cases it could be anyone's guess which way things would go. The right thing doesn't necessarily happen."

"That's exactly why I don't practice law anymore. I was at the top of my class, but that didn't matter. Blowing glass gives me a different freedom. Sure, it's not as lucrative as working as an attorney, but it's given me a creative outlet and the opportunity to make a decent living."

"Okay, so maybe it was a bad comparison."

"It was a good analogy. That's why it struck a nerve." He looked into her eyes. "You wouldn't have liked me when I was a lawyer."

"You're still you. The same person."

He didn't like himself as that person. "No. I was restless and cranky, not very pleasant to be around."

"I can't even imagine you like that."

They walked past the building and Flynn caught a glimpse of the men she'd heard talking on the dock. "Do you know those guys?"

Ford turned to look. "The one on the right looks familiar. Why?"

"No reason. I thought I saw them while we were walking through the property yesterday. I wondered if it was the previous owner."

"No. That is definitely not Winston. I'm not sure where I've seen him. Maybe at the Manic Moose." He stopped in front of the building. "I'll be right back."

"Okay." She sat down on a bench.

Ford walked inside the building and went to the office that had been set up to accept the bids in what used to be the break room. He'd had countless cups of coffee in this room before. It looked different with all of the vending machines gone and nothing but an eight-foot folding table in the center of it. Didn't look like a break room now, but he was definitely hoping for a break today.

"Hi. I'm Ford Morton. I came through here yesterday and picked up the bidding paperwork."

A young woman sat behind the table. "If you have any questions, you'll need to come back when my mom is here. I'm just filling in for her."

"Your first time to Alaska?"

"It is. Mom said it was a once-in-a-lifetime trip."

"She's right. Well, it wasn't once in a lifetime for me. I came here to visit and never left."

"Really? Where'd you live?"

"Tennessee."

"That's a big difference. I just live in Seattle."

"Nice city. I was wondering how many bids you have so far," he asked her. She was younger than him, probably still in college, if that, and very pretty.

"I'm just filling in, and the bids are confidential."

"Of course. I didn't want any information, just wondering how many bids had been made so far."

"Well," she blinked playfully, "I guess it doesn't hurt to share that information. We only have one bid so far."

Ford's mood soared. Hopefully, tomorrow morning when he asked, the answer would be the same. Fewer bids would surely increase his odds, and anyone really serious would have come to make their bid in person.

As he got closer to the entrance of the room, he saw Flynn pacing outside the door. She seemed anxious this morning.

When the door opened, she spun around and walked over to meet him. "How'd it go?"

"Fine."

"Did you place a bid?"

"No. I just asked how many had been made. They've only received one bid so far."

"That's great news. Less competition. All it takes is one dollar more to be the highest bidder."

She seemed more nervous than him. "I'm hopeful."

"Me too," she said.

Ford drove back into town. "I thought we'd eat dinner at the Moose tonight if that's okay with you."

"Are you hedging your bets so I have to fill your freezer with all that leftover food we bought? You know I'd cook food for your freezer if you just asked, right?"

"You'd really do that for me?"

"Sure. I love to cook, and you are treating me to an Alaska vacation. It's kind of the least I can do. Just tell me what you want. Anything southern you'd like."

"Careful. I'll take you up on that."

"I hope you will."

He pulled into the same spot his truck had been parked in when they came from the airport.

Missy came over with her usual bright smile and seated them at a corner table. "Someone will be right back with you, but tonight's special is crab bisque and hand-breaded fish bites. Can't go wrong with either one."

"She's not lying. I recommend the crab bisque."

"Works for me." Flynn pushed her menu to the center.

Chet walked over and slid into the booth next to Flynn. "Haven't scared the prettiest girl we've ever had here off yet, huh?"

Flynn smiled over at Ford. "Not yet."

"Not yet. Can you give me your best bottle of wine to go with dinner?" Ford asked.

Chet smiled broadly. "You know I can. I've got just the bottle."

"Thank you." Ford leaned forward with his elbows on the table. "Chet may not look the type, but he's got one heckuva wine cellar. Even went to some kind of sommelier class for it. Maybe he'll take you down and show you his collection."

"You never really know about people until you give them a chance to be themselves, outside of their regular environment," she said.

"Then I guess I'm really getting to know you. Can't get much farther from North Carolina than Alaska."

"True."

Her one-word response made him nervous for the first time. He'd thought things were going so well. Then again, the main focus had been on what he wanted. Chet brought the bottle of wine over to the table. He opened it, then poured it into a large clear decanter to let it breathe. Ford had seen him do this a million times, but Flynn looked impressed. "Just let that breathe until your dinner comes, and then you'll really enjoy the full flavor of it."

"I hope tomorrow night we're celebrating again," she said.

"Me too."

Chet grinned. "With champagne! And my treat. No arguments."

"Absolutely. If I have the winning bid, I won't be in any mood to argue. You could ask me for pretty much anything and I'd probably say yes."

She raised an eyebrow. "I'll keep that in mind."

He took her hands into his across the table. He didn't want to mess up what they'd started, but his focus had been on that bid. He rose from his seat and leaned over the table to kiss her.

Her lashes fluttered as she opened them and smiled. "I want you to win that building. I really hope this works out for you."

"Thank you. I heard someone say there's a good chance for Northern Lights tonight. As soon as we finish dinner, I know just the place to watch for them."

After dinner, Ford stepped out of the booth and slipped cash into the bill folio. He reached for her hand.

When she slid into the passenger seat, he held the door and then slid his hand behind her, leaning in close. "I'm so glad you're here to celebrate with me tonight."

"Me too," she whispered.

He breathed in her scent as he moved closer to kiss her. The deep, warm connection felt like a force of nature too. He wasn't about to ignore it.

As they came over the ridge he knew what was ahead, he'd seen it often, and the slight color shift that glowed was telling. Just another few minutes and it would be in plain sight. Excitement coursed through him, forcing him to keep a check on his speed, and as they took that last turn to where the clearing was visible, he heard Flynn take in a breath as the aurora borealis made its appearance. Her excitement was like one of those fires that jump from one point to the next, and it was like seeing it for the first time for him again too.

"That's the Northern Lights," she said. "Oh my gosh. It's more stunning than the picture." She put a hand up and forward as if somehow she thought she could touch it. Feel it. Be a part of it.

"It's always different. Like it has a mind of its own."

"Kind of does, since it's with only mathematical probability that they can forecast the likelihood of seeing them."

"Makes you feel out of this world in a way, doesn't it?" He swung the truck to the side of the road and hit the button to release the back door of the SUV. "Come on."

He jumped out of the truck and went to the back. She was just getting out when he climbed into the back and pulled a handmade quilt out and laid it down in the bed. "Get in with me."

Her giggle warmed him. He lay down with his head at the opening, and she slid beside him.

"It's so beautiful," she said, her words choked.

"Are you crying?"

"I'm sorry. I don't know why. It's just so pretty."

He rolled over and pulled her into his arms. "I love sharing this with you," he whispered. He moved his mouth over hers, devouring her softness. "You really are beautiful, Flynn."

"You make me feel that way."

"You make things feel so complete around here. I can't get enough of you."

She felt warm in his arms as they lay there watching the miracle of lights above them. She reached for his hand and gave it a squeeze. "This might be one of the best days I've ever had."

And if that bid went his way tomorrow, it might be the best week of his life as every single thing he'd ever dreamed of fell into place.

~

Flynn still felt stunned by the beauty of what they'd just shared. It had left her with a surreal feeling. The mood, the Northern Lights, the feelings of love—real love—that she could no longer deny. She stood at Ford's side as he opened the door to his house. "What a rush."

"What a day," he said. "You were the best part of it."

"Better than the Northern Lights?"

"Better than any aurora borealis." He closed the door behind her and helped her out of her coat. She shivered slightly.

"I'll start a fire. The temperature has really dropped tonight."

She curled up at the end of the sofa while he arranged logs in the fireplace. He started the log fire so quickly that she wasn't sure a gas fireplace could beat him in a race to make fire.

He walked over and knelt down in front of her. He kissed her. Soft, closed-mouth kisses, then slid his hands along her hips and scooted her down on the couch.

"What are you doing?" She let him guide her back on the couch.

"I'm making room for two," he said playfully.

Being here was like being in a dream. In a way that was true, because she was in the middle of his dream, and it seemed like a pretty good place to be.

A sensuous smile played on his lips, and then his mouth covered hers, brushing hers in a tantalizing invitation for more.

Anticipation swept through her as he settled one hand on her hip. His hands were big. Strong. He worked her much like he did his art—with confidence, strength, and innovation.

She lifted toward him, wanting to be as close as possible. Feeling his warmth. Wanting him to stay close.

But he backed off, leaving her wishing for more.

He stood in front of her and held his hand out. "Will you come with me?"

She wanted to so much.

He tugged on her hand and she stood in front of him. His hands ran the length of her arms, then encircled her hips, pulling her close.

All of the air expelled from her lungs in one wild gasp.

He planted taunting little kisses along her lips, her cheek, and ever so softly to the crook of her neck that sent shimmers as bright as the stars coursing through her.

"Sleep with me tonight," he whispered into her ear. Then he straightened and gazed into her eyes.

Flynn felt the rise and fall of his breath and the heat from his body.

He leaned forward and dropped another kiss on her forehead. A simple kiss on the forehead felt like being rescued by a knight on a white horse. "Please, Flynn."

"Yes," she said, letting him lead her up the stairs. They undressed and slid beneath the cool sheets. Her hands shook in anticipation.

There was no need to snuggle to get warm. Their bodies provided plenty of warmth.

"You feel so good in my arms," he said as she pressed her body against his.

Their embrace was slow and gentle, but the desire was hot and a little out of control.

His heart pounded so hard that she could feel it against her hand as she ran it up his well-toned chest. His hands explored her body, every curve she'd been aching for him to touch.

His kisses trailed down her body. She sucked in a breath, arching to meet his hands as they found their way, building her desire.

And then the colors that danced in the dark were brighter than those of the aurora borealis and just as breathtaking.

He rolled over, kissing her shoulder with a sigh. "You make me so happy."

"You have an amazing life here. Thank you for talking me into coming with you."

"Thank you for coming."

"I'm so jealous that you knew exactly what you wanted and made it happen."

"It's become a lot more clear lately. Since you came back with me." He kissed her on the forehead. "But I didn't know until my trip back to Boot Creek that you were the one thing missing. You've been there niggling at my thoughts since the day I met you."

"I didn't allow myself to even consider you like that when we met. I knew you lived in Alaska and that was impossible."

"And now?" He held her gaze. Eyes wide, but tears welling. She looked hopeful and terrified at the same time.

She closed her eyes. This felt so right. The safe feeling in his arms was more than she'd ever experienced. Love? Maybe the reason none of those past relationships had worked was because they really weren't love. "I can't deny what I'm feeling for you. This has been so fast and . . . unexpected."

He raised the hand he held in his and opened her fingers, placing a kiss in the palm of her hand. "I will always take care of you. I am in love with you. Stay with me here. When we go back to finish my residency at PRIZM, we can pack up your things and you can come back with me. Give it a chance. If you can make it through the winter, you can make it forever."

"I have the B&B to run." It was still important, but she'd be lying if she didn't admit that what she was feeling with Ford was exactly the way she'd dreamed she would feel with the man of her dreams. "It's allowing my grandparents to have their dream, and that's huge to me. I love them so much. Doing this is the only thing I could ever do that would make a difference in their lives."

"That's important, but if it's not your life's work, we could make it work. What if I help you get a management company to run the B&B? You could still handle the bookings from here, and the financials. You could fly down to Florida to visit them."

"It's so far."

"It is a long flight, but the air miles will add up quickly so you can earn free flights. Plus, it seems like I visit family more often now that I have to really plan visits than I used to when I was just a few hours away."

That made sense. One got lazy when there was too much flexibility, and if it hadn't been for Jackson and Angie's wedding, she might not have even seen her grandparents last summer. It had already been too long since she'd seen them. "We talk online a lot."

"You can do that from here."

Could she really make that happen?

He wrapped his arms around her and held her to him, spooning her as close as two could be. "Good night, baby. Happy thoughts and sweet dreams."

He squeezed her tight, taking a deep breath that brought her even closer. "I've fallen for you, Flynn Crane. I don't want to ever let this go." With one last kiss softly on her neck, she wrapped her hands around his arm and they drifted to sleep without another word.

When Flynn woke up it was already daylight, which meant it was late in the morning. And Ford was already up. In Carolina he'd been a late riser, but they were in his time zone now so she didn't really know what his normal was.

She climbed out of bed, and cool air hit her like an icy wall. She grabbed for the blanket at the end of the bed and hugged it around her. She looked at the clock on the dresser. Only seven thirty. Ford probably hadn't been up long, but judging by the size of the drifts outside the window, snow had been falling for a good, hard while.

Large snowflakes, as big as golf balls, landed heavily, smacking with a rickety splat against the windowpane.

Bids were due today. She wondered, would they shut down for snow in this part of the world? Northerners teased her all the time when she told them they shut down area schools for an inch of snow, but they weren't equipped or prepared for the occasional snow day in that part of North Carolina.

They had to get to town. That was nonnegotiable. He probably had a snowmobile or something, although she'd never really been one to enjoy riding on the back of a motorcycle or anything she didn't have control of.

Ford would figure it out, she assured herself, trying to keep from worrying about problems that weren't even hers. She had to figure out a way to tell him about what she'd heard. If those men were cheating, it would cheat him out of his dream, and she couldn't let that happen, even if it raised the chances that he might end up living a lot closer to her if that did happen.

The words he'd spoken were fresh in her mind. Comforting last night, they made her nervous today.

Could she leave Boot Creek?

She pulled the door closed and went out into the hall. From here the heavy snow clouds filled the wall of windows on the front of the house. Ford had already started a fire. His snow boots sat by the door.

A smile played at her lips. The boots. The fire. The sound of someone stirring in the kitchen below all felt so different than she'd ever imagined. She felt sort of like those clouds drifting. Heavy with something unexpected and special. One of a kind.

She went back into his bedroom and changed into the clothes she'd left there on the chair next to his bed, then went downstairs.

"Hey, I was kind of hoping I might catch you sneaking back downstairs naked."

"It's a little too cold for that."

"You're in for a treat. We had snow. Lots of it. Guess Chet was right."

"I saw."

"I made breakfast—your phone has been chirping like a pasture of crickets."

"Thanks. I'll check it."

He met her at the stairs. "Come here." He kissed her, then picked her up and put her down on the landing. "We might end up right back in bed if this snow keeps up."

"Do you hibernate all winter?"

"No. I get around some, but when I don't have to I don't mind hunkering down for a while."

They walked into the kitchen. He'd set two place settings, but there was paperwork strewn across the other half of the table. "I've been working on the numbers and some other stuff."

"You've been busy."

"I pulled together a list of all of the artists I'd like to invite to come here too. I'm so excited about this."

"Will we be able to get to town to place your bid, or will they allow phone bids or postpone it altogether?"

"I have no idea. I'm going to call as soon as someone is there."

She hoped they wouldn't go to electronic bidding. If she couldn't get into that office and look at the calendar, then she wouldn't be able to advise Ford with his bid. She should've told him about what she'd heard. The more she thought about it, the more awkward it would be to tell him now. It would hurt his feelings to think she kept that from him for her own benefit.

I have to make this work for him.

A sick feeling held in her gut. She pushed the food around on her plate. "This looks so good, Ford, but I'm feeling a little off today."

"No worries. Probably all the travel. Can I get you some toast?"

"No. Really. I'm okay." She got up from the table. "I'm going to go jump in the shower and maybe lie back down for a few minutes and see if I feel better. Will you come wake me up and let me know when you talk to the people at the auction?"

"No. You just rest. I've got this."

He had no idea. "I know you've got it, but I want to help."

He got up and walked over to rest his hands on her shoulders. "How did I get so lucky to find you?"

"I'm the lucky one," she said. "Wake me up. Promise me."

"Fine. Whatever you want. I promise."

The chirp from her phone echoed through the house.

"There it is again," Ford said. "You seem to be very popular this morning."

Flynn walked over and took her phone off the charger. She flipped through the messages as she walked to her room. Angie was dying to hear about the trip.

"Everything okay?" Ford asked.

She looked up. "Yeah. Angie wants an update."

He laughed. "Think she'll be pleased?"

"As pleased as Grandma's famous frozen sherbet punch!"

"Think your grandma is going to be pleased too?"

"You better hope so. She has a keen instinct."

"Note to self. Suck up to Flynn's grandmother."

"Good idea." She pointed toward the guest room. "I'm just going to go get cleaned up."

He'd let the silence steal the moment. "I'll let you know when I hear something."

Flynn opted for a quick text to Angie while the tub was filling.

Flynn: Things Are Great In Alaska. <3

Angie: Hey. Sorry For The Early Texts. Jackson Is Home For Lunch. He Just Reminded Me That You're Four Hours Behind Us.

Flynn: True. We Were Sleeping.

Angie: Together?

Flynn: Indeed. <3

Angie: I Knew It! I'm So Excited.

Flynn: Will Catch You Up On The Phone Soon. Thanks For The Advice.

Angie: Thanks For Listening For A Change.

After her bath she crawled across the bed in her jeans and T-shirt and closed her eyes. She was feeling better, but maybe she should feel worse if she didn't feel guilty about keeping that information from him. She'd miss Angie so much if she stayed here in Alaska. Jackson and Ford had remained best friends, but guys had different kinds of relationships than women.

Chapter Twenty-Three

Ford knocked lightly on the guest room door.

"Come in."

He pushed the door open and leaned inside. She looked beautiful lying there on the bed. The snow filled the room with bright light in a peaceful way that made her look almost angelic.

Flynn rolled over, her hair falling over her shoulder. "What'd they say?"

"They are calling everyone who picked up a packet. They want the bids in by noon. They're worried that the roads will be impassable later."

"We better get a move on then."

He'd wanted her to come, but had been afraid to hope for it after all that was going on. "Are you up to it? You can stay here if you want."

She jumped from the bed. "I'm absolutely coming with you. Give me four minutes." She ran past him into the bathroom. He sat on the bed and in minutes she opened the door and stepped out dressed in a sweater and jeans. She slipped her feet into her boots and grabbed her purse. "Let's roll."

"Ready in under four minutes? Don't make me fall in love with you again."

Her smile was devilish, and he liked it. "Prepare to be continually smitten," she said with a smug lift of her chin.

"My pleasure."

The driveway was icy, causing them to slip and slide a bit until they got to the main road. "If I'd known they were calling for snow I'd have left the truck down by the road." The snow had drifted pretty high in a few places, but someone had already scraped the main road.

"This isn't too bad," Flynn said. "This much snow would have shut down Boot Creek indefinitely." She put one hand against the dash and the other on the door.

"Main road is usually clear." He reached over and patted her arm. "I've been driving in this for a while. Don't worry."

She nodded, still looking nervous.

"Just about everyone up here helps each other during the winter months. It really isn't too bad most of the time." He hoped she could see how handling snow on a regular basis made a difference for a town.

When they got to the old building, there were several cars parked in front of it, but only a few in front of the other businesses.

He parked and they went inside. In the small room where the bids were being accepted five people stood over near a table. Some working on paperwork, others talking.

"I'll be right back," Flynn said.

He watched her cross the room and talk to the woman at the desk. They seemed to be hitting it off, smiling and laughing. Probably after hearing from Angie, she was yearning for some female chatter. A moment later when he looked back, Flynn was in the woman's chair using her computer.

Winston Ziegler walked inside, stomping snow from his boots. "All of you bidding on my building?"

"This is almost everyone. We're waiting for one more and that will be everyone with the exception of one bid that came in over the phone and we'll dial him in." The woman walked across the room, leaving Flynn behind. "Glad you could make it, Winston."

The conversation got louder as tension between the bidders eased with Winston coming in.

"Good luck, Ford," Winston said. "I'm sorry it all worked out this way. My foolish pride kept thinking I'd pull things out, but I was just in too deep."

"I understand. I hope things will turn around for you." Winston looked tired, haggard.

"Me too."

Flynn walked over. "Winston," Ford said, "I want you to meet someone." He turned and took Flynn's hand. "Someone special. Flynn, this is Winston Ziegler. You've heard me speak of him."

Flynn's face lit up. "I have. So nice to meet you."

"You've got a good man right here," Winston said.

"Thank you," she said.

Her smile melted the calm that normally ran through Ford. "I'm the lucky one."

"I've heard good things about you too, Mr. Ziegler," she said.

"Winston," he said. "Call me Winston."

Ford said, "Ziegler's been like an agent hand selling our work. Not only the art pieces but even the less artistic stuff like the household items that a lot of beginning artists worked on day in and day out."

"That's my job," Winston said. "At least it was."

"Can I talk to you for just a moment, Ford?" Flynn dipped her head slightly. "I'll bring him right back," she apologized to Winston.

"Excuse us." Ford stepped away. "Everything okay?"

"Can we step out into the hall?"

"Sure." He followed her out into the hall and she led him toward the front door then stopped. "I need to tell you something."

"Okay." What was so important that couldn't wait?

"Your bid today. How much is it going to be?"

He hesitated. They hadn't talked specific dollars. He'd only told her that he had money set aside. If she was going to be in his life, there was no reason not to share that information though. He looked over his shoulder afraid someone might overhear.

She must've read his mind, because she shoved a paper in front of him, but it already had a number on it. "Ford, don't ask me how I know," she whispered, "but can you make your bid over this amount?"

The number Flynn had written on the paper was $639,000.

Had she come across something on that woman's computer? He wasn't sure how he felt about that and he was glad she'd said not to ask, because he couldn't with a good conscience take action on an underhanded move. The bid he'd planned to make was only four thousand shy of that number. He could make that number with no problem. "I can."

"Then do it." She put both hands on each side of his face and kissed him. "I want you to have everything you ever wanted."

He turned and looked down the hall. "This might be ours."

"Yours. But I'll celebrate with you. I can promise you that."

"You'll be part of it. I want you to be."

She smiled and leaned into him. "We'd better get back."

The man she'd seen on the dock came in the front door and hurried past them.

"That must be our straggler," Ford said.

～

At three o'clock Ford and Flynn stood at the bar at the Manic Moose holding champagne glasses. Ford balanced himself on the barstool, holding his glass of bubbly high. He'd bought a round of drinks for the house and all eyes were on him.

"It's official. I just bought the old Glory Glassworks building. I'll be reopening soon. Join me in a toast!"

The room fell silent as everyone tossed back shots or sipped from their glasses, and then the bar exploded back into conversation and cheers.

"So happy for you," Missy said. "No one deserves it more. You going to stick around, Flynn?"

Flynn blushed. "We've been talking about that."

Missy looked happy about that. "I hope you do. It would be wonderful to have someone like you around here."

"Thank you," Flynn said, looking over at Ford.

Ford's lip twitched into a sexy grin. "It would be wonderful to have *you* here. Not someone *like* you. I kind of like the original."

"She likes you right back, mister," Flynn said.

"We're going to get on the road," Ford said as he put his empty glass on the bar. "Thanks for helping us celebrate." Sure felt good to say *us* and *we*. His world felt complete now.

Ford opened the door for Flynn and helped her in and then went over to the driver's side.

Her phone rang just as he started the engine. "Hey, Granpa," she said, putting the call on speaker.

"Hi Flynn."

"Is everything okay?" She mouthed over the phone to Ford, "It's my grandfather. He never calls."

"Yes. Well, no, but it will be," her grandfather said. "Just wanted to let you know that your grandmother took a fall. They're doing some tests to figure out what happened. Don't worry. They say she's going to be fine, but we're here at Regional Medical Center Hospital here in Florida. The one near the house."

Ford watched the color drain from Flynn's face. "I'll come. When did this happen?" she asked.

"Yesterday. Don't get all upset. I just wanted you to hear it from me and not one of the neighbors. Marty and Jill were here when it happened, and they were going back to Boot Creek. I figured it'd be all over town in a flash. You know how that woman loves gossip."

"She does. I'm not home. I'm in Alaska with Ford. You remember Ford from the wedding."

"Of course I remember him. Nice young man."

"The best." Her eyes twinkled as their eyes met.

Ford's heart hitched.

"Oh dear," Granpa said. "I hope it's not too late. Or is it early. How many time zones is Alaska from us? I don't know."

"Never mind, Granpa. Don't worry about that. I'll be on the first plane to Florida."

"No, Flynn. She told me not to tell you. She said that's exactly what you'd say. She'll have my hide." The poor man's voice was nothing short of panicked.

"Don't be silly. I need to be there."

"We're supposed to have an update in the morning. The doctor is supposed to come talk to us sometime between eight and nine. Call me back then. Okay?"

"Don't worry, Granpa. She's tough. It'll be okay." She hung up the phone and held it in her lap. "I need to get on the next plane."

"We're headed back on Monday. We could probably change your ticket to get you to Florida instead of Raleigh."

"I can't wait until Monday. I need to leave tonight."

A pang of disappointment shot through him. He wasn't ready for her to leave, and she hadn't made mention of him coming with her either. "Not sure when the flights run, but we'll need to coordinate the hop to get you to the airport from here."

"Who do I need to call?"

"I've got the numbers at the house. You can pack and I'll call to get things going."

She nodded and folded her hands in her lap. He could feel her concern all the way across the vehicle. He wished he knew something comforting to say. When they got to the house, she didn't wait for him to come open the door for her. She jumped from her seat and ran up the steps.

He opened the door and she stepped out of her boots. She went into her room to grab her laptop and came back out to the living room. She sat cross-legged and started searching for flights.

He called his buddy. "I need you to get Flynn to the airport. She's trying to find a flight out right now. Family emergency. What's your schedule look like?"

"My schedule is completely clear because the flights are grounded right now."

"Oh." His teeth clamped together. "How long is that expected to go on?"

"They're in white-out conditions up that way. Once the storm system moves along, they'll have some clean-up time. It could be a while."

Ford dreaded telling her that. He prayed a phone call to her grandmother in the morning would resolve the need to go.

Flynn looked like a teenager sitting on the floor using the coffee table like a desk. Her toes kept wiggling, probably the only way to burn some of the adrenaline that the worry had ignited. "Everything is completely sold out for tomorrow."

He hated seeing the worry in her eyes. "Let's get some rest."

She got up and walked over to him. "I'm sorry to be a downer. This is a big day for you. I'm ruining it."

"Don't be silly. This is life. My studio—damn, that feels good to say—will be here forever. This problem deserves your undivided attention. I'm with you, baby. We'll get through it."

~

At three o'clock sharp, Ford's phone honked like a fire alarm, or maybe it was more like the warning for a tornado. Flynn hopped out of bed in a panic kicking her foot against the nightstand and yelling at the inanimate object for getting in her way like it had been intentional.

"It's just my phone alarm," he said, trying to slow her down before she hauled butt outside. He turned off the alarm.

"Lord have mercy, I thought we were on fire or something. You need to warn a girl about that." She clutched at her chest. "One good thing about it. I'm awake now."

He pushed back his covers. "It works pretty well. Scares me out of bed every time, and I've had it set to that tone for over a year." He got up and pulled on his jeans.

"You don't have to get up. I'm just going to call and find out if there's an update on what's going on and then come right back to bed."

"You sure? I don't mind."

"Of course you don't. You're so sweet." She put her hands on his shoulders and sat him back on the bed. "I don't know what I did to deserve you, but I sure am glad."

Chapter Twenty-Four

Flynn went downstairs to grab a glass of water, but as soon as she stepped foot in the kitchen she smelled coffee. The light on the coffee-maker glowed. Ford had set the coffeepot to brew for three o'clock and the pot was almost done. That guy thought of everything.

She poured herself a cup of coffee, more to warm up than to wake up, then sat down at the table with her phone.

She said a quick prayer and then dialed.

"It's me, Flynn. How is she?"

"Good morning, sweetie. I didn't want to worry you."

"We're family. It's my job to worry. Did the doctor come?"

"Yes. Turns out she'd been feeling a little under the weather for a couple of days, but she never said a word."

"Is it serious?"

"Don't worry. She's in good hands. They've been running a bunch of tests to figure out why she's been so woozy feeling and all. So far everything has come back just fine."

"Do they think there's something serious going on?"

"I think they're just being cautious. We're getting older. She's in good spirits. Keeps playing it off, but I think she's a little worried. They did some heart tests."

Heart tests? Hers seemed to start a shuffle-ball change in her chest. "Oh my gosh. I'm coming down."

"Flynn, you don't need to do that. Your grandmother would shoot me dead if she found out I told you. Shoot me twice dead if she found out that I made you leave Alaska and that man she was so taken with last year."

"But . . ."

"I'm not surprised you're there with him. You know your grand-mother predicted you two would be a perfect match when she saw y'all walking down the aisle together."

"She might've been right."

"I told her it was just wedding magic. You know she gets all mushy at weddings, but sometimes that woman has a knowing about these kinds of things."

"It's been the best visit. I can't believe how different Alaska is from what I expected. It's a small town with different weather and really short days. It's not so different from Boot Creek."

"Your grandmother and I have talked about doing a cruise to Alaska."

"The ships bring in a lot of tourism to these places." Enough idle chitchat. She still didn't know anything and she wanted more than ever to be right there with them. "Will you call me or text me as soon as you hear from the doctor this morning?"

"We will, honey, but don't you worry."

"I love you."

"We love you too, Flynn."

She hung up the phone. If she'd been home she would've driven straight to the Raleigh airport and grabbed the first flight down to Florida. She'd have been there in a few hours. Being this far away gave her a feeling of hopelessness. A feeling of regret too. She wanted to be there for them. They'd always been there for her.

She went back upstairs. Ford had fallen asleep on top of the comforter still wearing his jeans. She didn't bother waking him. There wasn't anything to share yet.

Crawling back into bed, she snuggled up close to Ford and held on, letting her breathing slow to the rhythm of his.

She woke up to a kiss on the shoulder. She turned over and stretched, then grabbed for her phone. He hadn't called back yet. "Good morning."

"How'd the conversation with your granddad go last night?"

"Gran is still in the hospital. They are running tests to make sure there's nothing serious going on that led to her falling in the first place."

"That's promising though, right?"

"I'm worried." She pulled her arms across her body. "Granpa told me to wait, but I'm feeling helpless. I need to do something."

"What would you be doing right now if you were home?" he asked.

She shrugged. "If I did what my grandfather said to do, I'd be waiting and not worrying. But I know me. I'd be on a plane to see her right this minute."

"Well, you can do what your grandfather asked of you from here." He took her hand in his. "It's going to be okay."

She nodded. "Where are you going?"

"I'm going to head over to the shop here in a few. Take an inventory of things. Do you want to come?"

She considered it, but she was tired, and worried. She couldn't even think about shifting gears to that glass shop right now. She was probably more mentally tired than anything, but she wanted to wait on that phone call. "Would you mind if I stayed here?"

"No, babe." He pulled her into an embrace. "Go back to sleep, and call me later. I won't bother you so you can get some rest."

"Thanks."

"I love you," he said.

A zing like electricity went through her at the sound of those words. Not in the heat of passion. Not in an apology. Just because. "Ford, I love you too." So much so that the joy in her heart sent tears racing to her eyes.

She felt a calm when the front door closed behind him, and she heard the sound of his truck engine turn over.

Flynn checked her phone again. Still no update. She drifted back asleep until the special ring she had reserved for her grandparents woke her.

"Hello?" Her heart pounded from the ring and in hopes for good news.

"Hey, Flynn. We just got finished talking to the doctor."

"Are they letting you take her home?" She crossed her fingers and closed her eyes.

"No. Honey, they found a little blockage. They are going to do a little procedure to clear it. They said it's nothing to be worried about. Sounds like they do this all the time and she'll be up and racing around like normal in no time."

"Surgery?"

"A procedure," he repeated.

She wondered if that was more for his own comfort or hers.

"I'm coming."

"No. Honey, your grandmother was very specific about this. You need to stay right where you are. She said she feels fine and she has complete confidence in the surgeon. She'd rather you and that handsome man of yours both come down at Christmas or something when we can have fun."

She felt torn.

"I'm serious now, Flynn. She didn't even want me to tell you, but I told her I couldn't with a clear conscience do that."

"She better never keep that kind of stuff from me. I love y'all. I need to know these things."

"We're going to be just fine. They aren't doing the surgery until Monday morning."

She glanced at the clock. It was still early on Saturday. She could get there.

He continued, "I promise to text you throughout the whole thing."

"I should be there for you."

"Why? So both of us can sit on hard chairs and drink bad coffee?"

"Because we're family, and family is everything." And if anything were to happen she would never forgive herself. There was never a guarantee for tomorrow. Dad might have let his life fizzle to one of loneliness after Mom died, but it had only made her bond with her grandparents, Mom's parents, that much tighter. When Dad left, she'd needed them even more.

She wrapped up the call so she could think without her grandfather yammering on about what she shouldn't do. She never was good at being told what to do.

She tossed her phone on the pillow beside her, then got up and paced the room. Where were her priorities?

In the kitchen she spotted a small phonebook on the cookbook shelf. She took it down and looked up the Manic Moose. Hopefully that number would roll to Missy or Chet.

She dialed and on the fourth ring Missy answered. "I hope I'm not disturbing you," Flynn said. "It's Flynn. Ford's friend."

"Flynn. Hi. I'm glad I answered. That area code threw me. I thought for sure I'd be fussing out another telemarketer who didn't know they couldn't afford to ship to me here in Alaska."

"Never really thought about that."

"Oh yeah. Used to make me crazy. I'd get all excited about something and then they'd take the deal back or up the shipping on me. Anyway, what can I do for you?"

"I was wondering if you had the number for the guy with the plane. I need to get down to Florida. My grandmother is having surgery."

"I have his number, but he was just in here. He's not flying until Wednesday. He just went to help a friend with some damage from the storm."

Just her luck. "That's awful. For them and for me I guess. How can I get out? Can I drive to the airport?"

Laughter over the line was enough of an answer. "It would take you two days to drive there with this weather. Plus, even in fair weather you have to go around the mountain and that would take you a day on bad roads."

"I'm sorry I bothered you. I thought for sure there'd be a way out of here. I'm suddenly feeling like Alaska is a little too far away from the people I love. It's beautiful, but that might be a price I can't afford."

"I have an idea. Do you have a pen?"

"I do."

"Let me give you Louisa's number. That woman has the best connections. If anyone can get you out of here, she can."

"Thank you." Flynn's hopes rose. "Thank you so much." A single tear ran down her cheek. A tear of relief.

She jotted down the number and then called Louisa and gave her the details.

Just as Missy had said, that woman pulled together a plan in less than an hour. Rather than flying to Juneau where the flights were in delay status, she had a friend that could get her to Seattle. From there Flynn could catch a commercial airline to Florida and arrive late Sunday night.

"Thank you so much, Louisa. You don't know what this means to me."

"Sure I do," Louisa said. "Family is important. And I consider you part of our family in this town now. We all really like Ford. You've got a great guy there."

"Thank you. I know I've said it like ten times but I don't know what else to say."

"Say you'll be back," Louisa said.

Flynn laughed nervously. Could she promise that now?

Louisa didn't wait for an answer. "I'll be there in about forty-five minutes to pick you up and take you to Slim's place to catch that ride."

Flynn raced through packing. With her bags next to the door, she pulled a piece of paper from a notebook on Ford's counter and wrote,

Dear Ford,

I had to go. My grandparents are my only family. I have to be there. They are doing surgery on Monday. I didn't want you to leave your project, and I know you would have. You are so wonderful. Maybe I don't deserve you. Alaska is beautiful and you are the best thing that ever happened to me, but this is so far from my family, and right now they need me.

I'll call and let you know how things went. I'm wishing you all the best on the new glass shop.

With love,

Flynn

~

Flynn landed in Orlando and retreated to an airport hotel. There was no sense in trying to find a good rate, or something close to the hospital at this point. She just needed a bed and a pillow to rest her aching body.

At seven o'clock her alarm went off. She showered and gathered her things and took a cab to the Regional Medical Center Hospital.

When the cabdriver dropped her off at the front entrance, she spotted her grandfather walking up the sidewalk. What were the odds of that happening?

Thank you, God. She knew right then she'd done the right thing. She was in the right place, no matter what leaving Ford may have meant.

She paid the driver and then ran up to meet her grandfather. The look of surprise on his face was unmistakable.

"What are you doing here?"

"You know I had to come."

He shook a finger at her. "Your grandmother is going to want to kill me."

She wrapped her arms around him. "Won't be the first or the last time."

"It's good to see you." He squeezed her and for the first time he felt small and frail. If she was this worried, she could only imagine how worried he was.

They walked to the elevator and he led her straight to her grandmother's room on the third floor.

"Can I go in first?"

"Be my guest."

She opened the door and stepped inside. As soon as her grandmother spotted her she shook her head.

"I told your grandfather not to call you."

"Yeah, what was that all about?"

"I didn't want you to worry. I'm getting great care here. There's not a thing you can do that's not being done."

"I love you. I wanted to be here for you."

"The best thing you can do for me is be happy. I think there's something special going on with you and this young man."

"You're more important than that."

"That's just silly talk. I remember him from the wedding. He was quite handsome."

"He is super good looking, but he may be the nicest man I've ever known."

"So what's the problem?"

"He lives in Alaska."

"So move to Alaska."

"I can't do that."

"Why not?"

"The bed and breakfast. I would never let you down. And what if you need me? You wouldn't believe what I went through to get here. Some bad weather moved in and there were delays. I rode in a cargo plane from Alaska to Seattle to catch a real flight."

"Honey, that was just downright crazy. Hope they only charged you freight prices though."

That made Flynn laugh. Gran had a way of lightening the mood no matter what was going on.

"How are you?" Flynn reached for her hand. "I've been so worried. I feel so helpless right now."

"Stop fussing. This is exactly why—"

"Why she told me not to tell you," her grandfather said. "I told her not to come, Suz. I promise."

Flynn caught the pleading look in Granpa's eyes. "He did. But I didn't listen."

"I knew you wouldn't listen. You're just like your mother." Gran looked to her husband. "Real love is the most important thing of all, and if that means making some changes, that is okay. Isn't that right, dear?"

Granpa nodded. "A few compromises never hurt anyone. We made a few."

Gran smiled. "We sure did."

"I made a commitment to you to run the B&B. I won't let you down."

"We don't care if you don't want to run that inn. The legacy is in what it will give you. The freedom to live a full life. Like mine with your grandfather. I want you to have that and yours might not be that old house as a B&B. Yours just might be a life in Alaska."

"That's crazy." Flynn was juggling emotions.

"Is it?" Gran's chin set firm.

"We really probably shouldn't be getting riled up right before surgery," Flynn said.

"Don't be silly. It's a simple procedure. Not like my life is at risk. I'm going to be fine. Now you, you could be messing up the chance at a future with your one true love."

"Living in Alaska was never in my plans."

"Whose plan?"

"Mine. Remember me? Shifting from corporate America to running the B&B and finding a nice guy to raise kids in a small town."

"Honey, our plans don't matter. We had an escape clause. Remember?" Her grandmother pointed up. "It's his plan that counts. Alaska has small towns. Every state has small towns. And your plan hasn't been working out so well for you so far, has it?"

"Gran. That wasn't—"

"I'm just sayin'. Your plan might be a little too rigid. How's this Ford make you feel?"

Even just thinking about it the swirl of emotion made her tingle and feel lightheaded. And they had remembered the escape clause. Was this really meant to be? "Like I've been hit by a truck. Knocked senseless and off balance."

"In a good way. I can tell. He treats you right?"

"Oh he's a real gentleman. He's thoughtful. Old school. He makes me feel special."

"That's how your grandfather reeled me in. He made me feel like a real lady. Still does."

Flynn knew the feeling. "Yes. Just like that."

"He was smitten with you at the wedding."

That was silly. But he had said as much. "That was just an usher being polite to a bridesmaid."

"No. Walking you down the aisle is being polite. Talking to you through the whole reception is interested."

"We did spend a lot of time together that night, didn't we?"

"I'm surprised I seem to remember better than you do."

Why was that? Why hadn't he made an impression on her last summer? "It was Angie's day."

"And you had your guard down. That's how real love finds its way in."

"Why didn't I notice it then?"

"Maybe you were looking in the wrong places. Honey, you've tried to be the right one for so many. Love doesn't require that much work. It happens quick and unexpected, and it is okay if it breaks the mold. It's not one size fits all."

"She's got a point," said Granpa. "She knows what she's talking about on this. Just like your mom and dad. Didn't matter that it looked wrong to anyone else, it was right for them from the very first moment they saw each other."

"And like it was with us," Gran said with a smile.

Being with Ford was the first time she hadn't tried to change herself for a man. She'd been herself and things had worked. So well. Her days of being a chameleon were over. "He does make me happy in ways I never expected."

"Don't be afraid."

"The B&B was going to be my fairy tale. I love it. I really don't want to leave that behind. Plus, me running that is what is going to afford you that dream house."

"Don't you worry about us. We'll work that out. But you tell me. What good is the fairy tale if the prince is all wrong?"

Flynn thought about Brandon. About the other men she'd dated. And Ford.

"The B&B was *our* dream, honey. It's just geography. A safe landing spot. You know the difference, right? When you picture yourself without the B&B, how do you feel?"

"Like I'm letting you and Granpa down. Like I've put a lot of work into the place and I have so many wonderful memories there that I'd hate to leave behind."

"And if it was gone tomorrow?"

"I'd still have those memories, but I'd miss it."

The nurse came into the room with her parade of helpers. "We're ready to take you to surgery, Mrs. Crane." She turned to them. "I'm going to need to ask you two to leave so we can get this show on the road."

"Just a minute." Gran reached for Flynn's hand. "And how would you feel if you never saw Ford again?"

Devastated. That's how she'd feel. "I think I have a call to make."

Her grandmother smiled so broad that every wrinkle seemed to disappear. "We can go now, nurse."

Chapter Twenty-Five

Flynn wanted to make that call, to tell Ford she'd be back, but part of her still wasn't sure. She'd left without a goodbye and she couldn't work him like a fish on a line. That wasn't fair. He was a good guy. A great guy. He didn't deserve that.

She held off. There was time to make that decision.

She and her grandfather waited for an update on the surgery. As they sat watching television, all the news was about a storm system mucking up travel along the coast. It sucked to have your flight cancelled in Florida, where the temperature was hovering in the seventies with blue skies, only to be told that the problem was weather. But that was going to be the case for a lot of people today.

Mother Nature seemed to be trying to make a point.

"Mr. Crane?" A doctor in scrubs walked over toward them. "Everything went perfectly fine. She's in recovery now. Will be for a while, and then we'll move her back into her room."

"Thank you so much, Doc. That's great news. How long of a recovery will it be?"

"She'll rebound from this surgery way sooner than that broken hand."

"That seems wrong in some way, doesn't it?" Flynn observed.

"Kind of does. Her neck might be sore for a few days, and we'll keep her on a soft-food diet for a bit. I'll probably just keep her in here one more day and then you can take her home, Mr. Crane. Do you have any other questions?"

"So she's not in any danger?" Flynn needed the confirmation.

"Not at all. She did great. She'll be as good as new."

"Thank you."

The doctor walked off and her grandfather turned to her with a smile. "I told you she'd be fine. Now she's going to be fussing to get you out of here to go reunite with Ford. You know that."

"I do."

"You should leave now."

"Before I see her again?"

"Yes, that would be the best present you could give her."

Her phone vibrated on her lap.

Angie: Are You Okay? Ford Called Jackson. Said You Disappeared.

Flynn: I Didn't Disappear. I Left.

Angie: What Happened?

Flynn: Long Story. Gran Was In The Hospital. On My Way Home Now. Will Fill You In.

Angie: Call If You Need Me.

Flynn stood and hugged her grandfather. "Promise me you'll call if there's anything I can do for y'all. You know I'll fly right back down to help out."

"We're going to be okay. But I promise."

She took in a deep breath. The last few days had been an emotional roller coaster and she was exhausted.

She went back to the hotel to get her things. Standby was probably her only chance of getting out today, but by the time she got to her room, sleep was the only thing on her mind. Maybe tomorrow would be better anyway.

Lying on the bed, she brought up the website, which was showing nothing available at all. After nearly forty minutes on the phone with the airline, she wasn't any closer to getting home, and one thing was for certain—she was too tired to make the drive.

She was finally able to get confirmed on a five o'clock flight the next day, and would try standby in the morning. It wasn't a great plan, but at least she could sleep now.

~

The next morning, the terminal swarmed with grumpy people and cranky kids, and that wasn't helping her mood. Those people had probably roughed it all night in the terminal though. At least she'd gotten some much-needed rest. She put her earbuds in to lower the volume of her surroundings and tried to concentrate on the home magazine she'd picked up in the airport bookstore.

Angie: Do You Like Him?

Flynn should've expected that from Angie. She wasn't sure what answer she'd rather give. No, that she'd stuck to her guns and hadn't fallen for the handsome bachelor, or yes, that she had because Angie approved of Ford as a potential suitor. That was saying something too, because Angie hadn't liked any of the other guys Flynn had dated.

Was there a one-word answer to that question?

Flynn stared at the question.

Flynn: Yes.

Angie: I Mean Really Like Him. Like Love.

Flynn knew now that she'd overreacted to her grandfather's call. And leaving without discussing it with Ford hadn't been the right way to go about things, but she knew he'd have wanted to come with her and she just hadn't been, still wasn't, sure she could dedicate herself to a life with him that far away. Maybe just knowing how far away she was had freaked her out a little. But the truth was, if it had been an emergency, she would not have been able to get there in time, and that would have been a catastrophe.

On the other hand, Gran's lecture about the right man made things even more confusing. She barely knew Ford. Why did she think for one hot second that he could be the right guy? There were a lot of things going against them, and Alaska was only one of them.

Flynn: Too Complicated To Text.

Angie: Call Me.

Flynn: At The Airport. Headed Home. We'll Get Together There.

Angie: What Time?

Flynn: On Standby. Seven Thirty At The Latest.

Angie: Keep Me Posted. I'll Come Pick You Up.

Flynn: Thanks.

There'd be five hundred questions from Angie, but there was no one she'd rather see at the airport. Flynn flipped through her magazine. She stopped at a before-and-after feature about a home in Nantucket that caught her eye. A nursery to be specific. Well lit and painted the softest baby blue, with white furniture. Perfectly coastal. But that's not what caught her eye. Above the crib hung a glass mobile. Not exactly like the one in Ford's house, but similar in style, this one had orange seahorses, blue dolphins, black and white orcas, and pretty blue sand dollars.

She scanned the article. The artist wasn't mentioned, but it said enough—that the artist was known for his specialty glasswork and the piece had been contracted after seeing a similar piece while on vacation in Alaska. That was Ford.

Was someone up there trying to make sure that she was thinking about Ford today?

Her phone pinged again.

Gran: Are You Home Yet?

Flynn: No Ma'am. Weather Delay.

Gran: Sorry. Call Me When You Get There.

Flynn: Are You Okay? I Can Call Now.

Gran: Fine As Wine. Kiss The Prince.

But Flynn's prince wouldn't be there when she got home. Nope. She'd left him in Alaska. Poor Gran had been on so much pain medication she'd probably already forgotten that Ford lived in Alaska, or that Flynn had up and left him with just a note. You don't really fly clear across the nation after something like that without an invitation.

Picturing her life with Ford made her believe that love was all hers for real this time, but her life wasn't in Alaska. Megan had packed up and moved to California to be with Noah. She hadn't even hesitated, but then Megan was impulsive. And, worst-case scenario, she could keep on working on her candles no matter where she was.

If Flynn gave up the B&B, she'd have nothing. What would she do in Alaska? Even if Ford's house was big enough to turn into a B&B, that would be very seasonal. What would she do all winter? How would she earn money? She wasn't a mooch. That wasn't her style.

She'd have the money from the B&B if she sold it. Maybe it wouldn't hurt to at least talk to Chrystal down at Yates Real Estate. If anyone knew the market in this region of North Carolina it was Chrystal. Plus, she dealt in commercial properties often.

Was she actually entertaining going to Alaska?

She'd miss Angie, but since she and Jackson got married, they didn't really spend that much time together anymore. Billy would go nuts at the thought of seeing sled dogs.

What were her key questions about Ford?

She pulled out a notebook from her overnight bag and started a list. When they called her with a seat on the standby flight, her page was still empty.

～

Angie was standing at baggage claim when Flynn came down the escalator. "Thanks so much for picking me up."

"You look like you've been on a four-day bender." Angie reached up and fussed with Flynn's hair.

"I feel worse than that."

"You'll feel better after having a good meal and some rest." Angie pinched Flynn's arm. "I can't wait to hear everything about your trip."

"It's been a whirlwind. How much time do you have?"

"All the time you need."

Flynn grabbed her bag off the conveyor. "I didn't even get a chance to buy everyone souvenirs in Alaska, since my trip got cut short."

"No one cares about that."

"I thought you loved that shirt I brought you back from Hilton Head Island," Flynn said with mock insult.

"I did, but I'd have been just fine hearing the stories about the trip. You know that."

How many T-shirts from random vacations other people had taken does one need? "I know, but it's my way of letting you know I was thinking of you while I was away."

Angie sneered as they got into her car. "I was kind of hoping you hadn't had time to think about us. You really liked it up there though, didn't you?"

"I did. I can't lie. It was gorgeous and everybody I met was so nice." With the exception of the people trying to fix the bids on the building, but there were those kinds of people everywhere.

"And Ford?"

Flynn's nose tickled. She blinked back the emotion that threatened to tell the story before she was ready to. "Angie, he is the best man I've ever known. Everything feels so right. It's not about him. It's not about me. It's who we are together. Even little things feel special. A kiss on the forehead. The way he holds my hand. He trusts me with his secrets. I'd never felt happier when I was with him in Alaska."

"But?" Angie's brows pulled together.

"Stop that. You're getting that line across your nose. You'll need Botox."

Angie raised her brows. "Better?"

"Yes." Flynn sighed. "But it's Alaska. It is so far. I'd miss you. I barely know Ford. Why do I have such strong feelings for him?"

"When it's right, you know it. Remember how quickly things happened for me with Jackson?"

"I do."

"And I had the brakes on because of Billy. I was trying to be extra careful. Look how happy we are. I want that for you so badly."

Flynn reached over and turned up the radio. She couldn't have this conversation all the way back to Boot Creek. It made her sad to think she wouldn't be with Ford, even though she knew it was her own fault. His life was in Alaska. Why had she allowed herself to get swept into his arms? Why had she let him into her heart?

When they got to the Boot Creek exit, she had begun to feel back at home. There was comfort in the same old, same old. But Angie turned off toward her own house.

"Did you forget I'm in the car?" Flynn laughed easily. Wasn't like she hadn't let herself go on autopilot before.

"No. I'm going to take you to our house and feed you before you go home and collapse."

"You don't have to do that. I've got stuff in the freezer. You know me. I could survive the famine off of my pantry."

"That's true," Angie said with a groan. "But Jackson wanted to do this for you, since I'd done it for Ford when he came. I thought it was really sweet of him."

"Are you sure? I thought for sure he'd be mad at me for leaving Ford the way I did. I had to. You know that, right?"

"I understand, Flynn."

Only Flynn's mind went right back to her and Ford talking about how the only thing he'd really wanted that night was rest. Now she knew exactly how he felt. She also understood how hard it was to turn down such a nice gesture. She forced a smile.

"I'll take you home after we eat."

"Okay, I'm just going to leave everything in the car."

"That's fine."

They walked inside, and Billy came running across the room, hugging his mom and then Flynn. "We're going to serve you girls dinner tonight."

"You are so good to me," Flynn said, laying a loud smooch on his cheek.

He giggled and ran back into the kitchen.

"Hey, babe," Angie yelled. "We're here."

"Heard you drive up." Jackson poked his head out of the doorway. "You two sit down. I've got wine."

"Well, isn't this special?" Flynn sat down and pulled her wineglass toward her. One glass and she'd probably sleep until tomorrow.

Jackson walked in with a dishtowel over his arm like the wine sommelier, only it was a rooster dishtowel, and he was wearing a Budweiser T-shirt.

"Redneck wine guy?" Flynn raised her glass. "You sure I'm not going to end up with moonshine?"

"Girl, you should be so lucky. If you ever tried Uncle Bo's apple pie moonshine, you'd be hooked."

"I'll stick to the wine."

"Whatever the lady likes," he said in an exaggerated tone.

He poured a healthy glass for Angie. "I'm expecting you to make a play for the sommelier later," he said with a wink.

"He is pretty cute," Angie teased.

Flynn's heart ached. Billy ran into the room, his tennis shoes slapping against the hardwood floor. He hooked a finger into the air and Jackson bent forward. Billy whispered something to him.

"We'll be right with you, ladies." Jackson and Billy walked out of the room and Angie raised her glass. "To best friends," Angie said.

"Like family," Flynn said, remembering her conversation with Ford. Flynn took a sip of the wine. "This is really good." It made her think of the other night. A bit of her ached to relive that night and never let it stop. "Kiss the prince" echoed in her mind. If only it was that simple.

Chapter Twenty-Six

Ford stood in the kitchen with Jackson and Billy. "Do you think she knows I'm here?"

"No way," Jackson said. "Angie would never have told her."

"I hope I'm not making a fool of myself," Ford said. "If I do, this better stay between the two of us."

"Me too," Billy said.

"Yeah, the two of you plus me," Ford corrected.

"You're not going to make a fool of yourself, but promise me you've thought this through. I don't want you to have any regrets."

"I won't. I know what I'm doing." He was dumbstruck when he'd read the note from Flynn and realized she'd left without him. And as he softened the blow at the expense of his liver, not only had Missy and Chet told him he was crazy to let Flynn get away. Louisa had given him an earful too. She'd said, "You're an idiot if you let geography get in the way of your happiness. If Alaska is meant to be, you will both decide together to come back, but is it worth losing her now? Get your butt on a plane. Love will take you where you're meant to be. Don't dig in your heels and lose it all. It's not worth it. I've made that mistake."

When he'd told her he'd thought he'd finally found everything he wanted since he'd placed the winning bid on the gallery, she'd poked him in the chest with her finger and said, "Look here. You can end up like me. In the place you love, old and all alone. It's not all it's cracked up to be."

He'd drank so much that night that he'd had to sleep on Chet and Missy's couch Saturday night. He woke up with the worst hangover. Although Chet assured him the pain he was feeling was only half hangover. The worst part was the broken heart.

Chet had poured him a stiff drink. Hair of the dog and all that mess, but it had helped.

He hadn't even bothered to drive home. Instead, he made a couple calls. A few hours later he had a plane ticket and a plan.

Thank goodness for friends.

Ford turned the fried pork tenderloin over in the cast-iron skillet and gave the white pepper gravy one good, last stir. Billy smashed the potatoes. A few lumps let you know they were homemade. No harm in that.

Angie stepped into the kitchen and looked back over her shoulder. Ford, Jackson, and Billy all stared at her. "What?"

"You're supposed to be out there," Ford said.

"I know, but you're taking so long I started to think you were changing your mind."

"No way. I'm ready." He used a fork to take the meat out of the pan and lay it on the platter. "I don't know how I'll ever thank you for this."

"Just make her happy," Angie said. "Don't you dare break her heart."

"Not going to happen. I think I knew there was something there that night at your rehearsal dinner. I never realized it was that strong until I had the chance to think about it not being there."

"I'm not one to talk. Katie still swears when Jackson and I saw each other that first day when I took her out to Criss Cross Farm that she could feel the sizzle between us. Neither of us realized how intense it was. Maybe it's just so far-fetched that you don't allow yourself to believe it. But it was true. We had something special, and I wouldn't trade it for the world."

"I don't want to lose Flynn before I even have a chance to make her happy."

"You're really serious about this."

"Completely," Ford said. And the worry that he'd had as they waited to hear when Flynn would be back, and even when she was on the way here, fell away. "Let's hope she doesn't break my heart. Now, go sit down."

Angie walked toward the door and then turned and blew a kiss.

Billy caught the kiss in the air and blew one back to her.

Ford high-fived Billy. He couldn't wait until he and Flynn had one of their own to share every happy moment in their lives with.

Jackson went out first with the bowl of greens.

"That smells good," Flynn said, and then she looked up and her mouth dropped open as Ford stepped into the dining room with the platter.

"I promised I'd make you my fried pork tenderloin."

"You did," she said quietly.

"I couldn't break a promise to you."

She blinked as if she wasn't sure it was really happening. Then she looked to Angie. "You?"

Angie shook her head. "Not me."

Ford put the plate on the table. "I won't ever break a promise to you. I love you, Flynn."

"But this is so—"

"Fast. I know. It's fast, but it's right."

"Your whole world is in Alaska. Mine is here."

"My whole world is not in Alaska. You're not there." He spread his arms wide. "I spoke with the second bidder. If I want to sell, they want to buy that property."

"But that's your dream."

He laid a box in front of her. The white satin ribbon was wrapped around a plain cardboard box. She slid it off and took off the top.

Billy ran to her side. "What's your present, Aunt Flynn?"

She pulled back the cotton. Four compartments separated the items. Each wrapped in bubble wrap.

"Please tell me you want a life with me. If you say no, I've got nothing. I think I knew the day I met you."

She lifted her left hand to her face, sweeping at the corner of her eye. She unwrapped the bubble wrap, recognizing the shooting star shapes that had been carefully wrapped. The blue and orange colors shone through the bubble wrap. She could guess what those were. She pinched her fingers at the corner of the wrap with the hint of pink under it. Fluffy cotton candy clouds.

"Those are so pretty," Billy said, reaching a finger toward one but stopping short.

"You made these," she said.

Ford nodded. "I made the last one yesterday. PRIZM let me come in for an hour to make them. Three was my dream. Four sounds even more perfect. I want to spend my life with you, Flynn. I can do that here in Boot Creek."

"No, Ford. You'd regret giving up your dream. I can't let you do that."

"You can't not let me. I want to be with you. We'll keep my house in Alaska. We can stay there a few months a year. We'll figure something out. Are you willing to give it a try with me?"

Kiss the prince.

"I am, but I'm not sure staying here is the answer."

"What do you mean?"

"I'm willing to discuss it, compromise, come up with the right answer for the two of us."

"Giving up the B&B?"

She nodded. "My grandmother is a wise woman. She asked me what good was having the dream house, the castle, if you didn't have the right Prince Charming."

"Am I your Prince Charming?" He'd make any sacrifice to be with her, even give up the chance of having it all in Alaska. It was worth whatever it took for them to be together.

"Forever, I hope."

Ford took her hands and she stood in front of him. "Me too. I want you to come with me to Tennessee. I'm way overdue mending fences at home, and I want you to meet my family."

"I'd love that. And it's Pop-pop's birthday."

"You remembered?"

"Of course I did. It's special to you."

"And you're special to me too. I really want you to meet him."

"We shouldn't put that off. We never know how many tomorrows we'll have."

"He's going to adore you." He held his hands out, palms up, and she laid her hands in his.

"Flynn Crane, there are no guarantees how many tomorrows we'll have, but I can promise you this, I want to spend every single one of mine with you."

"And I'll be yours until tomorrow . . . every single day."

Acknowledgments

Special thanks to Pam Murray and her family for inviting me to join them on a two-week vacation through Alaska. It was a trip of a lifetime, and it was during our glassblowing excursion that the hero of this book came to life for me. Who knew there was something so strong and sexy about blowing glass?

And to all of my friends who succumb to my sometimes close-to-crazy enthusiasm to try something new, or drop everything and go somewhere . . . thanks. It's those moments of a lifetime that help me bring fresh stories to the page and ultimately to the reader. Without y'all, it wouldn't be nearly as fun.

To my Montlake team: Chris Werner, Jennifer Glover, Krista Stroever, Jessica Poore, and the whole gang over at Montlake Romance, y'all make this Montlake Girl feel like she can do anything. Thank you for helping me become a better writer with every single book and for making this dream come true.

I'm truly blessed to be surrounded by a wonderful extended family who loves and believes in me. Thank you for the sacrifices you've made as I follow this dream. I love you all.

And to Dakota, my chocolate Lab, who lies faithfully at my feet through every draft, naps with me when I'm exhausted, and snacks with me through the edits—there's a percentage of royalties that will be tagged for doggie treats just for you!

About the Author

Photo © 2016 Adam Sanner

USA Today bestselling author Nancy Naigle whips up small-town love stories with a dash of suspense and a whole lot of heart. She began her popular contemporary romance series Adams Grove while juggling a successful career in finance and life on a seventy-six-acre farm. She went on to produce works in collaboration with other authors, including the Granny series. Now happily retired from a career in finance, she devotes her time to writing, antiquing, and enjoying the occasional spa day with friends. A Virginia girl at heart, Nancy now calls North Carolina home.